# THE DREAMS

## REVISED EDITION

### B. MICHAEL FEE

To my wonderful family

and

Pasquale (Pat) Emiro

1923-2013

# Prologue

Ashley woke up to his name being called.

"Yes?" he said, "Yes?"

He waited a moment, clearing his head.

He could not see anything.

"Liz?" he tried reaching for her, whispered…"Elizabeth? I think we've lost power… are you awake?" He tried reaching again but his arm touched nothing but empty space.

He was not in his bed he realized. Wherever it was, it was completely, utterly black. No illuminations or slivers of light, anywhere.

He barely took a breath for what seemed like many minutes, waiting… but there was nothing. It was overwhelming. No sound, no light, nothing.

He stuck out his tongue. "I can taste it, gawd, I can taste it" he said out loud…"feel it on my skin." He remembered a term his science advisors had used once, "dark matter." He wondered. "Is this it? Has something happened to the world in the night?" He did not know enough…but *whatever* it was, it was complete, and *he* was in it. Held in the totality of it. That was it, he thought. "I am held in this total, unyielding, blackness… a kind of sensory deprivation experiment." His mind was spinning with possibilities.

By his reckoning, he was standing up, but he couldn't be certain. He turned, or did what he thought was turning, all there was, everywhere, was the enduring pitch. He realized, suddenly, that without a frame of reference, without something *firm*, he could not tell where was up or down or if he should move or what he would find if he did. His eyes were open, he at least knew that. He could feel them blinking on his face. But what this dark was he did not know...nor if there was anyone else here with him. He remained still again. He was listening for breathing...he could not hear any, as before, there was no sound of any kind.

"Is there someone here?...*hello?*..where is everyone?... *HELLO?*"

But there was nothing in return.

"They are the same thing" he said to himself, "blackness to the eyes is the same as silence to the ears...a kind of sensory desert...nothing for the brain to process, nothing to respond to...nothing. I am in a kind of nothing." He thought about that for a moment. "in a kind of nothing." What could that possibly mean?

His wonder was tipping to anxiety...a growing uneasiness because he could also *feel* something...undefined, but here...something *about* this dark. It was more than just an absence of light, it was something tactile, a presence, even something *alive*...

He discovered then that no movement occurred when he "told" his arms to move..."oh gawd, my legs too...I can't move, or see, or possibly hear".

Then he realized...he was only talking in his mind...no sound was coming from his mouth...did he even have a mouth?...he realized too that he could not be sure that he was blinking anymore either or if he even *had* eyes.

But he *was* aware...and had no idea what had happened to him. It was then that he remembered the words from scripture..."the earth was a formless void, and darkness covered the abyss"...he suddenly felt cold and afraid.

"Where am I?"...

There was nothing particularly unusual about Coughlin O'Malley's first half-hour at work this Friday morning, it was 5:30 am EDT when he entered his office, the customary Friday all-everything bagel with lite cream cheese in hand, and, as always, he had picked up all the overnight messages and newspapers at the West Wing entrance desk as he came by. Coughlin O'Malley, affectionately known as "Cough" by the President, was Chief-of-Staff for Stephen Ashley, 47th President of the United States. This morning, the routine for the President was a little relaxed, and he was not to be briefed until 6:30 am, so Cough sat down with his bagel and coffee to get a head start on things...while skimming the overnight "accounts of interest," O'Malley found 2 which would require attention...one regarding a "sudden illness" keeping the Chinese Premier from attending an important Communist Party function to-day...O'Malley noted to send "well wishes for a full and speedy recovery" from the President and the people of the United States, and another from the official spokesperson for the Socialist Republic of Vietnam... the President of the SRV had suffered a "stroke" in the night...O'Malley would ask Secretary of State Jack Stanley to respond appropriately, and likewise the US Ambassador in-country...

Mrs. Julia Freitas, the President's secretary, was just getting settled, at 6:10, as O'Malley crossed through the Oval office from his office into hers. "Good Morning Mrs. F,"...Freitas smiled,

"Something I can do for you Cough?", not looking up, working her keyboard.

"I think we're going to change the timing for Senator's Collingsworth and Bidswell....we need to push them back 15 minutes or so...there is a call to the German Chancellor the President will have to make...so let's push the Senators' to 10:30..."

Freitas logged it, and said she would notify the Senate offices.

O'Malley headed back for the COS office when his beeper lit up...

"POTUS sick...call Dr. Gaiter". Dr. Gaiter was the President's personal physician assigned from Walter Reed Medical (the President's decision to opt for WR instead of the usual Bethesda Naval Hospital), and a top-notch diagnostician.

O'Malley called Gaiter's cell from his office,

"Morning Doc, what's going on?"...

"We can't wake up the President" said Gaiter,

"I've been up here for 20 minutes, and Mrs. Ashley and the Secret Service have been trying for 30 minutes before that...we *CAN'T* wake him up"...

O'Malley shot into action. He flew into Freitas's office,

"call all the staff...and the VP's COS...the VP is still in Brazil, so call Jim Snell, and get him over here...15 minutes in my office...everybody."

Freitas began hitting the buttons. O'Malley tore into the First Family's residence, and was met immediately by the Service second-in-command exiting...

"Phil, what the hell is going on?"...

"You talk to Gaiter?"...

"Yes"...

"things haven't changed, he's like in a coma or something"...

"Oh God...no...Stephen...a coma"...O'Malley's eyes began tearing up despite the adrenaline pouring into his bloodstream...he slowed into a fast walk as he met a series of additional agents at new positions within the residence. Dr. Gaiter was at the desk in an access corridor just south of the President's bedroom. He was talking animatedly into the phone. O'Malley grabbed a Kleenex from one of the lamp tables and swabbed his eyes...he needed to switch to COS mode...fast.

"I've got G-Protocol 6 I'm following" said Gaiter, "and that means you guys sending somebody whether we need them or not", he was talking almost too fast for the human ear to pick it all up...G-6...O'Malley was trying to think...G-6 is a type of medical crisis response protocol...he would have duties to execute directed by the protocol...he'd have to check as soon as he got back downstairs.

"Doc"...O'Malley waved his arms, which garnered quizzical and concerned looks from the agents...the Service, should the President become compromised, assumes a different psychological model...no one, no matter who or what position, is considered "benign" until answers begin emerging...so O'Malley, despite being Chief of Staff, became, what the intelligence and security community called "neutral personnel" and accessed the President only with Service present at all times.

"Doc...can we talk a second?"...O'Malley was giving him the time-out sign.

Gaiter was done anyway, and stood up.

"Cough, come into the bedroom"...

The head of Secret Service, Peter Barrett, was present, Mrs. Ashley, the President's personal agent in the residence, Allan Wheeler (Wheeler also assumed the role of "watcher" of all WH contacts...he was discreetly fully-armed, and had a level-7 rating for hand-to-hand combat disposi-tions...he had both the training and the instincts to meet any in-close threat opportunity), and Dr. Omer Jackson (Gaiter's second), his black bag open, was taking readings of blood pressure, listening to cardiac rhythm, checking respirations, etc...all were normal.

"I've examined his eyes, looking for any sign of swelling or bleeds, we've done elementary neuro-tests...Cough, everything is normal except he won't wake up...I've applied several traditional pressure point thrusts (Service didn't like it, but) but so far nothing...we've sat him up (which made him smile for some reason), wiped his face with cold water, all the external attempts have, as you can see, failed...I've sent for some inject-able meds to try and arouse him and reverse what appears to be a kind of general anesthesia...and there are neuro-folks coming for further eval"...

"What kind of meds, Doc?"...

"Well, I'd say Narcan for one, we have epinephrine here, and insulin, but I just did a Quickstik sugar on him...he's just where he should be...the Narcan is a reversal agent for barbiturate induced coma..."

"You think that's what's wrong here?"

"I don't *know*, Cough...I don't **KNOW** what's going on here" Gaiter ner-vously raised his voice, then took a few deep breaths, and continued...

"I just want to have as many available options as is prudent."

O'Malley kept his gaze on the President...

"He just looks like he's sleeping very soundly, even snoring a little...what about the readings again?"

"WNL" said Jackson absentmindedly as he checked the President's fin-gernail beds for signs of cyanosis.

O'Malley looked at him.

Jackson caught the focus of the COS's attention from the corner of his eyes...

"Oh...sorry sir...within normal limits that is."

"OK"

Cough was crunching scenarios in his head, writing things down, "Dr. Jackson, I'd like you to join me in my office as I speak to staff...please give them an update...Dr. Gaiter, what exactly are your instructions for G-Protocol 6?...I'll pull mine when I get downstairs"

Gaiter told him the Presidential physician was to contact appropriate specialists from the list...

"G-6 is essentially a procedural neuro-plan then, that right?" said O'Malley, Gaiter affirmed.

"Ok, anybody else?...absolute secrecy?"

Gaiter shook his head no then yes, "and secret service intervenes once I make the calls...I have made 3 calls...there's 2 more to make"...

"OK Doc, let's put a hold on that for the moment...can we bring in, inconspicuously, some state of the art monitoring equipment?"...

"Cough, I don't believe you have authority to put a hold on G-6...this protocol is under Service command"...Barrett interjected.

"Yes Peter, you are right of course...I'm just thinking we can stagger this a bit"...he turned to Gaiter, "which one of these specialists is closest?"...

"the Boston team", Gaiter looked at his watch..."they should be here by 8:30 or so..."

"I guess I'm wondering why not someone closer?" said O'Malley,

"Johns Hopkins or Bethesda? What is the criteria?"

Stephen Ashley was not only his Commander-in-Chief, he was O'Malley's long time personal friend...he wanted to know why a specialist who could be minutes away, wasn't already here.

"Are they even on the list?"

"The President's personal physician makes that call, Cough. If it's determined that the President is in no *immediate* danger from an assessed condition, then options for specialty protocols are entertained. If Dr. Jackson and I could not agree, then we would already **be** at Bethesda ... but the flags are not there. We can deploy a protocol in other words. The WH protocol's identify the best current minds in the field, they are kept current by a sub-team at the SG's office..."

O'Malley took it all in...nodding along in agreement.

"ok...Boston, you say?...and you and Dr. Jackson will be here, one of you always in attendance..." he turned to Barrett, "before we know it, we will be up to our chins with all kinds of people as the executive branch hunkers through this...press, extra staff, all the VP's people..."

He turned back to Gaiter, "do you think that 3 specialists are adequate for the moment?...given our emergency proximity to Bethesda or Walter Reed?"

Gaiter rubbed his forehead..."yes...I think so Cough...especially with Dr. Jackson and myself already here...that's 5 of us with only one patient..."

Barrett wrote in his pocket log, writing the time down... "ok then Doc, if you think we can place a hold, then we're good, the Service is good with that."

Gaiter returned to O'Malley's question about the monitoring equipment and nodded, "yes, we can"...

O'Malley had to think what he was referring to for a moment..."right... what exactly would that be?"....O'Malley had his omnipresent pocket notebook out, and wrote everything down.

"Let's see, a standard visual and audio-alarm electro-cardiograph with respirations, periodic blood pressure cuff for auto-readings, oximetry, a couple of volume IV systems...we already have a crash cart here...with cardiac meds, laryngoscope for intubation, ambu bag, defibrillator, all that's initially needed for resuscitation efforts in a sudden cardiac arrest........it's right over there."

Gaiter pointed to a red multi-drawer wheeled cart with a defibrillator sitting on top of it...paddles at the ready...

"We've already placed the paddles on his chest to check his electro-cardio rhythm for abnormalities indicative of recent cardiac events...but nothing looks irregular...Dr. Jacksons' sub-specialty is cardiology, in case you didn't know that, and based on the digital readouts and paper stream, both he and I agree, the President is in NSR or normal sinus rhythm" . Gaiter re-focused on the crash cart. "Every floor has one of these carts by the way, the Service knows where they are, and all agents are trained in addition to select permanent White House staff...the additional equipment we're talking about is always on stand-by at The Reed or Bethesda if needed, I'll call to get it over here."

"Alright, you're telling me the President is not uncomfortable, not likely in danger that you can determine from readings...he's" and he checked his notes, "he's WNL, and he *appears* peaceful...let's get the monitors in here and those few specialists, and hold things steady for a while...the President is in the best hands given what we now know I would say... no need to send shockwaves through the capital just yet...and I'll take **full** responsibility for this cautious intervention plan...and beep me at the slightest change...agreed?" O'Malley took measure of the faces in the room...

"Ok then, I've got some executive branch stuff to take care of...

And let me know when those specialists get here?"

"Cough, I have drawn bloods already to determine a few things..."

"Like what for instance?"

"blood sugar, a formal level...not just a Quickstik...the presence of certain cardiac enzymes, narcotics, poisons...routine CBC, a few other things..."

"You think the President has had a heart attack in the night, Doc?"

"Well...it would explain a few things, even though we can't see anything unusual when we take a reading with the defibrillator."

"when will you know for certain...?"

"not more than a couple hours"

"Ok..." O'Malley had written it all down...they would need this information for the inevitable press briefing..."but the monitors and stuff?"

"I'm on it"

"Sounds like we have it rolling...and however this turns out Doc, the timeline starts"...he looked at his watch..."the timeline starts, now"

"Understood" said Gaiter

And Allan Wheeler also made note, so there was now 3 validations of the beginning of formal responses to the President's condition.

Peter Barrett and O'Malley were often in conflict about logistics regarding Presidential itinerary and line of authority decisions, but he did have to admit, Coughlin O'Malley was one of the most effective and efficient chiefs-of-staff he had ever worked with...he would give O'Malley a longer leash until he was given reason not to...but, as he had learned, O'Malley rarely gave reason to pull back that leash...but Barrett had *his* responsibilities, and would carry them out, if he needed to, in support of the office.

Dr. Gaiter was already, almost absently, making additions to the items he would need to set up a fully functional monitoring scheme in the President's bedroom...and then he turned as O'Malley was heading to the door..."but Cough...I have the authority in matters like this...the Service may have the protocol, but the welfare of the President is my province...*I* will make the call to move him if the situation warrants...at the moment, I agree it is not warranted...as the President does not appear to be in danger, so let's gather more data."

"Agreed" said O'Malley, "he looks more peaceful than I have seen him in months, Doc...but hell yes, more information...and you *definitely* make the call."

Allan Wheeler, who was listening anxiously to Gaiter and O'Malley discuss next steps inserted himself forward, as only Secret Service can do, and joined the conversation...

"Mr. O'Malley, Dr. Gaiter...I recommend the USMC Heli-1 at E-condition amber: medical stand-by, if I might..." Wheeler had been by Ashley's side literally since before the election...O'Malley looked at Wheeler...

"Yes, Allan...that's a good idea...make it happen. Thank you."

Wheeler started speaking into the transmitter on his wrist...

"All set, sir", and returned to his vigil.

O'Malley then went over to the First Lady..."she's spent...hollow" he was thinking..."just teetering forward and backward, rocking in place"...

"Liz...do you have a moment to talk?...or would you like me to come back?"

"Yes, Cough, come back please"

Mrs. Ashley looked completely drawn and solemn...

"In a little while then...maybe we'll have tea"...and O'Malley turned softly and exited the bedroom. As soon as he was out of earshot down the hall he dialed up Li Ming, the COS for the First Lady, on his cell...

"Yes Mr. O'Malley?"...

"Has Mrs. Ashley had her meds this morning?"

O'Malley came to the top of the residence stairs...

"No sir, not yet...just waiting for her to return to the office"

"Please go to the bedroom and bring her back...I do not think she is doing well...understandably, but things might get much worse, and she should be getting her medication support...ok?"

"Yes sir...on my way"

In an instant, the brilliant voice of Italian tenor Andrea Bocelli, bountifully filled the room...his early 21$^{st}$ century rendition of Domine Deus, the aria from Rossini's ***"Petite Messe Solennelle"*** opera...Jared Faulkner had a special cell service which routinely changed his cell jingle using artists he himself had chosen...it was updated constantly. Bocelli was nearly finished as Faulkner, barely awake, began fumbling for his phone. Faulkner rubbed his eyes, looking for the clock...it was only 3:02 am... the Clinical Investigation he was authoring and had fallen asleep reading went flying... "what the hell?, I'm not on call tonight"...he could function on 4 hours sleep almost anytime, but tonight, was exhausted from a particularly demanding clinical and OR schedule the previous day, and didn't have precious time to waste on middle of the night phone calls, whether prank or otherwise, so this was nothing but annoying, and he was ready to let the caller have it...

"Jared" said a voice.

Faulkner immediately shook off his slumber, *and* annoyance...the voice on the other end of the line was Dr. Malcolm Bennett, Chief of Neurology and Neuroscience at Stanford University Medical Center, Faulkner was on Bennett's 'first call' team should a determined crisis situation arise... and it had...

"we have an A2 situation..."

Dr, Jared Faulkner had been scheduled to oversee a procedure at 7:10 am, a type of neuro-corrective surgery he was rapidly becoming recognized in as a world-class specialist...but that procedure had been cancelled by

Bennett. A1 would have been an in-house emergency, A2 was everywhere else.

"There should be a car waiting for you outside ...give a look", in fact, as Faulkner passed through to his living room, there were 2 cars idling out there...

"I see them" said Faulkner rubbing his eyes again..."looks like a state car and a dark suburban or something"...

"That'll be the Secret Service I expect" said Bennett..."look Jared, don't pack anything, it'll all be taken care of, just dress, take your I-Med laptop and M-tablet, and get out there as fast as you can...you can wash up on the plane...you're going to D.C. Dr. Gaiter, the President's personal physician called at 2:30 our time..."

Just then, the chimes on the front door clanged, and Bennett finished by telling him that equipment he might need was already being loaded at the airport, and he would be briefed on route,

"Keep in touch"... said Bennett, then added ..."if you can", and hung up.

Everyone was there except the VP's COS when O'Malley came in with Jackson.

"Morning everyone, we have a situation... this is Dr. Jackson, for those of you who have not met him, from Walter Reed... Doctor"

O'Malley stepped back to behind his desk. Jackson then described what the current status of the President's condition was as they had determined, there were, understandably, a few gasps... and sobs.

"He is in every way, except one, in very good shape... he is not, and has not been, conscious, that we are aware of, since last evening around 11:50 when he retired with the First Lady... beyond that, all we can say with assurance as of 3 minutes or so ago, is, he continues sleeping at this hour"...

"Sleeping?" asked Mike Jennis the WH Communications Director incredulously, "what do you mean, sleeping?".

"Just that" said Jackson, "the President is sleeping...soundly...in no discomfort that we can presently ascertain, but specialists and equipment are on the way."

"Well, why don't we move him to a medical facility... what's the problem?"

O'Malley spoke then, "the President *will* be moved, if conditions warrant... at the moment, they appear not to... all vital signs are within normal limits, no bleeds have been found, he is responding to external stimuli exactly as he should, like reflexing, facial grimacing when shouted at, that kind of thing, he does all this with one very noted exception... he remains unconscious... Dr. Gaiter has sent several vials of the President's blood for analysis to Walter Reed, results are expected shortly, faxed to the med office upstairs... as Dr. Jackson has said, specialists will be arriving here presently, with a higher level of expertise in neurology... let's give them a chance for a full neuro-examination, complete with equipment tests, *before* we go green to a medical center... we have loose ends to tie together, and serious work to do as far as determining what is causing this condition... all of you need to address today's normal work as quickly as possible, then be prepared for this current situation as it further evolves... so let's get to it... one more thing, this is a total lock-down situation... no one speaks to the press or sources until we gather more info here... understood?"

Everyone nodded... O'Malley knew that if the President was moved for whatever length of time, the Ashley Presidency would be effectively over... the Vice-President would pounce to consolidate power, move all his people in, and all Ashley's out..."after a respectful period of time"... O'Malley was thinking 3 days...most likely, less...he finished as Phil Bailey (Bails) the Secret Service second in command at the WH came right in...

"Langley wants to start a complete review with the Service regarding every detail of the President's schedule starting last night prior to the President retiring, and working back from there..."

"OK" said O'Malley,

"I can have Dante pull everything for review down to the Sit Room... plus, we'll have total secure information access...I'll send him down right now to get things going..."

"Maybe the President has had a reaction to something he ate or drank?" Jennis wouldn't quit with the questions..."is he diabetic?...my uncle is, and this kind of thing can happen I guess..."

Jackson answered, "the President has no known history of diabetes in his family, is not falling into discernible risk, but we have checked that previously, and we are checking again now with the bloods already drawn",

He looked at his watch...

"Good" said O'Malley, and ended the meeting..."we all have things to do people...I'll call you back periodically as needed. Thank you".

The team stood and started leaving the office...

"Jill", press secretary Jill Monroe, "a standard flu release please...and going into the weekend, that's perfect...if anyone wants details, Dr. Gaiter can speak to the press later this morning..."

"This is a wait and see situation Jill. I don't particularly like the idea of deliberately giving misinformation, but the only thing we know at the moment is that the President is un-arousable...possibly from a virus... *that* as yet has not been ruled out...so we are in uncharted territory here." O'Malley was uncomfortable with deception. He did not like it when *he* was deceived, and struggled with it when confronted with doing it himself.

"Yes, I understand." said Monroe, "we'll work something up sufficiently vague and send it quickly to you for clearance." She looked at her watch.

"Give me ten minutes."

"Thanks Jill." Monroe started toward the corridor.

"... and Jill, this could get pretty rough, in short order...expect the White House reporters, if they get a whiff of anything skewed, to be all over your office. There have been strange reports bubbling out of other countries this morning, which frankly, I don't know what to make of.... my advice is just to stay frosty, ok?"

"Got it" said Monroe, and left the office.

Stephanie Angelo was already on-route to Washington, having received the call from the Neuro-Chief at MGH in Boston just before waking up... Dr. Angelo's specialty was neuroscience, more specifically, neuro-biology and anatomy with a sub-specialty in neuro-genetics, and had been running a lab at MGH for almost 3 years.

"I would have gone myself" said Ed Winthrop, Chief of Neuroscience at the General, "but I'm still on the mend from that damn hip replacement...Dr. Angelo is my first choice, no question."

With medical degrees from Dartmouth and then Harvard, a residency in the prestigious Blanev Neurology Center in Austria, and breakthrough research at MGH, she was a star on the rise, a brilliant physician. She was getting briefed by Jackson and the Secret Service on secure channels as they flew the military corridor from Boston to Washington...

"Yes, yes, and you say no evidence of any bleeds at all?" she typed into her laptop..."pupil reactivity?...flexor 1 and 2 tests are negative?...and no tremors however slight in the extremities?" she burrowed into her database link to the General...

"Ok, who is with him now?...do they have a portable EEG yet?...ok...we will need that right away...no need to shave his head for first runs...what else has been done?" she was speaking with Gaiter who filled the spaces Angelo was looking for.

"How close to Washington are you?"

Angelo looked at the Agent, "when will we be getting there?"

"10 minutes to landing, then another 5 to disembark, 10 more to the White House"...

She went back to the secure line, "25-30 minutes we will be there, please try to get that EEG done before I get there, thanks...oh, and digitally record it please, we may want to ship it out for DCA (diagnostic-comparison analysis)...thanks" and hung up.

Angelo made additional notes after the conversation, including initial impressions of the President's condition...heart attack or stroke, and if stroke, likely in posterior regions of the brain.

The agent across from her looked straight ahead...nervously, but coldly too... "these guys must be at the hair-trigger right about now"...she thought.

Dr. Gaiter had just finished another full round of vital systems checks when he noticed the President's eyelids began fluttering wildly…"he's dreaming" he said to himself…in fact, the President was consumed in a completely new trough of dreaming…as yet, unknown to science. His body remained completely motionless in the upstairs family bedroom of the White House in Washington, DC…while his mind (and more) was somewhere else altogether.

Stephen Ashley came to with a start. He was leaning heavily against what appeared to be the front of a corrugated metal work shed. It was rusted and neglected. It was also just one room and functioned as a house for an extended family of nine. Pans clanging sounded like someone was cooking inside. Ashley thought it might be early evening by the looks of things. And it was humid. Unbearably so. His clothes stank, and were torn in many places. He had no shoes, and stood ankle deep in foul excrement ridden mud. Human waste mixed with wet slimy earth and all manner of other trash. He gagged, stepping on somewhat drier ground.

A group of boys, 10 or 11 year olds, came running by, laughing and shouting in Spanish.

"Where am I?" he called as they ran by.

"Hombre blanco el stupido" one of them said, laughing and giving him the finger.

In fact, he was in one of the horrific slums on the western edges of a major South American city…near the mines. He looked up the long alleyway the boys followed, and moved that way. The air was thick with awful smells and crying. He passed more and more of the dilapidated shacks with alleys splintering in all directions. An impoverished maze of misery. A small naked child was sitting in the fetid mud putting handfuls of something rancid to his mouth. Ashley threw-up at seeing it.

The slum went on and on. After an eternity of walking the long snake-like passage, it was now dark. He heard several shots, a woman screaming, then more shots, and silence. He walked faster and fell out onto what appeared to be a main artery of transit. It had a semi-paved road in serious disrepair, and numerous aging but colorful 2-story cement store-fronts of bars and prostitution houses. The boys he had followed were horsing around in front of the brothel hoping to see something lurid. Men were drunk or smoking crack in the alleys between the buildings.

Ashley turned when he felt a sharp pain in his back.

"Signor...give us your money"

Two men, both smaller than Ashley, stood smiling with very bad teeth. One had a knife, the other what looked like an ice pick.

Ashley reached into his pockets and turned them inside out.

"Nothing"

"ring...chain...?"

The man with the knife was moving it around menacingly.

Ashley looked at his fingers...his rings were gone.

"no, no jewelry"

They both started to circle around him, moving their weapons with precision. Ashley was getting nervous...even scared. He could not watch both of them at the same time. One in front, one behind. The man with the knife, in front of Ashley, suddenly slapped him, hard across the face.

The blow jarred him, igniting his sweaty face. The man held his hand up, starting laughing, taunting, as the tip of the ice pick ran up and down his back. Ashley had no military service, and had virtually no self-defense skills, but he quickly stepped to the side and put his fists up...ready for their next move.

Just then, several emergency and military vehicles raced around the corner, almost hitting them. The knife and ice pick were put away in a flash. Both men now smiling and waving at the men in the trucks.

"What's going on?" hollered Ashley keeping his balance.

"Cave in at the mine" shouted the driver.

Abruptly, everything changed. Everyone started running, including the two men shaking him down. They were trying to keep up with the vehicles.

As the cries grew, hundreds of people filled, and headed down, the road. He watched as men emptied from the bars, prostitutes scampering to keep up.

Now he was alone in this awful, awful place. He wondered what had happened to him that he was now in a place like this. This did not feel like a dream.

"Is this hell?" he thought.

"*AM I IN HELL*?" he yelled it out while he turned in a tight circle. No one answered. He considered yelling it again. A gust of very hot wind kicked up dust into his eyes and mouth. He began spitting...and it hit him...he was acutely aware of *everything*...he stood still, trying to sort it out in his head. "I am *reflecting* on what I am hearing...and *thinking* about the surroundings, *responding* to them"...he looked around again to make sure those thugs were really gone...

"I can even smell the whiskey" he gave a second look...

"no, something is very wrong...this is *really* happening...I have to get out of here..." and turned in the direction where the military vehicles came from, and headed quickly down the darkened road.

Secret Service also had responsibilities in the G-6 Neuro Response Protocol...to vet the inevitable replacements that would occur from the original list...neither Dr. Faulkner, age 33, nor Dr. Angelo, age 32, were primary list choices...the Chairs of the departments were, so Faulkner and Angelo's backgrounds were in play, and they had to be cleared. Neither an unusual nor, in this case, a difficult task, as both were recipients of grant monies from the NIH, but Faulkner was primarily listed as a surgeon, and that needed clarification. So calls were made as to why he was sent instead of someone else...the White House did not request a surgeon as such...and that might trouble things a bit. Dr. Bennett cleared it up in one sentence,

"He's both, many of these folks at the top do multiples of things exceptionally well, Dr. Faulkner has privileges as both a neurosurgeon and a neuroscience researcher. I'll send his latest accomplishment list..."

He was also something of a rock star in pushing radical neuroscience research...he was on several international teams fusing multiple branches of medicine and physical design nano-technology together, ambitiously pursuing better 21$^{st}$ century tools for improving clinical outcomes. Jared Faulkner was a student of the information age, and the more information, especially in brain research, the better.

Stephanie Angelo's plane landed precisely as the agent had said, 10 minutes. They were off the jet and in the suburban suvs' in less than 5 minutes, and now on route to the White House.

"The news has not leaked yet " Dr. Angelo was thinking...

"No one in the Capitol knows…no one in the **country** knows" she looked at the Service agent, wondering what *he* was thinking…all sorts of scenario's starting marching through her mind…could our Chief Executive be a victim of a man-made organism of stealth? Bio-terrorism? (she had seen a movie a few years back with George Clooney as a government researcher in the Center for Disease Control (CDC) or somewhere who had to figure out a cure for the President, a victim of bioterrorism, against the clock as she recalled…and Clooney was, not surprisingly, successful)…did the Secret Service fail to protect the President?, the nation?…what if this was a high-tech targeting action by a foreign government or group?…and she calmed her mind down by reminding herself that this appears to be stroke or neurological failure of some kind…not a crises precipitated from external means.

"I have to stop, I'm thinking a little bit like my brother" she thought.

The vehicles did not move faster than surrounding traffic, nor gave any alerting signals that they were "VIP" personnel, and entered the grounds of the White House, stopping at the Secret Service entrance to the West Wing completing an 8-minute trip.

"Doctor" said the agent from the plane getting out and opening her door, "the equipment you requested in-flight is following after" he checked his watch, "less than 20 minutes it will be here."

She knew she could rely on that estimate, and went in…

Coughlin O'Malley was on a secure line to the Capitol Building, the Speaker's Office. "He's comfortable, everything that the doctors *can* measure without being invasive, is, or will be, right here...there are specialist's on route, and equipment...I'll make sure your office gets an update regardless, every 30 minutes or so...(O'Malley made another mental note to have the WH Communication office pop out updates every 30 minutes to high-level government figures for the immediate foreseeable future)..ok then...if you have any questions, Mr. Speaker, send them by secure fax to Mrs. Freitas please, and we'll do our best to address them quickly...but for now, that's all I have...and, at least for now, the press has not been made aware...we are drafting a statement...so please Mr. Speaker, no leaks...at least until we release our statement?"

The Speaker said this was a national security issue, and on a NTK basis only (Need To Know)...there would be no loose ends from the Capital... O'Malley accepted his wishes on behalf of Congress for a favorable outcome, and hung up.

He called Dante Espinal to make sure the Situation Room was focused, and got a beep from Service....

"Exploring possibilities...when r u free?"

He called Bail's... "where are you?"

"In Pete's office with the Chief and Jeremy Fitch from Langley...we want to pound the ground to look for possible explanations" he paused, then went on, "if there are any...who, what, when, where...that sort of thing... this may be or may not be useful, depending on what the specialists find out, but we need to act as if something untoward has happened, and try to nail it down if we can...so we are going to the SR, can you meet us there?"...

"Yes...give me 10 minutes".

He checked with the Comm Director, a press release was issued that the President's formal schedule had been cancelled for the day due to what appeared to be flu-like symptoms...Dr. Gaiter would be issuing a more detailed statement later in the morning. That's good, thought Cough, but we need to get on that formal draft of the actual circumstances, and circulate it for comment among staff...he called Jennis to get that officially going and then pulled his Plan 6 from his safe...he scanned it as he walked to the Sit Room...

"Chief-of-Staff of the President, was, on behalf of the administration and the American people, to contact the leadership of our major allies, through the Office of the President, with assurances that the constitutional process would be formally initiated once a conclusive diagnosis was determined by G-6 diagnosticians...it was *with certainty* that the constitutional steps be mentioned so as to allay allies possible unease."

Jeremy Fitch already had a CIA power point of names, meetings, food, beverages, even medications which officially had been logged regarding the activities of the President in the last 48 hours up on the room's big screen, one of the smaller screens was showing a CNN crawler that the President had the flu scrolling across the bottom. Fitch was speaking as he came in.

"So nothing in...oh, hi Cough" O'Malley nodded..."so nothing in the last 2 full days show anything unusual in terms of unofficial contacts to the President...so we will have to be certain about **personal** contacts here in the White House and food, etc., before we start looking beyond it...so please look at your briefings in front of you and confirm we have everything down..."

The team was reviewing when Gaiter hurried into the room...O'Malley stood up, Gaiter was ashen...

"Doc...what's happened?...has something *happened* to the President?"

Gaiter held up his hand, shook his head no...and took a moment to compose himself...

"One of the calls I have to make...one of the calls I *made* I mean...was to Dr. McMasters, he's a dual-citizenship researcher from Ottawa, one of the best in the field, he was on his way and he called me...his plane had been officially turned around", he paused, looked scared, "Cough, the Prime Minister of Canada is unconscious."

The blood drained instantly from the room. No one spoke while the sounds of the words soaked into them...

"the Prime Minister"...the other head of state in North America was now down. Jeremy Fitch got on his cell immediately to get confirmation from Langley.

It was only the beginning.

Within 2 minutes, Fitch got confirmation.

"The RCMP (Canadian Protective Policing Detail) has acknowledged... it sounds like the same thing...they can't wake him up. This changes the equation. We need to get Justice in, and NSA...the stakes are entirely different...this cannot be treated as a coincidence...something's going on..."

O'Malley left the room, heading for his office. Gaiter catching up to him,

"Cough...what the hell is happening?"

"Well, I was hoping you would be able to tell me, Doc...you still might..." Gaiter took a deep breath.

"Yes, I expect the Bureau and Service will want full blood screenings and toxicologies now, in addition to what has already been sent...and full viral and bacterial ID's...I better get ahead of it"...

"Yes Doc, and word of this **<u>cannot</u>** get out...I do not want to stress that enough...not until we secure the VP...under law, in the line of succession, he is or will be the acting CIC while the President is incapacitated...and that", he checked his watch, "is underway as we speak...you get that blood chemistry stuff off...thanks."

The doctor headed back into the residence. O'Malley stood on the stair landing... "incapacitated"...he didn't like that word...didn't like what it was beginning to taste like...

"O'Malley" he said to himself, "you'd better get this right"...and headed to his office. It was 8:49 am EDT, officially almost 9 hours in from when the President retired.

Dr. Angelo's personal agent escorted her right through the checkpoints and on up to the hallway outside the President's bedroom.

"It was a pleasure, Doctor" said the agent, "please wait here for either Dr. Gaiter or Dr. Jackson to bring you in" and headed back toward the stairwell.

Angelo looked up and down the corridor...6 agents, 2 on cell phones, 1 at a desk computer just south of what she presumed was the entrance to the President's bedroom. She walked to the desk. The agent paused, looked up, and locked hard, uncomfortable eyes with her.

"Yes Dr.?...something I can do?"

"No. thank you...just a bit nervous I guess..."

"Yes ma'am...understood" and returned his focus to his task.

The bedroom door opened then, Dr. Jackson emerged, extended his hand, "I'm Dr. Omer Jackson, second attendant to the President. Please, come in Dr. Angelo."

He took her coat, stepped aside, followed her in.

"The First Lady has just gone to her office, I'll make sure she knows you're here...she's anxious to get something more than what we've been giving I'm afraid, even with the equipment."

The monitors O'Malley had requested were here, and the President was wired up for the basics, cardio rhythm, respirations, oxygen saturation, and had an IV in running with basic saline...Jackson had also left access for venous blood draws, already had used it in fact, sending more vials to the Reed for analysis, he sent an arterial blood gas too, just to cover the bases...Angelo looked at the President, then at Jackson...

"He's smiling...wait"...and got much closer, moving to the left side of the bed..."no, he's definitely smiling"...it was contagious in fact, and she smiled too...

"I'm expecting some equipment Dr. J...can somebody check on that?"...

"Yes, instructions are to bring it post haste...Service will check it of course, but they know the urgency..."

Angelo opened her bag (that too was checked on the plane) and pulled her stethoscope...as she started her examination, she placed the diaphragm on the right carotid artery of the President, then the left...she was listening for "anything unusual"...but there was nothing.

"He appears to be a very fit man" she said pulling the covers down to his waist...she auscultated his heart and respiratory motions...she glanced up at agent Allan Wheeler as she palpated the President's femoral arteries...

"Agent..."

"Wheeler ma'am, Allan Wheeler"...

"Agent, the President is in his altogether here, might I ask you to swing to this side of the bed for a couple minutes?...this way, you can protect the President's privacy by shielding him from the doorway as I finish my exam..."

"Yes ma'am, certainly" Wheeler took the new position as Angelo pulled all the covers off.

Getting a couple of instruments from her bag, she started at his feet with a series of maneuvers testing neural communications...reflexes and such, general indicators of neural integrity and basic brain health...watching his entire body as she manipulated it, and found nothing unusual...she re-arranged the bed linen, and focused on the President's head.

"Thank you Agent Wheeler" Wheeler returned to his position, facing the door.

"Doctor Angelo", Jackson was speaking as he came back in from a cell call..."the President's COS has asked for updates and summaries of the President's condition..."

"Of course...and can we discreetly get some pajamas on the President at some point?" said Angelo, "and yes" she said turning to Jackson, "I'll enter whatever findings into my laptop...we have software which will frame and index everything, I'll add comments....also, I'll instruct my drone agent send them every 30 minutes...I'm breaking into the monitoring stream using this wireless connection...it's pretty standard at The General...I've already added a transmitter..." Jackson was impressed...

"I'll ask if there is some line you can tap into and send it straight to the Sit Room"...

"Great...they can get the monitor transmission in real time, and the software can provide interpretation...terrific".

Jackson got motioned to the door...

"The neural scanner is coming up, sir" said a voice.

"Dr. Faulkner is due to land in 46 minutes..." Angelo spun around...

"Which Dr. Faulkner?"...the Service agent stepped into sight...

"Dr. Jared Faulkner ma'am...flying in from ..."

"Stanford" said Angelo finishing the sentence.

"Yes ma'am, do you know Dr. Faulkner?..."

"Yes, I know him, or rather, of him.....he's very likely the most provocative thinker in the field at the moment...boy, you guys are connected" she smiled, and turned back to the president.

"I'd better get that EEG started...the first runs will be from the standard EEG in use today, we have a beta-model which is magnitudes more sensitive...but we will have to wait for that." Angelo wheeled the bizarre looking contraption over to the bedside. "There is absolutely no danger to the patient, to the President, when we take these measurements. I will be attaching multiple electrodes to his face neck and head held in place with non-allergenic adhesive." So she attached them all over his head, and after plugging the machine in (it could run on batteries), she ran a pilot calibration, then, after a brief pause, ran 10 minutes of actual brain activity tracing.

Jeremy Fitch and Phil Bailey had scrutinized the President's schedule, contacts and consumables (in the process, vetting the WH food service and culinary staff again) all the way back to Sunday 10:30 pm when the Presidential contingent returned to the White House from a conference weekend in New York at the United Nations. The International Economic, Climate and Human Rights Initiative was the most ambitious international conference in a decade. More delegations participated from more countries than ever in the history of the United Nations. Kings, Princes, Prime Ministers and Presidents were in consultations and signings of multi-party, multi-state agreements all weekend.

There were state sponsored dinners and speeches, caucuses of voting-blocs forming and re-forming, all driving toward the much anticipated final signing agreement...the Climate Restoration Accord... but frenetic lobbying by the world's growing economies derailed the accord in the final hours. Energy needs, and costs, once again trumped all considerations and it's disagreeable embedded harsh global penalties were finally seen as too restrictive. The scientific establishment had "not made the ironclad case", the world's energy producers claimed through embedded diplomatic channels, and energy consumers would not sacrifice despite the growing and alarming signals...besides, there were more and more "cleaner technologies" in use...the world needed everything it could muster, what with 9 billion or so human beings.

One of those alarming signals being a steady increase in ocean level now measured at **11** centimeters in Bangladesh...driving hundreds of thousands further into the country inland and dislodging more waves, millions, of human beings with each passing year. The President of the United States had once again maintained a position which effectively neutralized the more ambitious ministers to pull a significant global change effort together. Ashley was not particularly impressed with the US position, but domestically, the US was slowly and surely putting the technology pieces in place so *it's* energy needs would be met completely and independently from any other nation or economy with majority pieces now in "green technologies" or as some were calling them, "*our* internal emerging economies"...and after months of discussions and preparations, the US did not see the need to de-stabilize the poorer, less independent nations with economic catastrophe. In the end, at least now, it was all about economics. Despite the failure to agree however, there were several lower level agreements of significance which regionally would continue and accelerate the existing alternative energy revolution and conservation efforts, and great progress was made on a new, far reaching, human rights initiative.

Little progress however had been made to end the multi-state African War ...there was scant intervention beyond a superpower alliance and

UN initiative to slow the flow of arms...every treaty had ended in ruin, state civilian/refugee populations were constantly under the growing shadows of conflict and death...and so far, the world community had been unable to agree how to stop it. The nightmare was in its 28th month...with countries at the shifting edges even now being desperately drawn in. The United States had sponsored several iterations of multi-nation ceasefire plans and one firm peace accord with the Democratic Republic of the Congo and its neighbors, Uganda and Rwanda...all tumbling to failure.

After reviewing the emerging global pattern, Fitch believed that something had happened *here*...in New York...something they would have to tease out of a wider picture...whether this was a direct assault on the President, or on an aide who would confer at close personal contact with the President was an unknown, but another reason the conference went to the top of the interest list was the Canadian Prime Minister...he, and the entire Canadian diplomatic PM delegation, were at the conference.

The Justice Department had worked for weeks on the UN conference. Given the size and scope, the New York State Police, local NYPD, Secret Service, coordinating with individual delegations (some here for the first time), extended personal protectors for ambassadors and participating country leaders. There were hundreds of FBI agents and federal marshals intermixed with UN and individual state security personnel...President Ashley was committed to absolute conference security despite the fractious global conditions..."not on my watch" is what he specifically said to O'Malley during the lengthy preparations...Fitch now believed that something vital had been missed...and the world, and most painfully, the North American alliance, was now paying for it. He would ask for immediate and thorough medical evaluations of all personnel who had been part of the Presidential delegation...and contact Canadian intelligence, asking them if they hadn't, would they do the same with the delegation from Canada.

In the months leading up to the conference, a mountain of new passport requests needed investigation, special foodstuffs had to be cleared, even some animal clearances...the point being that virtually every participant had to be vetted. No human being who did not receive prior approval was present...or so the authorities believed.

Frank Willow, the Secretary of State's COS was on the phone to O'Malley, it was 11:16 am EDT.

"We're coming home early, Cough...the meeting with the Egyptian President has been re-scheduled to when he comes to the state's in July... So what about that re-match?...this time I'll kick your ass"...

O'Malley immediately asked for details,

"Why was the meeting shelved Frank?"...

"Some matter of urgent family business is what they said...and that's fine with us...this has been a killer 10-days...first the conference in New York, then over here for 5 days, we're happy to get the EO"...

O'Malley was still stuck on the reason for the cancellation...but let it go to ask, "How is the Secretary?...his health?"...

"Fine, I guess...all of us are tired though...we'll catch some Z's on the flight"...

O'Malley stiffened...

"Ok, see you back in Washington, Frank..."

Cough called Fitch, "State is returning early from Egypt...cancelled meeting with President Nassaram...I would like some inside info on this...can you get?"

Fitch said yes, and would contact his source.

"I'll get back to you shortly".

Cough was in his office to make some discreet calls within diplomatic channels...he was beginning to sweat a little...he did not like the looks of the possible emerging picture...he would call Britain first, then Japan, then Israel...and hope he would not hear anything having to do with "illness" or "vacationing" regarding the country leadership...

He would also call the US Ambassador to China for discreet but clarifying details on the nature of the Premier's illness.

Jared Faulkner M.D., Ph.D. was just pulling up to the West Wing entrance when his car was waived forward...the Vice President had returned by military transport from Brazil, and was just coming in behind. Faulkner was not a big fan of this administration to tell the truth, he did not care for the distaste that the Washington power base seemed to have for funding pure research...investigative medicine might lead somewhere, and might not, or it might take years, because even with today's tools, his craft remained an *art form* to some degree, a phrase which had been used relentlessly in slashing NIH financial support through grants and such, bottom-line: funding had been getting skewered for the last 2 years...he was cutting lab tech's and IT folks, this was personal with him, and this Vice President had much to do with fomenting the miserly positions... yet military spending was at an all-time high...49 % of every tax dollar went to support the military in some way...it was indefensible as far as Faulkner was concerned, and he had spoken to that end in several of the advanced neuro-anatomy classes he conducted at Stanford.

"Dr. Faulkner, we'll just wait a moment until the Vice President is in the White House please..." his assigned agent was listening to the chatter on his earpiece...then, after 2 minutes...

"OK sir, we have the green light"...Faulkner was brought in the same way Stephanie Angelo had been, with no abbreviation at the front desk ...proceeding right to the residence...the VP had gone down to the Sit Room for a complete fill in.

Vice-President Hadley Willis was a career politician...starting as a representative in state government, state senator, then governor...a networked path steeped in power and ambition...he was not the President's first choice for running mate (not even his second) but he could swing the election for the party because of his regional power base...and that's exactly what happened.

The entire southeast voting bloc went Republican, and the election was over.

For the last 22 months he had been chiseling power away from the President by having Republican congressional and specific government department channels (like Defense) dialed in through him (reminiscent of another recent Republican administration)...

Stephen Ashley had already privately decided not to run in what was sure to be a very competitive cycle this coming election, he had had enough (it was an election he now wished he had never agreed to)... which left the door open for Hadley Willis, and now, with the President "incapacitated", he could effectively give things a trial run...speak to the nation...get some legislation saddled up which he had been secretly working with like-minded colleagues in the senate...the country would be supportive and understanding, as they always were when unexpected transitions occurred within the executive branch...and Willis was a master manipulator...yes, he could exploit this sympathy by the American public...and he *would* if given the chance...yes, this was going to work out just fine for Hadley Willis.

Everyone stood as the VP entered the Sit Room.

"Thankyall, an be seated evrra one...I wan tuh hear it awl now...from thuh beginnin...I'v been briefed a course, but give me everythin ahgin please..."

Mr. Willis on occasion lapsed into his syrupy Mississippi drawl.

Jared Faulkner was brought into the President's bedroom, his mobile neural PET and fMRI scanner wheeling in behind...Dr. Angelo was at a three quarter turn, back to the door sitting on the edge of the sofa, just starting to run her EEG interpretation software on the Apple laptop, she had wired President Ashley up to a basic EEG as soon as she finished her general neurologic exam...Jackson touched her on the shoulder...

"Oh...yes...Dr. Faulkner" she stood, turned, and extended her hand, "Stephanie Angelo, MGH"...Faulkner was entirely unprepared for her beauty, which she clearly tried to subdue...no make-up, rich long black shiny hair loomed back and up into a kind of ponytail flop at the back of her head. "This woman is striking" Faulkner was thinking...earthen brown eyes perfectly shaped and spaced, alluringly placed on a face with slightly high cheek bones and understatedly full lips and all blended together with an extraordinarily smooth complexion. He couldn't take his eyes off her. Jared Faulkner had worked, over the years with his share of beautiful women, nurses especially, but Stephanie Angelo was simply breathless...he was mesmerized by her. By her form fitting thin black sweater and shapely casual grey slacks...

"Doctor?" said Angelo, "You have an exceedingly long handshake, even for **our** profession" and smiled. Faulkner hadn't even noticed...he was completely lost in those bottomless earthen eyes.

"Sor-r-ry Doctor...I don't usually do that, I apologize" releasing her hand.

"Perfectly alright...I've heard a lot about you" and smiled again. "I'm glad we've had a chance to meet."

Allan Wheeler, who had taken all this in and knew exactly what Faulkner was thinking, looked to the floor and grinned broadly.

Faulkner nodded, tried to look away, embarrassed, then looked over at the President...motioned for the scanner to go to the other side of the bed...he quickly took in the monitor screen, and the readouts. He then put his professional hat on as best he could manage it.

"You've done an EEG then, Dr. Angelo?"

"Yes...just running it all through the EE-Synch software...here...take a look"...she sat down placing the laptop on the long mahogany coffee table...

"Gorgeous table" said Faulkner still standing, "looks early 18th century", he ran his long elegant fingers over the 200 year old master scrollwork... Angelo noticed immediately...

"I'm afraid I don't know my colonial era craftsmanship very well" said Angelo smiling, but now appreciating the piece...

"This being the White House" said Faulkner, "likely made for one of the early President's...Jefferson or Madison perhaps...Philadelphia was a craftsman's hotbed I believe" and rattled off even a few well known artisan names from that period, "and New York...this is an exquisite piece"...

Even Agent Wheeler was paying attention...

"Fascinating" said Angelo...locking eyes with him again.

"Oh, ok, here it comes"...the graphical readouts were digital and would automatically brake at any anomaly...the software did not stop thru the entire run...Angelo read the software first run conclusions...

"Normal, with high activity levels in the Beta regions" (the Beta wave readings gave a strong measure of attentiveness)...the President's were measuring high to very high normal..."doesn't exactly present like the observable condition...but there it is"...

Faulkner asked Angelo to bring frame index 006:26 up again...he noticed something...a "ridge abnormality" he called it...she brought it back up...

"Yes, there..." he pointed to an unpronounced variation in an inflection, then another, three cycles later. Angelo looked at the tremor in the single upward tracing at 006:26, then the other one...

"Artifact?" she asked.

"Perhaps...but whatever it is, this may be indicative..."

Faulkner turned, looked hard at Stephen Ashley...

"Doctor" he was talking to Angelo without visually addressing her..."do you recall if anyone was speaking during the test?"...Angelo thought for a moment...

"No one spoke" she looked at Allan Wheeler, he nodded to confirm..."just the 3 of us in the room...no one spoke"...

"Ok" said Faulkner, "let's run it again please?...this time talking to the President...then again when Mrs. Ashley joins us...if we could?" Angelo nodded and graphically marked both sections which showed the variation with a note to the team back at MGH...

"What might this be?"

Faulkner spoke again, to no one in particular...

"In my experience, this is a highly unusual reading...the President needs to listen to someone speaking, and someone he knows...and pose a few questions to him...and we need to measure his brain's responses while it's processing all that."

Coughlin O'Malley and WH Chief Legal Counsel Paul Carson were pulling at the line of succession legalities in his office...

"Look, Cough, I know you are not fond of the VP, but you basically have no choice...there is precedent established, the 25th Amendment for gawd sake..."

"I know, I've read it...but the President is **not** dead, Paul, and Omer Jackson just called to tell me his first EEG results are normal to high normal...mind telling me how a high normal EEG reading fits section 1 of the amendment?...look, I just want to delay this transition until we have irrefutable evidence he is unable to continue...he never signed any authorization document, so we are in a no man's land here I think...I mean jeez, Paul, the VP is down in the Sit Room right now, and he'll have Jim Snell moving into my office before the sun goes down...I need a legal avenue to delay...to stall this...give us time to find out what the hell is going on, that's all...ok...can you review our constitutional options... and give something I can chew on here?"...O'Malley held up his hand for a moment... "an advisory opinion, Paul...written by the CLC for the White House...specifically addressing the line of succession pathway and plow into it the different legal definitions of incapacitation in light of current science...section 4 of the 25th amendment has, in my opinion, exploitable loopholes...this has to have substantial referencing and I'll get it signed by the Attorney General after your signature of authorship... Paul, remember, all I need is a delaying tactic...I need something that will be a serious legal stonewall, well thought out"...Carson considered it for a moment...

"Willis will have to get all the Secretaries together to vote this...if the 25th is followed properly and that'll take time...ok...delay huh?...to keep the VP from running the show?...alright...I'll jump into it...I'm not exactly thrilled by the idea of Willis getting antsy with the full throttles of power either Cough, ...ok, we'll run with it"...

"All I want...thanks...and Paul...we need it 5 hours ago"...

"Understood"

Carson exited the office as O'Malley's secretary buzzed his urgent line....

"Ambassador Williams, Cough, calling from Beijing"...

He imagined the temperature at least in the mid-nineties as the sun seared into his back. As he came to, he was hanging, in a climbing harness, on a sheer rock face, 1000 or so feet above the ground…

"WHOA…" he was looking over his left shoulder and clutching fast the very taut rope. His heart was pounding in his chest….he was *not* a fan of heights. The landscape was nothing but cliffs and deep ravines…he realized suddenly that there was talking below and above, and even what sounded like yelling or crying…he was suspended there, hundreds and hundreds of feet up…in a series of blue nylon straps, with little metal hooks on the waist belt and a cache of multicolored fabric rope tied in the back…one of those straps had a metal clip to which Ashley was tethered, fastened to the shear wall…he looked up, but started to spin some, and grabbed the rock face… "there's got to be twenty climbers ahead of me" and at least that many, looking down, between his legs, hanging below him…some of the climbers were clinging to the rock, others, like him, were just dangling there, spinning slowly…"and we're all strung together…wait", he thought, "I've seen that on the Discovery channel or National Geographic or somewhere, what is it called?…rappelling?.. no…belaying?…I'll have to remember to ask O'Malley"…and spoke it out loud…

"I'm not sure there is a name for just being strung together Mr. President… tethered maybe?" said a voice just above him. Ashley was startled…"At least I'm not familiar with it…unless it would be a tandem line…you know, for safety"…it was Petr Jorbin, the President of Finland, but Ashley did not recognize him with his helmet and climbing gear on…"Over the years", Jorbin said, "especially in my youth, mountaineering was an enjoyable hobby of mine…not now of course, but I remember some things" and felt a jerk on his line…"ok, we're all moving again…up we go"…Stephen Ashley was being pulled a little too by his harness as he reached for a handhold…then a foothold.

"I'm sorry", said Ashley straining a bit, "where is it exactly that we are?"…

"Ya" said Jorbin pulling himself up again, "none of us knows."

4:36 pm EDT...one of the streaming monitors in the Sit Room was carrying CNN when the news anchor delivered this, "CNN reports that South African leader Mutumbe Oko is "medically comatose"..." and "opposition leaders have called for new elections"...The Vice President looked at his blackberry for messages and hardly paid any attention...

"Ok, I'm headed tah the residence tah see the President"...he stood up, they all did, and he left.

O'Malley was coming down the 2-story staircase as Hadley Willis was going up...

"Mr. Vice President"...

"Cough"...and both kept on going...but Willis turned on the landing as O'Malley neared the bottom...

"Cough, I want Jim Snell to get with you at the earliest convenience to work out transition details..."

O'Malley said nothing...just nodded and kept moving toward the Sit Room. Lower level staff had now been pushed to the chairs lining the wall...the Situation Room had had 2 significant overhauls in the last 15 years...the needs of the executive branch for real time, up to the second information from an always on global community, whether it was meteorological, agricultural, economic, political or military activity, this need to know, and more importantly, to *do*, dictated the 2 transformations... the last one brought supercomputer crunching power in addition to regional real-time multi-screening of diplomatic and/or military summary report options...24 hours a day...the latest holographic software was also piped to the room...information was sent on a constant cycle because on any given day, two to four staff members were in the Sit Room sifting the possible important global developments. In addition, the need for the President to have audio-visual access to every American embassy, and every in-country American ambassador on multi-split screening was now necessary in such an always-ready, always in motion, world community.

The enhancements to the Situation Room now delivered that capability.

CIA and Justice had taken over the room...they were connected on secure audio and video to Langley of course, and the Hoover building, but the nerve center was here, the White House. William Sacks, Chief Investigative Officer for the International Bureau, chaired the FBI effort, he actually supervised a considerable staff both stateside and overseas... but was pulling together the latest pieces for the Homeland Security chief, Barb Jefferson, he was doing this under the newly assigned mission name: **<u>Aladdin's Lamp</u>**.

## Operation: Aladdin's Lamp.

In June of 1995, President William Clinton signed Presidential Decision Directive 39 which outlined which US agencies would play key positions in dispensing responses to terrorist attacks either within US borders or against US interests abroad. The State Department would lead any overseas response, and the FBI would do the same inside the US. A terrorist action was any which utilized nuclear, biological and chemical materials. President Barack Obama would add further, any economic action, covert or overt, taken against US banking, financial, commodity or securities institutions or systems. PDD 39 was in play now. CIA, FBI, NSA decision makers all believed that terrorism was at the root of this expanding nightmare. Protocol would be followed. In addition the DHS (Department of Homeland Security), a relatively young federal agency, created by President George W. Bush in response to the attacks of Sept. 11, 2001 on the WTC, Pentagon and Flight 93, had authority to coalesce and orchestrate any federal response to a mainland attack was at its highest alert status. Homeland Security was hovering at the fluid center of this crisis until more facts became clear.

"We have official confirmation from Israel, Prime Minister Nouriel Jacobi is 'in a coma-like condition'...cannot be aroused...my source also says the Israeli's have gently shocked the PM after everything else had failed to bring him around...President Ileah Corzon of the Philippines is 'not to be disturbed' with an 'unspecified illness'...Greece, Italy, The Republic of Georgia are all privately, thru diplomatic channels confirming something similar...but there are far more unofficial leads now appearing and indicating this as a global takedown, a worldwide calamity...this 'event' actually started yesterday along the Asia-Pacific rim with the commencement of the new day...so we are not" he checked the international times on the various monitors, "only 12 plus hours into this as we might have thought, we are a full 28 hours...however this thing is being executed, and this is my *personal* assessment, it is behaving it seems, if I can even use that term, with a kind of alignment with the 24 hour rotational cycle of the earth...bending around the globe...or at the very least a delay-action virus or bacteria or man-made organism"...

Barbara Jefferson, who was an administrator, not a scientist, was incredulous and immediately asked for possible explanations.

"Our goal Madame Secretary, is coordinating with the most powerful, most plugged-in, intelligence agencies in the world...we *are* one of course, and we are <u>already</u> exchanging as much information as is prudent presently, and the FSB believes they have found a few threads hidden in the just concluded UN Conference...we are meeting with them, the Brits, France and the Chinese, in addition to Canada and Israel...we are deliberately keeping this meeting closeted for the time being, but working groups are popping up on their own as more and more services share outcomes with their counterparts...this is comprehensive...what looks like a global assault on leadership...unprecedented in any era...cooperation and I dare say even suspicion is the guidance I can offer at the moment... but as far as exactly explaining what or how whatever is happening is happening is...frankly...beyond anyone at the moment...the intent, with our international colleagues, is to narrow the field of vision...eliminate causes...Jeremy has the current details and will walk us through them..."

The eyes in the room swung to the CIA man...

Now it was Fitch's turn.

"Thanks Bill. What I *can* say with assurance is the Agency has never schemed a hypothesis quite like what we see playing out here...neither has DARPA, the Bureau, or any of the think tanks we normally work with...but we have several teams working it now, with a premium on time...so let's see what these folks come up with, and apply some logic to it. When I say we have *never* schemed a scenario quite like this, it's true...

however, the Agency did game-out contingencies should Kennedy and Kruschev both be rendered non-players through some intervening action during the Cuban Missile Crisis, but we have reviewed conclusions and actions from that game-out, and dismissed it's applicability here". Fitch continued, "There is nothing credible to report from the powers of the global intelligence community (that includes us of course...many of them want to know what *we* might know, etc, etc.)...but the best possible lead geography is right here we think...in Manhattan...the United Nations. Starting 9 days ago, and lasting for 5, as you all know...and some of the people in this room participated...was the largest single gathering of global leadership in history...

And those unable or unwilling to attend themselves, had representatives here who then went straight home to report results and commitments to them...undeniable threads lead straight from New York right back to every capital on the planet...and to every leader.

This cannot be ignored, and is not...we have a round the clock team from the Bureau, with the power of the NYC terabyte supercomputers, crunching images, data, faces, suspicious or radical persons and groups who can be identified as having attended or participated in some way in this conference...there was, as always, a kind of security post-mortem on the conference...which was, is underway, at the Bureau, all aspects, and I mean *all*, and the Bureau, as I understand it is cautiously optimistic with the findings...this is because nothing of note occurred by way of overt untoward action at the conference as yet discovered...but it is clear now that we missed something, something very big... so the team will be looking at all that data again, and sifting the collected measurements from the hundreds of 'sniffers' scattered around the city...trying to find what the security folks may have missed the first time...both during the conference, and in the post-mortem that might be meaningful now. So, in our opinion, Madame Secretary, NYC and the UN in particular, is the nexus...I also want to say that every member of every delegation is being vetted <u>again</u>...something of this magnitude could not be carried out singlehandedly...at the very least, regional saboteurs would be necessary, as we see it...but it is all on the table now...nothing's out, as we say."

It was CIA, Fitch reported, that had asked in conference at Langley earlier in the day, questions as to whether we really know that *all* these identified leaders are really down?...and in that same line of thinking, what if this calamity has been orchestrated by a single government or cabal of leaders attending the conference?...if more than one delegation were involved, that would likely increase the chances of success for whatever was the designed intent...Fitch brought this up as an fyi to those in the room. What was problematic with the pursuit of intelligence to confirm *this* possibility is getting total verification...some of these governments were untrustworthy, even hostile...so a plan was needed to that end. Fitch laid out other provocative questions as well...but he and the agency were correct...verification was impossible.

This open-ended unknown made everyone in the room understandably uncomfortable...and agreeing there was an urgent need for the kind of plan Fitch spoke of.

It wasn't until Fitch had finished taking questions that his memory jarred loose a classified document he had read last year from the Army's Chemical and Biological Research Team..."Marker DNA Sequestered, Target Agent Delivered via Nano-particle".

"Madame Secretary, I just remembered a rather exotic paper written last year by a Dr. Helen Crosby, I believe...she's with the Army's CAB team at Ft. Dietrick...it might prove useful to review. I'll have Dr. Crosby join us here asap."

O'Malley met Fitch just prior to the Sit Room exit.

"I know that look, Jeremy...what line are you tacking here with this Dr. Crosby?"

Fitch looked left and right before answering, letting several junior staffers leave before speaking.

"Cough, there are ways to deliver, or at least *in-theory* there are ways, virtually any kind of toxic agent to specific populations only, right down to specific **persons** only...I had completely forgotten her brief on it. As I recall, if, and I'm reaching here, because to tell you the truth I understood only about half of what she was talking about, the genetic material is available, scientists can mark or target, any organism they want, and isolate their target from the entire surrounding environment... using a nano-particle as the delivery truck. I thought it was theoretical stuff, you know, positioning the research for more liberal funding...but now I'm not so sure." Fitch just kind of shrugged and added, "I'll dig up that research paper if you want..."

O'Malley nodded. "Yes, please...you think this has a ring to it?"

"We won't know, or at least I won't, until we get competent people in the room to have a go at the concept..." He looked at his watch..."I would like to have her located and here in 6 hours or less...and I'll make that clear to Service when I link up...they can use DOD for back-up if necessary."

Fitch left the Sit Room, heading to his poached West Wing office, to do exactly that.

Within 22 minutes, Dr. Helen Crosby had been located, with her family, at a local restaurant in downtown Frederick, Maryland...about 45 minutes outside of Washington, DC. The conversation at every table was centered on the global leadership reports:

"It has to be terrorism" from the booth behind Dr. Crosby

"I read a science fiction book that dealt with exactly this kind of thing... everybody in the town was taken over by some kind of alien life form...

it was a test before they took over the world..." from the booth across from them.

"I'm about halfway through my meal..." was what Dr. Crosby was saying on the phone to the Secret Service when they pulled in. They inquired at the desk where Dr. Crosby was located.

"Dr. Crosby, ma'am, may I speak with you in the foyer please"

She followed him into the waiting area which was conveniently empty... "May I see your credentials please ma'am?" The agent took little time confirming against his readout.

"If you'll be kind enough to follow me ma'am, we have an urgent need for your attendance in Washington" the agent gave no details inside the restaurant.

"I will wait 3 minutes for you to conclude your dinner engagement...I'm sorry ma'am, we are on a very tight timeline." Crosby hurried back to the table...she kissed her husband, and her daughter...

"I have to go, official business...I'll call you when I can...love you both", and was gone.

Dr. Crosby was one of the senior research scientists in the National Interagency Confederation for Biological Research at Ft. Detrick, a sprawling 1,200 acre military biomedical experimentation and analysis facility in Frederick, Maryland. Detrick had a rich history in designing, testing and enhancing military applications of biological organisms... Crosby was an authority on delivery vectors, and that's what Fitch remembered...the exquisite freighting vehicles. Dr. Crosby would be thrust into a near-impossible position of determining what, if any, had been used on the President.

Stephen Ashley was actually getting the feel for this, and with the help of Petr Jorbin, they had moved up the very tough rock face an additional 20 meters or so...and Jorbin was helping the climbers immediately above him as well.

"Once we move to the next secure position, I can support you some from here" he said, "and then you can support Ufi Granjeau, just below you, from your new spot and so forth...it all works if we are helping each other...ya?...you cannot climb without such dispositions...or, how do you say...without such helping hands...it's critical" ...the sweat was pouring off Ashley....the wind was ever so slightly picking up, and as he pushed himself off the rock face a bit to determine how far from the top they were, he could not see any end to it, any top to the cliff...and beyond that, it looked to him like more climbers were up there now...many more...just then, as several climbers above Jorbin were beginning to move again, a tremendous commotion came up from below...hollering and yelling... Ashley could not make it out, but it was getting closer...and louder...men were screaming now...Ashley instinctively clutched and braced himself as best he could...Jorbin too was gritting..."it is a free-fall I think...someone has lost their hold and has pulled several others with them...the climbers below us will be unable to hold the weight...they will all go...then us... then those above us...it will happen very fast now I think"...Ashley was terrified...falling...from here...no...no this cannot be happening...someone higher up yelled for Jorbin to get his knife out....

"Cut the rope Petr...cut the rope below you...do it...it is the only way... hurry...we will all be killed...***PETR...the rope...CUT IT***"...the urgency was strident...pleading and frantic...

Jorbin, an immensely powerful man, was breathing rapidly...looking up, then down...climbers were slipping off now not 60 meters below him... he took his knife out...placed the razored edge on the skin of the rope... and took it away...he locked eyes for a moment with Ashley...

"I will *not* cut it" he said almost in a whisper to himself...Ashley reached for him just as the relentless upward force from all the falling bodies strung together below, overwhelmed them, ripping Ashley, Jorbin, and the others, off the safety of the sheer rock, hurtling into total, deadly, freefall.

O'Malley was getting a hellfire of printouts on his secure-line printer... he began scanning them...

"*Catherine*" he called to his secretary without getting up...

"Yes Cough" she answered without getting up...both were extremely busy as the Executive Branch had taken on crisis control tempo...Catherine was, at that moment, on the phone with the Labor Secretary, giving him the latest on the rapidly widening situation...

"The AP is now reporting this" said O'Malley..."not here, in Asia, they have the Israel story already, several countries in Africa are reporting their President's or Kings or PM's as sick or near death ...even Europe... we'll be getting calls any second"...

"Yes Cough, I'm with Eugene right now"...

O'Malley continued, "any press, refer them to MJ (Comm Director Mike Jennis)...call Jill and ask her to come over on the double please...and please alert the staff that due to the global nature of this thing, expect to work 24/7 for a couple days at least...so get the sleeping bags out... no doubt we will be having meetings and conferences round the global clock..."

"Yes I will Mr. Secretary" and she ended the call and began connecting with Monroe's office.

"Already on it Cough...Jill first, then the staff" said Catherine...

O'Malley allowed himself a little smile…"the woman is a powerhouse…I don't know how I'd do this job without her" he said to himself, and went back to the mounting printouts…

Jill Monroe had been the Press Secretary from the beginning of the Ashley Administration. Very competent, a balanced sense of humor, attractive, and impeccable collegiate and journalistic credentials…she had handled virtually every blip on the radar screen in this administration with aplomb and without egregious error…to the appreciation of her boss…but was considering stepping out of the way sometime in the next 3 months…this "event", whatever it was, was now the biggest story of her, or anybody else's young career…and she would likely be the point person for the administration no matter where this went. It was shaping up, as an NBC analyst had just finished saying, "as the biggest global story since World War II…possibly ever."

"Jill", O'Malley moved around his desk to the armchair as Monroe hurried in to his office, "please…sit"

"How is the President?" …

"Nothing to report beyond what you already know…have you been up to the residence?"…

"No…I wasn't sure it was proper…or allowed by Service"…

"Well, it is and it is…after our chat I'll go up with you"…

"Thanks…I know about the AP, they're not the only ones either…"

"Yes, I see that…CNN is into it now…and both the London and New York Times…it is apparently worse than we had been told or notified thru diplomatic channels…NBC has cracked it open on their network… leaks have sprung from every capital on the planet…the networks will be pulling regular programming off to give end-to-end coverage...so much for trying to keep this quiet for a bit"

"I have a map on my wall, Cough...and I'm putting push-pins into the countries we have official, or back channel, and now news accounts of... the map is loaded, every part of the world...what the hell is going on?"

"That's what we have the CIA for...and the other intel services, that's their charge...and they are on it...pulled out all the stops...our job is to account to the civilian population, try to project a kind of assurance if we can...there is no policy or politicking in this...and from here, it's keeping the President comfortable and secure until this thing passes"... and then he added, "*if* it passes"

"I am having reports from the neuro-docs, Gaiter, and from Fitch sent by...his FPC (for public consumption) report...you'll have to read these quickly, and have your office put out a press conference notification to your regulars...try to keep it to 45 minutes or so...I'll ask Dr. Gaiter to be handy as well...we cancelled this morning's PC because of the President's flu story...so maybe the regular's took an early weekend...but I'm just wishfully thinking I'm sure...with this seeping out from every government now...well, they'll be back here pounding on the door... questions?"...

"No sir"...

"Okay then, let's go see the President"...O'Malley led the way back thru the Oval Office heading toward the residence.

The Mossad, (Institute of Intelligence and Special Operations) of Israel, had an additional, separate, avenue they were following as they believed they had had "prior warning" in some of the intercepted phone chatter a week prior to the conference...this single transmission did not change the security plans for the Israeli's as they traveled to and attended the conference, but it was the last part of the message, lifted into one of their internal security reports that now garnered their attention...they were backtracking fast to nail it down...and Fitch knew nothing of this...

Examining the file, Ehud Lessar reviewed the intercept, time index 171 hours prior to the UN Conference in New York..."...*yes...this time we will kill the dog, and take them all if we can...*"

"*and take them all*"...these four words...he swiveled in his chair to look at the world map on the opposite wall...he stood then, and left the building...he would get in touch with Mustafa (a code name), his link on the inside of the Palestinian Authority Security Service, but not from his office...he would drive...at least 5 miles away...then park, and call.

He double-checked the time making sure the call did not interfere with Islamic prayer time, mindful of the particular solemnity of this day's events...it did not.

"Mustafa...Blessings on you and your family...how are your children?"...

The man on the other end was pleasant but tense...

"There is great unrest on the inside here, my friend...the coalition leadership wants nothing to do with taking the presidential role...they are afraid...so the government is weakening at the edges, with radicals ready to step in...Zaheb Aswari is like the others, dead but not dead...chaos is around the corner I fear"...

Ehud agreed with him...stress was showing in the Knesset too... right-wingers were arguing this was God's finger on his sinful children...

"But, we are waiting Mustafa...holding the firebrands off...as you too must do...there is an explanation...that is why I am calling"...

"You have news of a cure then?"...

"Not yet...but, we may have a link to who has done this to the world... about 7 days before the conference in New York, and it was good to see you there, my friend, we acquired a cell phone message..." and he gave the message to Mustafa...

"We know the approximate location of origin"...and he gave him that... "your jurisdiction"...he waited, Mustafa said nothing.

"I will send by official secure line the complete details, but we cannot intervene...your side will have to pursue...I will call you in 2 hours time after the details...shalom...and Mustafa...we are brothers in this now." and ended the call.

Mustafa's real name was Sari Abdallahi and his affection for Lessar was genuine. Years back when Lessar was a young military IDF officer, he personally intervened in the indiscriminate killing of Palestinian live-stock (owned by "the cave dwellers") in the South Hebron hills by radical Israeli settlers. The settlers were systematically poisoning the livestock, goats and sheep, owned and herded by the poor and nearly destitute cave dwellers. When Lessar, stationed at the nearest outpost heard of such a thing, he confronted the men responsible. A gun battle ensued, and when it was all over, Lessar had killed 6 of his own people.

"They are the worst of Israel" he was quoted as saying. "The threads of peace unravel in our hands when such men do things as this. I do not apologize." It was a stellar military record which saved him from the military court. The public outcry was more positive for Lessar, although he did receive death threats. It was then that he attracted the eye of the Mossad.

They wanted "full bodied" agents, men and women who were not afraid of the larger, the greater goal, and to put their life in the balance. He was exemplary as a military officer, with exact munitions experience, and even some commando op excursions. He would be contacted once the furor subsided. And he was.

Lessar was an instant, if minor, hero to the Palestinian people, and not forgotten by Abdallahi, whose families had their livestock killed. Abdallahi would watch Lessar from afar at first, but when Lessar contacted like-minded Israel citizens for reparation monies, even the government, as a gesture of his seriousness, Abdallahi knew this was an honorable man. Their friendship began then, as Sari was the spokesman for his families and others. It had only grown with time.

As Lessar made his mark inside Mossad, rising to senior agent in the Political Action and Liaison Department...during this same time, Sari Abdallahi was also training and learning the military/commando activitites for the Palestinians...Lessar had even given him a name to get him started...and moved up in the Palestinian ranks. Prior to his death, Yasser Arafat had appointed Abdallahi as secondary diplomatic aide for Fatah in their relations with Jordan. An important and complicated post. Abdallahi became a sub-level information conduit...often handling the thorniest pieces of negotiated agreements. He became indispensable to the first elected President, Mahmoud Abbas early on, because of the breadth of his personal contacts, (and surprising understanding of the Israeli possible responses via Lessar), rising to the position of special advisor to the President...but things had changed with the following election, and then this one, with Zaheb Aswari elected...Abdallahi was forced ever further down the diplomatic column, as other men took larger and larger roles...but Jordan *was* still his primary responsibility... and Jordan would suddenly become the most important location on earth...and only he knew it.

The Russia secret security service, the FSB (latest incarnation of the KGB) said they also had cryptic information...from Chechyn rebels...or, believed to be Chechyn's...using Ingushetia, the tiny Muslim republic on Chechnya's western border, as a strategic base and "safe place"...separatists, killers... "we have information" the Russian Ambassador shared with Jeremy Fitch on a secure line, but it was a lie..."we would ask for a meeting...this seems to point in many directions, and if true, could unravel this global calamity..." Fitch hastily agreed...

"We will patch in from Langley, you are welcome to join us there Mr. Ambassador"...

"Thank you Jeremy, we will come"...and with that, the Ambassador ended the call to begin the arrangements...the best intel agencies working anywhere were invited...it was not a long list...Britain, France, USA, China, Israel, Russia, and Germany...Canada would be included as would Japan and India...this video conferencing call would span X time zones, but few from the intel services were sleeping since these dominoes began falling, and this would be the first international cross-governmental attempt to actualize a plan in real-time...if they could.

Israel, officially, would not admit to any investigative avenues they were following, but would sit in, and be supportive, on the Russia call. The Israeli's had "their people" in place close to the Kremlin decision makers, and from what they were hearing, the Russians had been waiting for the right moment to "settle old scores"...some, older than a generation. Although, as far as Israel was concerned, *any* intervention against global radical extremists was welcomed, but this was revenge, going back to two party confrontations in the 20$^{th}$ century, during the dissolution of the United Soviet Socialist Republic. Those were difficult days for the Kremlin, but no more. Russia was clearly the risen dominant power in all of Europe once again...flush with prodigious revenues from their oil and gas reserves, Russia's military was re-built, and dissenting voices were silenced, just as in the old days, and this "crisis" served some very old purposes.

As the scheme quickly came unfurled in the Kremlin, no military or FSB option was "off the table"...this might be the last best chance for old scores to be settled...so something quick...something devastating...a tactical nuclear device...or even biologicals, delivered in multiple locations for maximum population exposure. Opportunity was clearly knocking, and forces within the Kremlin were eagerly ready.

O'Malley took the Vice President's COS Jim Snell aside in the corridor...

Snell was walking back and forth across the hallway O'Malley and Monroe were taking to the residence...getting upset with someone on his cell call...

"Jill, I'll be right along, just have to check something with Snell"...

O'Malley asked for a moment...Snell ended the call...he took Snell by the elbow...

"Jim...we don't know yet a damned thing about what's going on"...an inner voice caught him, changed his direction...

"No wait, let me clarify that, rather, **HOW** it's going on...we just got word that Slovenia replaced their PM, who was,...*is*, in coma, (or whatever they end up calling it) with the constitutional member next in line in their government Viktor Blushenka or something like that...so he gets officially installed, goes in for a nap, which seemed to be his custom every early evening 5:30 or so their time, and now they can't wake **HIM** up... whatever this is Jim, it seems to track whomever is the *acting* or official head of state...a cautionary note to the VP...he could be affected if he starts in any kind of official capacity..." Snell looked at him in astonishment, "O'Malley, what are you talking about?...how is the fucking Executive Branch supposed to run?"

"What I'm talking about is give a gawd damn call to Slovenia if you want confirmation...the word is spreading like wildfire...this will paralyze the functional workings of the global governmental community...people are petrified to be named the new leader...call the embassy in Slovenia, John Lilja is our ambassador..." He passed Snell the number.

Snell left to do exactly that, but called Hadley Willis on his cell as he walked...

"Sir, we may have a transition complication...fill you in" looked at his watch, "in 10 minutes" and ended the call.

He glanced back at O'Malley for a moment who was heading up the staircase with Monroe..."huh" he shook his head, and rushed to his office.

Snell was a snake in human skin. A long history with Willis in and out of government, mostly on the edges of propriety, and legality.

He conducted the VP office just as Willis wanted it...a pit of fear. Willis always had the perfect out when others objected to the strong arm tactics...

"Well, ah know itz a lil rough...but Snellzee gits things done by gawd... but awl speak to 'im for ya...count on it."...all of which he had no intention of doing...keeping folks guessing as to where they stood with quite possibly the next President of the United States was just how Willis wanted it.

Yes sir.

Faulkner had been asked by Gaiter and Phil Bailey to speak to the assembled Cabinet and Legislative leadership (Treasury was still out of the country), now assembled in the Situation Room, and was, after his introduction, just beginning his summary …

"We have completed a battery of tests, gauged to measure electrical activity and continuity of signaling in the various portions of the President's brain...if you open the report in front of you, ladies and gentlemen, I'll help you to make sense of it all as I bring these other slides up on the screen"...there was a question before he even started...

"Dr. Faulkner", it was Commerce Secretary, Abraham Whorter...

"These elementary physical tests you and...Dr. Angelo is it?"

"Yes, she's here from Boston"...

"These tests, is there one you might demonstrate please? I'm from the old school, I want to **see** it...you know, feet on the ground kind of thing."

"Well...that's a bit unorthodox I guess but...sure, I think I can manage it" Faulkner scanned the audience, found an attractive young staffer sitting against the far wall brought by the CDC Chairman (who was here because of hypothesis questions regarding possible routes of transmission, contamination vectors, and communicability gestation periods...nothing was, as yet, out of scope for the investigative community)

Faulkner went over to her...

"Hello...Ms.?"

"Walker...Michelle Walker"...

"Yes, Ms. Walker...might I ask you to stand a moment" she stood...she was wearing a pant suit..."great" he thought...he half-turned to the seated dignitaries...

"One of the responses we expect our brains to execute for us is arousal when external physical stimuli are acted upon us...if I may..."

He placed his left hand firmly cupping Ms. Walker's left anterior/posterior shoulder muscles, the deltoids in the front, supra and infraspinatus on top and the back, asked her to remain calm, and took his right hand and reached down and took about an inch of flesh of her right buttocks and squeezed forcefully with his thumb and index finger...Walker shrieked and jumped...

"Just as any of us would"...said Faulkner smiling..."thank you Michelle, you're gluteus nexus will likely purple up a bit in a day or so...but all in the line of duty, eh"...he returned to the podium...

"the President showed no such similar response ...to your question Mr. Secretary"...

Walker was several shades redder and more than a little embarrassed, but had settled back in to her seat...

"This is called deep-pressure stimulation...not used in all neurological examinations, but it helps to confirm a few things...nerve endings in the muscles are agitated...they should send electro-chemical signals or impulses back to the brain via the spinal cord up and terminating in the areas of the brain appointed for arousal...*we* are conscious of the pinch, even in sleep we will respond at some level, turning, pulling away, and so forth...the President *appears* not to be, and I say that with consideration, he *appears*...which is curious because all the higher brain functions, especially the ones associated with consciousness, the ones we have measured in fact, are exceptionally active and intact...it almost expresses as an override of some kind...a report earlier by Dr. Gaiter confirmed that the President *was* responding appropriately to reflexing, and auditory stimulation earlier...so this may represent a slight change"...

The question prompted Faulkner to bring up the EEG records he and Angelo had been running...

"For example...first, I'd like to thank Dr. Gaiter, standing at the back there, for piping us in" Gaiter nodded...

"And by the way, this is a remarkably sophisticated technology set you have here", gesturing to the surroundings, "very impressive...but as I was saying, this is the first run of recordings Dr. Angelo, (he checked his notes) excuse me, Dr. Jackson had run about 7:45 am this morning... Dr. Angelo's screening software does a nice job of highlighting abnormal readings." The images moved across the big screen."...Faulkner was pointing as he spoke...

"Other than the slightly high REM sections here, nothing out of sorts... and these graphics are not in your reports there, only our conclusions... this second one will show differences..."

The moving digital images looked just like the first...Dr. Faulkner watched the peaks and valleys of the bands of lines, and then stopped the image...the deflections were evenly spaced, no aberrant high points or low points...

"This section right here"...he was up close to the screen now...

"This is the section where we initiated deep-tissue stimulation with significant pressure on the President...the same test which sent Ms. Walker jumping off the floor and squealing" Faulkner glanced at her, smiled...

"Michelle's was the classic response to DPS...and this...is what the response of the President **should** have looked like..." he clicked in an overlay...the differences were dramatic...

"President Ashley's response, here" he framed a section of the readout with his hands, "looks basically, well, unresponsive...very unlike the control reading...as you can see...*however*, and I must stress this, Dr. Angelo and I are not prepared to diagnose this condition as coma" the audience looked startled, but Faulkner continued...he chose **not** to show, however, the slight inflected "ridge abnormality" he had pointed to with Dr. Angelo... (the ridge abnormality would later be seen in all the global leadership, and at increasing frequencies...the inflection would later be known as the Angelo-Faulkner Shift...because they had first documented it's characteristics, appearing at the apex of REM specific wave activity, and corresponding with incremental increases in white matter congestion. It had never been documented before).

"As someone from the administration has previously asked me, let me take a moment and make a few comments about sleep itself. I am not a sleep specialist per se, but much overlap occurs in neuroscience, and sleep *is* a fascinating subject...so, o.k., what is sleep anyways? Well, much controversy swirls as new findings are released for peer review on the subject, but while early research examined what deficits occur when sleep is deprived, and there are genetic conditions, like chronic fatal insomnia, which emerge later in life confirming end results, but current research has focused on the *process* of sleep...what is happening in the brain during the two dominant states of sleep, REM and non-REM, which you've all heard about before...primarily two things, at least in the adult population: REM sleep is a state where certain neurotransmitters are completely turned off by the neuronal communities...the mono-amines...and those of you taking SSRI pharmaceuticals, serotonin is a mono-amine...research confirms a constancy of mono-amine release de-sensitizes those receptor neurons so important for learning and mood balance...REM sleep seems to allow them recovery time...which is critical. Non-REM plays it's part by lowering metabolic demands, metabolic rates, total brain temperature, giving damaged cells much needed repair time...so, both conditions are necessary for different cellular recovery operations...Stephen Ashley is sleeping, make no mistake about that...and he is spending more and more time it seems in the REM environment..." Faulkner knew he was losing some of them, but wanted it on the record..."alright then, let's proceed through the report..."

Dr. Helen Crosby had arrived and was ushered to the Situation Room where she heard about thirty per cent of Faulkner's report and post commentary questions.

The updates ended and all but a few of the attendees remained behind. O'Malley introduced Dr. Crosby to the security and governmental personnel allowed. This was top secret, classified at the highest levels...so NSA folks efficiently but politely had cleared the room.

"Dr. Crosby"...O'Malley came up and shook her hand. "You have been briefed on the ride over, so, what can you tell us about possibilities?...The situation with the worldwide leadership (with a few non-confirmations) seems to be the same...and the people in this room and elsewhere have to try and figure out how this has happened, and then, more importantly, what can be done to restore or reverse this condition. We are not just talking about the President we are talking about the global leadership. So, having said that, how can you help us?" Crosby looked at them. "Well, without wasting time about describing our work, let me just say that my team, and they all have the highest security clearances, will need about 10 cc's of blood from every individual starting with the President, and his entire entourage. The agents shared with me the point of focus, at least for the moment, the UN last week...that means we'll need blood, VERY CLEARLY marked, from every person in the President's detail... right down to the driver(s)...all samples to be on ice and brought to the labs at Ft. Detrick...and as we have no idea what we are dealing with we will drive all material into BSL-3 (BioSafety Level 3) and the regimens therein first...and if need be, BSL-4...I'll start calling my team to assemble. If there is a vector organism or particle, we will find it. Now, let's get started." O'Malley was already on the cellphone to Dr. Gaiter.

"We have the complete list, double and triple checked of those who attended the conference from the White House and other agencies... we will get the bloods and start getting them to you." Dr. Crosby put her hand up in a STOP position. "No, let's change that process...please send the individuals *to* Ft. Dietrick...the more I think about it, we want to extract the samples under the *most* controlled conditions...for safety sake. Anyone who cannot make the trip, we will send a special van and personnel to **them** to acquire the blood."

"OK, Doctor, that sounds better... do we need to read your article for any reason?"

"I don't think so at this time...it will only distract you from other things... Let us do our piece of this and get a report as soon as possible to you. OK?" O'Malley nodded..."any questions from the room?". There were none. "Alright then Doctor, it looks like we have a plan. Thank you. And needless to say, no talking to the press...they will get their briefings from the White House only for the time being."

"Understood"...and she left for her offices making cell calls escorted by Service agents.

When Ashley came to he was on his back, heaving, out of breath and soaking wet...everything was total chaos... sails, torn and shredded, were slapping freely, wildly...he was on some kind of sea vessel...old, wooden, with rough thick planking on the deck...very cold ocean water sloshing all over the place...in and out of the gunnels...and it was night...nearly totally black.

He was having great trouble even getting to his feet...and he wasn't the only one. Men and women were scattered everywhere...trying to hold on to something, or secure something down, as the vessel lurched and pitched in the rough seas. He crawled to a piling of heavy roping and steadied himself to his feet...the wind cut into his face and eyes with hard salt spray...**"WHAT'S GOING ON"** he hollered out...someone grabbed his shoulder...

"we need you at the cannons"...Ashley turned...men were scrambling in the tiny lantern lights to set the monstrous cannons in their places... the phrase "loose cannon" was just bubbling up in his mind when one of them sideswiped him off his feet..."aaaaahhh" he grabbed his upper left leg and just rolled out of its path in time as it came back again...

"get up" said a voice, "we need you ...***now***"

Ashley took the man's hand and forgot his leg...and helped get the cannon back in its place...**BOOM!**...he saw a flash of light way off in the dark...and then a whistling whine and ***SSSSMASH***...whatever it was blew a huge piece of the decking splintering into the night..."quickly" said the man apparently directing things..."**FIRE!**"...and 2 cannons up toward the starboard bow crackled in the dark...now the whistling was heading away from them and...*SSSSMASH*...they hit solidly whatever it was that was out there...Ashley was holding a rope on one side of the cannon that had crunched him moments earlier...another man...no...a *woman* was holding the other side, she looked bloodied up too...and very much like Patricia Fitzsimmons from Britain...3 others were loading and priming the cannon..."okay...move it to firing position"...they pulled on the ropes and pushed as the cannon seated into its bed...they did not see the flash from the other vessel...but they heard the terrifying high pitched whine as the other gun screamed it's rain of death...*SSSSLAM*...the projectile destroyed the rail and opposite front end of the cannon cradle Ashley was roped to...his counterpart, the woman went skidding across the deck crumpled in a heap..."fire" said a voice in the wildness...there were only 2 men supporting the cannon now, along with Ashley, and one of them struck the fuse up...the cannon shuddered out it's deadly cargo as it pitched up and back...more yelling from the starboard section...they were getting ripped to pieces...the entire vessel pitched violently back and the water rushed in pushing the limp woman right on to Ashley's feet...she looked up at him...

"Stephen" she said, struggling for breadth... "what...in God's name is happening?..."...gasped, and said no more.

John McMasters, MD, Ph D, was attending to the Canadian Prime Minister

Phillipe Morneau, his team and the team from Britain had been exchanging notes, comments, ideas, possible intravenous drug administrations, approved or not, etc, to treat this thing...Patricia Fitzsimmons, the British Prime Minister was also an insulin-dependent diabetic, and without information about what had befallen other leaders from outside the ministry, her doctors immediately suspected she had descended into diabetic coma, and took blood, started IV's, began fluid administrations heading in a direction of diabetic coma-reversal, but had to put the brakes on, when all her blood chemistries returned within normal limits...as word spread, first from the intel services, then the official diplomatic corps, and now the global media...the British had contacted a few of their closest allies, including the US, and were presently collaborating with Canada on some kind of medical procedural response... they were having the same luck as Gaiter and Faulkner and company... nothing was coming up on any tests except, high to very high Beta wave activity...the same as Stephen Ashley.

McMasters called Gaiter...

"Yes John....how is the Prime Minister?"...

"Unchanged....but comfortable....I know one thing, he is **NOT** going to be happy about some of the things we've been doing to him up here.... when...I mean **IF**...he wakes up...and President Ashley?"...

"Yes, about the same...what can I do for you JM"?...

"We've been thinking about a collaborative med team video conference… with the Brits and a few other state teams…would the US join?…yourself and Dr. Faulkner…perhaps Dr. Angelo as well?…we could compare data we have acquired…"

"Yes…I'm all for it John, I'm sure both Jared and Stephanie will be as well…who will coordinate?…the only place we can do this at the White House would be the Situation Room, which is heavy with intel folks at the moment, but let me give you Dante Espinal's cell number"…he pulled a notebook from his suit coat pocket…gave McMaster's the number…

"Ask him to set a block of time for the medical side of things…I'll get Coughlin O'Malley to clear it…sounds good…give us a heads-up a couple hours before the call…ok?" McMasters said that he would…

"This whole thing just doesn't make any gawd damn sense…let's hope we can figure something out…because the cable media are already pulling in their bank of 'journalistic doc's' to give their opinions…at least we can bounce that out through official channels…that we are working together…sounds better all the time…thanks John" and ended the call. He left to find O'Malley.

Stephanie Angelo was losing steam…she needed a nap or something… everything was catching up with her…"Dr. Jackson"…Jackson was out in the hallway, but re-entered the bedroom…"Yes"…"I need a place to lay down for an hour or so, but I want to sit-in on the press conference coming up"…she looked at the time block on her laptop…"I believe Mr. O'Malley said 9:45 or so…is that right?" Jackson nodded…"but after that, isn't there a bunker or something under the White House?…"

"Yes, and excuse me for not making provisions earlier…I'll get right to it"…"Thanks, I'm hitting the wall a bit, and I didn't sleep much last night to boot"…"Actually" said Jackson, "so am I"…"we need relief…I'll see to that too…no reason why I can't nap in the bunker…there's 20 or so beds down there…showers, facilities, and so forth….I'll have refreshments brought down from the kitchens....you haven't eaten for 8 hours at least...I know that...not even fruit...and I must apologize, Dr. Angelo, I'm afraid we have not been the most gracious host's today..." and then Jackson hurried out to get it all arranged.

Ehud Lessar called Mustafa exactly 2 hours after delivery of the details.

"this group is known to us" said Mustafa, "very passionate...we have a contact on the inside...not the deep inside, I am trying to reach him...if they had representatives at the UN Conference, they did not attend from here...this is a local group...with threads to Syria...and Jordan."

"Jordan...?...this might be possible" said Lessar..."yes...Jordan could be possible...a good cover...Damascus is sifted on every member of their delegation ten times ten...and the Syrian President is reported to be *ill* as well...that is our report...but Jordan, yes...Mustafa, please send details in the normal manner...our people will review...contact me at any hour... blessings to you and your children" and ended the call.

The details were sent promptly...the fax patched in always from a different cell phone...*Fire of God* was the group's name...it was a relatively unknown terror group...even Mossad had little on it...and nothing on numbers...but there was a trail now...a beginning...an edge leading to Amman perhaps...to the Jordanian delegation...they would scrub the list again, which they already had...but now they would scrub it against Mustafa's list of local and wider group members...he had Jordanians, Syrians, Lebanese names...Mossad agents began the painstaking follow-up of alias's and false names...this would take time...but if the Israeli Prime Minister was the target, and others were also taken down, then this group had done something no one thought possible...

"There are 7 terror groups internationally claiming responsibility for these actions"...a Mossad agent was leaning around his desk and speaking into Ehud Lessar's office..."2 we have never heard of...and this is not concentrated it seems, in religion...one is an environmental guerrilla group...based in Thailand...and an anarchy cell in Germany...all over the place...we may never find out..."

"No...we may not...but know this...whoever has done this has a terrible weapon...I see no safety anywhere...we must find them...and fast"

The sun was coming up soon...and no one had slept since yesterday... Lessar called his team together and ordered them to get 4 or 5 hours right now...and he would do the same.

Jill Monroe had never held a press conference in the East Room, The Brady Briefing Room had always been her home turf, the ER was reserved mostly for Presidential Press Conferences...but not tonight, Monroe was the show, in fact, she would now be *the* face of the Executive Branch, until this resolved, one way or another ...

O'Malley's hope that only a few journalist's would attend had completely crumbled when the global affirmations started pouring onto the cable and network news tickers...this world story pre-empted everything else... her conference would be held live, at 9:45 PM, EDT...**LIVE**...she was as well prepared in what she did as O'Malley was in his job...and she would need it...she opened with a statement.

"Ladies and Gentlemen. An event of unprecedented and historic proportions has befallen the citizens of the world...from all reported accounts and confirmations, the global community of leaders have been separated from conscious existence, and we have, as yet, no idea how or why. All attempts to change the course of this condition have failed, here and everywhere else.

The states of the world are responding to this crisis, this trauma, with restraint and caution...there is quite possibly no one who knows how this will end. Here, at the White House, the President has in attendance several physician's, both personal, and specialist...his condition remains unchanged...this, 20 or so hours in as it affects the President, 33 hours at last count when using a global reference...the First Lady is with the President and their daughters are with grandparents at the moment...I know you will join the staff in keeping the entire family in your thoughts and prayers...I have asked Dr. Gaiter to give the medical statement, and he will remain as we open the conference officially to questions".

Dr. Gaiter sketched for the assembled journalists, a sharp, detailed composite of the President's condition...concluding with the key phrase, "the specialists agree that based on conclusions to conducted tests, the diagnosis should not...and let me repeat...should not be categorized as coma"...the room exploded with confusion...

Jill stepped back to the podium..."Yes Mr. Ruland", John Ruland, senior WH reporter for Reuters News Agency received the customary first opportunity..."Thank you. News reports from all over are repeating again and again that leaders are in coma...how is it that this is the consensus disorder of so many, but not here?".

Monroe responded, "While the physicians have compared results with some of our closest allies, we are not in a position to comment on the medical status regarding other state leaders...we believe that that is best conducted by attending medical personnel...in addition, we may be dealing with variants of unconsciousness, as has been mentioned...so we would encourage examination of each instance of this event as it has happened and not to generalize if it can be avoided"...she turned to Dr. Gaiter, "anything to add Doctor?"...Gaiter stepped forward..."only that I have also reviewed the EEG results, which we have taken 4 times today... all brain activity is showing normal to high normal"...

"*Jill*"...it was CNN White House correspondent, Sara Donleavy, "how is that possible? ...as Dr. Gaiter has stated, the President is unconscious... how can he have normal to high normal EEG results?".

Monroe stepped to the microphone again, "Yes...that's correct...normal to high normal...and to the second part...we have no idea."

"Who are the other doctors?" Monroe gave the names and institutions...

"What, if *any* other tests can be run?"..."Dr. Faulkner will be running neural scans with a prototype neurological diagnostic tool...a few infra-structure changes are needed to support its operation, and results will be shared, if we have them, first thing tomorrow"...and so it went...questions of who, what, when, and where, from every angle until 11 pm EDT...

"ok...last question"...a European journalist, representing the French paper Le Monde, stood as he was chosen for the question..."does the American government believe this is a terrorist act?"...the room grew tense, quiet... Jill Monroe glanced at O'Malley, standing in the back,...Monroe paused, deliberated her words..."it is considered a possibility...yes" and collected her papers, ending the conference...reporters jumped to their cellphones and laptops, leading their stories with the "possible" terrorist thread.

Ashley was freezing cold as he suddenly came to. He was still at the cannon station as the horrific battle continued. The woman, who lay at his feet, slid away from him as the ship listed sharply leeward..."we are sinking" someone yelled..."the ship has been blown out at the water line ...the ocean is pouring in"...another screaming cannon blast sent more bodies flying...the ship groaned loudly and shifted again as the cold sea rushed into its belly...there was no one manning the cannon now... Ashley locked both arms to the rail and swung to the left..."Mr. President Ashley" hollered a voice...Ashley was peering through the mayhem toward starboard trying to find the owner...it was Jorbin...just then, Ashley was slammed from behind by a wave as the ship pitched hard, nearly dislodging him...Jorbin was having his own problems trying to keep his feet ..."*I am thinking*" he shouted..."*there is a reason for this...a reason...*", he was trying cup his hand over his mouth...but he never finished...the vessel that had been firing, rammed fully into their side, splitting the sinking ship apart...sending all hands into the cold dark rage of the sea.

An unsettling thought passed through Stephanie Angelo's mind as she lay on her bunk in the 4-person stall beneath the White House..."what if *I* don't wake up?" she propped herself up on her elbows..."what if this is a transference illness of some kind?...a bacterium or GE bug (genetically engineered virus)?...all these state leaders had been shaking hands with each other...kissing on the cheeks...but why is no one *else* affected?...we haven't heard anything at all about the diplomatic staff's...maybe it is an organism requiring gestation of some duration...maybe there will be more?...maybe there *are* more, and we just haven't heard about them yet... I'll have to remember to ask Mr. O'Malley about the diplomatic corps attending the UN Conference with the President...are they all accounted for?"...she discounted the Slovenia story, she just did not believe it...there was no logic to it...but what possible common thread could there be?... she knew that governments and private laboratories around the world were tinkering with organisms and delivery mechanisms for all kinds of applications...and microbes were naturally, and frighteningly, morphing into formidable and sometimes apocalyptic killers, but she had never, in all her work and familiarity with the journal literature, ever came across any condition quite like this one..."we need to confirm spinal cord health and brain stem integrity...this, whatever it is, could be originating in the spinal cord"...she would discuss this tomorrow, to see if tapping the spinal fluid would be a prudent clinical test...the promise of it showing something was clearly worth consideration...and she relaxed a bit then, laid back down and told herself that if this was an organic biotic agent driven condition then it *likely* was a gestation illness and others **would** start getting it, maybe they already were, but it wasn't being reported yet...if that was true, then **she** would be unaffected for several days at least...after all, she had repeatedly touched the President...yes, a few days...yet still...and slipped off into a sound sound sleep.

It was now 12:39 am EDT, Jared Faulkner wanted to run the neural scans which they could not run earlier because the combined transmitted diagnostic information required significant bandwidth, swaths of gigabits (terabits if he could get them)...the WH communications crew (part of the larger WHCA, the White House Communication Agency...reporting to the WHMO which is basically responsible for the necessary structural supports for the President, Vice-President, etc.) had been working since early evening to get the feeds needed for the scanning outputs to work...they had deployed "bend-insensitive optical fat pipes" directly to the President's bedroom, with the proper connectors for Faulkner's neural multi-scan machine to link up with...the fibers were patched to a light guide cross-connect panel in the telecom closet servicing the Situation Room...and all the awesome crunching information power contained there. Faulkner had injected himself (after consulting with Bennett) with an experimental drug he was trialing in his lab...a sleep deprivation mixture which allowed 72 hours of continuous and alert activity with no side effects...when the drug wore off, you simply re-assumed your normal circadian rhythms. He had done this several hours ago. He had already discovered, that, like a hospital, the White House NEVER sleeps...so, in order to provide the best possible attention to this unusual situation, he decided to stay up around the clock...running tests under various conditions, etc. It only made sense to him.

Faulkner, with assistance from 2 Service agents adjusted the President's position, supported his upper torso, and slid the portable scanner over the President's head...Jack Platt, one of the service agents remarked that the scanner reminded him of Star Wars...a survival helmet of some kind...a likeness not lost on Faulkner..."it does, in fact...yes...I agree...I even have the theme music as my phone ringer on occasion back home..."

Faulkner retrieved a hand towel from the bathroom that was part of the larger suite…"the President's neck needs an ever so slight hyperextension" he rolled the towel three quarters…"this looks right"…and slid it under Stephen Ashley's neck…"there…that's about perfect"…and went to the LED dominated pedestal controls…the 3rd of the President's personal physicians, Dr. Eliot Weinstein came into the room to log vitals, but turned to listen to Faulkner as he spoke…"this scanning machine is the culmination of 12 years of miniaturization research believe it or not…this was not the original intent, to build this…we took the knowledge-base and ported it to neuro-diagnostics…and worked with Cal-Tech and MIT to explore the possibilities…in the end, the designers have incorporated all the functions of scanners 10 times the size…an incredible achievement…reduced for portability…for the battlefield, routine neural diagnostics on med-surgical floors, pediatrics…even community clinic or first responder environments…it will transform how neurology and neuroscience is practiced…and all of it is nanotechnology driven…atom sized devices making pioneering-edge revolutionary functional connections in this baby…we have 6 prototypes…they are being tested in various trials at global locations…we affectionately call them BK1 thru 6…BK for Boris Karloff, the iconic twentieth century actor who portrayed the cinematic creature in Mary Shelley's classic Frankenstein",…he turned to the agents, "you're familiar right?"…they nodded…he looked to Weinstein, "Yes…I like Boris Karloff" and smiled broadly…Faulkner continued…"see, I have a soft spot for the 1931 version…these units can show us physiological and chemical-electrical processes with unprecedented clarity… something, I dare say, if Dr. Frankenstein had, he would have realized the monstrous abnormality he was unleashing on the world"…Faulkner was making adjustments at the pedestal as he spoke…"not only that, but when we're testing, all the data is sent thru special telecom feeds back to Stanford…to the 2 supercomputers, Tweedledee and Tweedledum for upload and analysis (Weinstein smiled broadly again)…special software runs comparisons against a substantial control bank of information, information results of testings of hundreds of specific neurological conditions...normal, extra-normal, and aberrant...and we, the docs and researchers, review everything...this little gizmo hopefully is *THE* significant first step in mobile neural diagnostic analysis...". Faulkner was clearly energized by his work...he barely took a breath.

O'Malley had just entered the room as Faulkner finished. "I have one question Dr. Faulkner, is there any danger to the President when you run your tests?" Faulkner responded as he wobbled and walked in circles in the bedroom..."N-n-o s-sir...I have been tested m-many t-times myself" sputtering and smiling. He stopped and extended his hand.

"Just a little kidding, Mr. O'Malley...the President is in no danger whatsoever, sir. Let me explain what this contraption does and why I have brought it."

O'Malley was not exactly amused and would pull the briefs on Faulkner and Angelo (which he had not yet read) as soon as he got downstairs. The COS got beeped and stepped back...Faulkner waited as O'Malley texted.

When he was done, he looked up and Faulkner began.

"Have you ever had an MRI Mr. O'Malley?" Faulkner had settled himself into a no nonsense professional attitude, and O'Malley liked it immediately.

"Yes, I have...on my shoulder."

"And the film was reviewed with you?"

"Yes it was."

"Then you know that Magnetic Resonance Imaging accurately depicts anatomical conditions and states. It serves as an impartial and static window into tissues and bone. The clinician can then evaluate options for treatment of the interpreted condition. I trust your MRI provided the information sought?"

O'Malley nodded.

"And a treatment regimen was pursued?"

O'Malley nodded again.

"Excellent...and how is the shoulder now?"

"Good as new."

"In the case of the President, the BK will process multiple slices at various axial increment positions...in degrees. Because we don't know what we are looking for, we are looking for everything and anything. Dr. Angelo (he still couldn't get her out of his mind) and I will give on-site opinions, and then we send the images on to both Stanford and MGH, by agreement, for comprehensive team evaluations. Each team is composed of specialists and sub-specialists all dedicated to some aspect of neurology... so we are loaded with leadership quality intellectual moxie. In addition, the Stanford team will run these images, with the help of the twin supercomputers, against all known or aberrant conditions. Whatever is wrong, if anything **IS** wrong with the President, **we** should find it."

"In addition, this is an MRI, which requires radiation exposure and penetration...

Typically the machine needed would be the size of this bed and room to perform this task, but because of years of development and numerous proprietary processes, the NanAtom Technologies company, working directly with Stanford and others has developed a nano-shielding process which both protects everyone here, and algorithmically compresses the radiation levels needed to fractions of previous levels. As I said earlier, I have been tested many times myself, and my radioactive exposure is well within norm...it is an elegant solution for 21st century applications.

Any questions?"

O'Malley was listening intently...jotting a few things down. "Yes, Dr., just one question...how long, end to end, will this likely take?"

"Well, we could get lucky and discover something right away...confirm it, then issue a diagnosis statement, and, based on that, and some review, hypothesize possible causes, and beyond that, treatment hopefully. If we are not lucky, and we run the shots through the whole process, then many hours may pass...best I can tell you on that Mr. O." Faulkner had a penchant for abbreviating names and let what he was thinking slip out.

"Excuse me sir, Mr. O'Malley I meant"

O'Malley nodded, thanked Faulkner and everyone else, took a few steps closer to Stephen, paused, then turned and left. He was headed for his office to review the background files on Angelo and Faulkner.

NYPD and local FBI officials had been running the video from 11 different primary camera feeds of the thousands of marchers that had gathered for the weekend UN Conference of The International Economic, Climate and Human Rights Initiative...this was and was not the kind of usual mix of marchers...most were protesters, but some were not, some international organizations were supporting the conference and the likely far-reaching accords which would certainly follow...these folks were showing their approval...and the usual raft of reporters...but *they* were not the marchers that Shep Collins and his colleagues were now looking at, *had* been looking at, and isolating digitally to transfer to the FRR databank (Face Recognition Resource)...in the years which followed 9-11-2001, New York City had re-trenched it's infrastructure like no other city...it was now the most technologically monitored major city on earth, Pittsburgh was a kind of 24/7 experiment because of breakthrough robotic applications from Carnegie-Mellon, and because of it, came a total recovery from the misery of the dying big steel years in the 80's and 90's...Pittsburgh was the robotic R&D and manufacturing capital...and Boston/Cambridge was a close second with MIT experiments everywhere, but New York was now like no other major metropolis (cameras, real time monitors, chemical and biological "sniffing" cubes, and robotics...small unobtrusive "flyers" zooming from one end of Manhattan to the other...thousands of them...for security and other purposes, traffic monitoring, schools, even the extensive subway systems...but the most useful tool to security was something foreign, moving in and about New Yorkers on the sidewalks...artificially intelligent robots or "bots" as the locals called them...a kind of hybrid of the Segway transporter with superior gyro-technology for stability and speed, and a 5ft segmented polished steel cylinder with multi-rotational part axis and 20 optical scanning instruments and chemical/biological samplers...it was independent, self-sustaining, and self-protective and in constant 2-way data-stream mode with the terabits, gathering and acting on information...and there was one in operation on virtually every block on the island)...and Shep Collins and his team were scrubbing *all* these information threads...deciding and sending huge packets of digital data to the parallel-processing multi-stage terabit quantum computer vault in a secret location in the city...since the Bureau had determined that **<u>Operation: Aladdin's Lamp</u>** should review the marchers, not more than a dozen hours ago, the local team had organized, delegated and was now sending significant data to the terabits...an extraordinary achievement in such an amount of time.

"I don't need to tell you, Shep, what circumstantial evidence *might* mean here, because no one knows...but, if there is the possibility of some kind of connection originating during the index of time around the conference, we have to try and find it...24/7...so get 3 teams together to run this...no let downs...smooth transfers...all that" it was Collins' branch director, Bill Livingston..."we're on it sir...no hiccups"..."let us know if those machines even *sneeze* with anything...we want to see it...ok, get at it...good luck" "Thank you sir" "...and Shep, everyone is looking...the whole damn world is getting wigged out...so the sooner the better..." Collins said they had already started, and ended the call. Standard procedure **before** the UN gathering was to look at video, review suspicious activity, run images against known "faces of interest"...another series of teams had actually done that, and all of the data they had collected and prepared reports on, would now be reviewed again...banked against any possible shred of information which intel teams from around the globe were now sending...the task was colossal.

O'Malley pulled his briefs on Jared Faulkner and Stephanie Angelo as soon as he hit his office. Catherine was gone, her office dark. No disturbances. He turned his pager to vibrate.

He always wanted to know, no matter what the situation, who he was dealing with, and physicians, especially such highly regarded and focused physicians, were mysterious creatures to him. He wanted to know about the person behind the stethoscope...so he pulled the file on Jared Faulkner and began reading.

Jared Faulkner was the 3$^{rd}$ son in a family of 6. Both parents successful California lawyers. His mother's career interrupted only by childbirth. They had nannies, cooks, and went to the best private schools available... and being from Santa Barbara, most of the boys surfed, including Jared.

They were all good, his oldest brother Jonah competing and winning many competitions. Jared was always tinkering with his boards...skinnying them down, lengthening them in the shop...he loved designing and re-designing all manner of mechanical and electrical objects, robotics being both his favorite high school subject and favorite high school club... competing in state and regional competitions. It was clear to everyone that Jared Faulkner was going into some branch of mechanical engineering...most likely robotic engineering, and tinker his way to stardom with some hot-shot start-up, he was that good.

O'Malley looked up from the page, and thought about Faulkner doing exactly that...and let his mind wander a bit before returning to the bio put together by the FBI and Service.

Everything changed in this dynamic just after graduation from the elite California high school Oldcott Academy. Jared was home for the summer before heading east to Carnegie-Mellon University, one of the top robotic engineering schools in the nation. He was testing his latest surfboard concept but was having trouble keeping his balance as the board was very thin across the middle. Twenty or thirty surfers were enjoying the 6 to 8 foot swells along a quarter mile or so of beach. There was another surfer about 10 feet off to his front and right as a good swell picked him up but again he didn't get up. The other surfer was paddling forward just ready to jump up when the left front of his board and body exploded from the sea. He had been attacked by a great white shark mistaking him for a seal. The shark had all of the surfer's left arm up to the shoulder in its mouth and with shocking speed and power shook the arm completely off smashing back into the sea.

Faulkner did not hesitate, driving his board right to the screaming man. The ocean was bright red and Faulkner could see gushing blood coming from what was left of the man's upper arm and shoulder. Without thinking he detached his safety line from his ankle and board and bound it around the man's mangled limb...he tied it as tight as was humanly possible to stem the bleeding. The man was losing consciousness. Another surfer came in from behind and the two of them got the man completely on a board and finally to the beach where Faulkner took yet another safety line and secured a second tourniquet as an ambulance came screeching into the parking lot. People were screaming and getting out of the water, but Faulkner was unnervingly calm...he had been clear thinking and commanding through the entire terrible ordeal. The paramedics told him he saved the man's life for certain, and indeed he had. And he went to the hospital. Met the man's family. Met the doctors. Followed the man's progress and robotic prosthesis.

His life had changed forever. "This is where I'm supposed to be" he told his parents.

Jared Faulkner was an average student, except in math and physics, never really showing much interest in anything else...but that was all changed now. He tore into medicine, screening specialties as he went until finally confronting the brain. "An ocean of mystery" he called it. He was now 33 yrs old and had lost none of his mechanical engineering passions (he minored in it at Stanford)...even regarding the human body as **the** marvel of mechanical engineering...but neurology had him now. And he was one of the best young neurologists in the country.

O'Malley sat back...pictured the scene in the Pacific. The panic and horror of it all...the immediate intervention of Faulkner...being in the blood red water with a man eating creature likely only meters away. He stood up and shook his head. He put the brief aside. He knew all he had to about Jared Faulkner now...and poured himself one last cup of coffee.

He pulled the Stephanie Angelo file.

Stephanie Angelo came from "the other side of the tracks" than Jared Faulkner. Born and raised in a suburb north of Boston, Amesbury, Massachusetts, a population of about thirty thousand. She was the eldest of two children born to an alcoholic DPW employee and a retail gift shop clerk. Her childhood was speckled with family tension and argument, and occasionally violence when her father really got hammered. He generally targeted Sheila, his wife, with Stephanie's brother, as he got older, invariably stepping in between and absorbing a few blows. When the drinking was marginal however, life could be near normal, even happy, at Angelo house. She excelled at high school, even lettering in two sports, track and soccer all four years...but they were not good years for her brother. A year younger, Anthony Angelo was showing early, baffling signs that something amiss was going on in his behavior and his thinking. His father dismissed it all as "growin up", his mother though was clearly worried. He would hit all the high marks in school one quarter, then fall close to flunking out the next.

On the night of her Junior Prom, dropped off very late, 1:30 am in fact, Stephanie found Anthony, naked and shivering, in the bushes along the side of their house. He was petrified, but didn't know of what. She got his bathrobe and supported him into his bedroom, tucked him in, soothing him in her soft empathic voice, then slept outside his door, all night, to make sure he was safe.

But then he would be fine, or seemed to be, for weeks, even months. This was a puzzle which she had been living with which garnered more and more of her intellectual attention. She read everything she could find on mental illness. Even drove him to a mental health clinic at the local hospital when his symptoms were particularly florid. He trusted no one else. Bipolar disorder was the diagnosis (she had actually suspected that), and medications were given, prescriptions written out and so forth. Her father dismissed it again as "more foolishness".

Stephanie graduated valedictorian of her class giving the commence-ment address on a particularly turbulent afternoon at crumbling Landry football stadium in town..."a fine metaphor for my life" she was thinking at the time. She threw the traditional gauntlet down to her classmates about "making a difference" with their lives and "to contribute to the betterment of society" and how great their families had been, etc...and then she shocked them all by telling them exactly what she was going to do..."I am going to study medicine. My focus of study, after the usual pre-med and internships, etc. will be neurology"...her goal would be dis-covering and then unlocking the illnesses of the human brain. No one in Amesbury High School history had ever said or done such a thing... but she would.

O'Malley paused then and brought the 32 yr old doctor from Mass General Hospital into his mind. A rare beauty in any field, she com-manded a man's attention as soon as she entered the room...and she had been upstairs, most of the day, keeping watch and conducting tests on the most important man in the free world. She was both precise and comprehensive, something O'Malley appreciated. He liked her. Shapely and casually dressed, and quite possibly, at this very moment, despite all the power positions swirling around her, having the most important job in the place. He was glad that Faulkner and Angelo were here.

He continued reading on her medical training and internships and stable guiding hand on her brother.

"Yes" he thought, and closed the brief, "this is someone we need here at the moment...someone the *President* needs here."

Faulkner sent the first, preliminary test runs, downstairs, to the supercoms resident in the White House Situation Room...the number of people had dwindled some, but it remained a hotbed for vetting reports from all over the planet...what was reported, what was checked, contacts to our embassy's, and so on...Faulkner had his laptop with him, and logged in to the access tunnel which the communications folks had provided with clearance from O'Malley...he had already sent the data directly as the President's test was proceeding...now, he wanted to see it...had everything "arrived" properly?...any "missing" pieces of information...he sent the signal to the UHD screen to his left...35 inches of ultra-clarity...then, the test data began to flow...Faulkner's intensity focused as the slices and patterns materialized and plodded slowly through the screen...he remained fixed and motionless for 15 minutes... then, the screen went black, the results finished...Faulkner furrowed his brow, stood up...he would forward the data to Stanford...with his initial comments...PK1 had delivered clear and comparative images and electricals...the measurements were not giving him what he expected, but Jared Faulkner's mind was working this now...and as a springtime artic bay clogs and clears of jams and dams of ice, so too, Faulkner's thinking. He would, as was his way, take all the data in *again*, let it roll around, look at it from as many directions he could, and then determine something. He was at the frontiers of neurology and neurosurgery, he only got the toughest cases, the most resistant, the impossible to understand...

After a scant 5 hours sleep, Ehud Lessar had contacted Mossad agents in Jordan with the information Mustafa had sent...he asked for digital images once they had located the Fire of God cell in Amman...and this was the highest priority...he did the same for the Damascus agents and Beirut...identify and deliver...they needed to run analysis...perhaps even share the information...above all, they needed to place the membership in New York...at the build-up to the conference, and possibly the conference itself. Lessar himself was at the conference, and he was draining himself trying to imagine how this thing could have happened...right under his nose, right under all their noses.

An hour later, a Mossad agent entered Hariri's Bakery in south Amman, buying 3 small loaves and a sweetcake...he displayed no technology whatsoever, yet, every man in the small table section inside, the bakers themselves, and the young men standing around outside had been recorded digitally each in turn as the agent walked in, lingered some, exchanging pleasantries and facing every direction slowly...hardly raising suspicions, and leaving a donation for the local charity as he left...sending his blessings to the baker and his children...as he left, one of the young men just outside handed him literature...which he gladly took, invoking Allah, and sending His praises...15 minutes later the images he took were on their way to Tel Aviv.

Ufi Granjeau was the democratically elected President of Cote D'Ivoire (Ivory Coast). His country was one of the countries which was going to benefit most from the recently signed Human Rights Initiative...they had, like so many other of the African states been torn internally for years...armed factions...tribal strife...and mostly, corruption ... corruption was how most government officials supplemented their meager salaries....but Ufi had been elected on a platform promising to combat the conditions which spawned the corruption practices...he had promised to the world community, especially to the Secretary of State of the United States, and the US Ambassador, to dedicate 50% of his time to improving the unacceptable practices which compromised human rights in his country, and he asked that the US attach a special envoy to his interior ministry as an observer..."unprecedented" said a State Dept. official..."President Granjeau is applying all appropriate energies to his promise to the people of Cote D'Ivoire to establish sweeping improvements against significant odds...criminal, institutional, a graft ridden business community...but we will support his efforts as best we can... and encourage more of the African nations to measure his success as a useful model, a paradigm for change"...Granjeau was seeking significant US assistance and guidance, and would disguise nothing in his efforts to establish accountability and prosecution, and level as much of the playing field as he could economically...but he was unconscious now...opposition leaders were wasting no time seeking to have new elections after a proper period of national mourning "for our fallen leader"...Granjeau's doctor's did not have the sophisticated technologies available to leaders of countries like Britain or Japan, but they could keep their President comfortable...and safe...the Presidential Guard was in full force around the residence, and in 24/7 mode. On the eve of the second day of the

President's condition, Cote D'Ivoire doctors observed in their patient something new, something as yet unreported in the medical briefings from other countries...Ufi Granjeau's left hand began moving...and to his team of physicians, it seemed to them to be deliberate.

Faulkner was reviewing the latest literature in a side conference room when his cell chimed with another Bocelli selection...he let it play out and then answered it...

"Jared?" It was Dr. Mahoney sitting in for Bennett..."we have the first contributions from the comp's and the members of the team assembled...a skeleton crew actually. Shall I pipe them to the address you sent?" He gave nothing away, Mahoney never did.

"Yes please Dan...I'm anxious to have something concrete for the COS and the attendant Doc's here at the White House..."

"Okay, am sending now...give it few minutes. Anything else we can do at this end at the moment?"

"I don't think so Dan, please thank the team for me. Goodnight."

"Goodnight Jared".

Faulkner considered the conversation. He wasn't exactly close to Dan Mahoney, nobody was as far as he knew, but there was a hint of disappointment in his voice...Faulkner would bet on it. He wouldn't jump to conclusions, but he tempered his expectations...he suspected the professional review and comparisons would yield little or even nothing...he had a "gut" feeling that this would somehow baffle them all...but it was fleeting, and he returned to his reading.

He made a note to himself that he would also need the best telecom optical engineer available...he knew someone now at Bell Laboratories and would call him early in the morning, after submitting his name, etc.

to O'Malley and the Service...as they would have to vet him. He would not interact with the President, but would be vital to Faulkner's teams as they set up the BK's on agreed upon world leaders, and how to advise them to get the information out. He would direct an international IT ad hoc group to insure a smooth flow of recorded information all at the same time, all to the same place. He would ask for none other than Dr. Sabeeh Ehsani, a Bell Labs Nobel Laureate, whom he had met with several times during the design and construction of the BK concept. No one else could make this happen, Faulkner was certain of it.

Gaiter, Faulkner and Eliot Weinstein were gathered in the 3 chairs closest to the front most screen in the Situation Room....McMasters and the med team in Canada, the counterpart teams in France, Japan, China, Germany, Britain and Israel, were all isolated in split positions on the largest projection surface the room had...Russia would join the next call.

McMasters ran the conference. "Thank you all for joining this important exchange...I realize the extraordinary sweep of time zones we are dealing with as we meet, and quite honestly wished it were different...but...(and he did not finish)...well...we all have the latest medical analysis sent to the group by fax about 30 minutes ago...there are truly few differences in either chemical, electrical, or observable input from all our patients... after subtracting diabetes, epilepsy, 2 cases of benign cardiac arrhythmia, we are looking at composite information which looks remarkably similar...I wonder if we might share a more detailed summary with each other, and we are recording this in Ottawa, if anyone else is, I just want to be candid...if no one has any objections, we can start..." and so Dr. McMasters and Dr. Touray took turns giving the full sketch of what they had done in assessing and responding to the Prime Minister's condition... and each of the eight teams, in turn, did the same...Gaiter, who had barely got any sleep spoke mostly for the US team, Faulkner chiming in on neuro-particulars, Weinstein taking notes...the call was 55 minutes old before McMasters opened the floor for questions.

China's Doctor Yeng Fu asked the Israel team about whether or not they had run a heavy metals test on the Prime Minister's blood..."they had not" they said, "only the American's and the Japanese then?...besides us?...we have found more than just trace amounts of cadmium in the Prime Minister's blood, more toxic to brain tissue than almost any other

metal...neither the American's nor the Japanese have found this metal...
but may we ask that all teams run this test please...in fact, a battery of
heavy metals testing, and share on our next call?"...everyone agreed they
would, and McMasters then set a follow-up meeting, for 12 hours later...
more questions, more clarifications, more test comparisons...France was
examining tissue samples for viral and bacterial contaminants, not just
blood..."quite honestly, it was the first thing we did...a viral agent, as we
have learned from our diplomatic mission in Sudan some years back, can
be both surreptitious *and* deadly...but so far, we have found nothing...
and our pathologists are now looking for more exotic contaminants..."...
Israel was initially suspicious of radioactive exposure..."there have been
many global cases in the last decade"...but that, so far, had turned up negative..."what about DNA-analysis?" asked McMasters..."I think an analysis is prudent, and then, a complete comparison of all our findings"...
the team agreed it should be done. Then Faulkner, wondering aloud,
asked if anyone would object to measuring brain function with his new
scanner..."there are 6...they are being tested in international locations
at the moment, some of those locations are very near to some of you...
if I can co-ordinate, would you care to run scans in real time, assuming
your current circumstances can support the bandwidth?"...Germany
had already run some neural scans, as their PM was in hospital, with
access to both fMRI and digital EEG readers..."ok" said Faulkner, "but
let me show you the results we recorded last night on President Ashley"...
Faulkner accessed the data stream and punched it onto the main piece
of screen..."can you all see this?"...Japan was the only one who could not.

"Fascinating" was Dr, Jeremiah Paley's response (chief of the British
team)..."you can see right here..." Faulkner was using a screen pointer
to identify what he was referring to..."hyperactive REM flushing...huge
bands of electrical and perfusive activation which, frankly, I have never
seen before...I'd like to know if there are similar readings in your cases...
my suspicion is 80-90% chance we will see the same things...and if that's
the case, what the hell does it mean?...not to step into science fiction or
anything" said Faulkner, "but...I have to say, the thought has crossed my

mind that what we might be dealing with is a prion like, or prion based illness...hence undetectable by any clinical methods we now possess...a post-mortem is the only way I know of...having said that, please note that we are not measuring deterioration of the brain in Stephen Ashley, we are measuring an **expansion** of brain activity...so whatever this is, it is **stimulating** the brain at the moment...what remains open, is what is the physiological endgame here?...very much still an unknown I'm afraid... ok then, as regards the BK's, I'll contact our research labs and see who can bring what, where...and fast"...

McMasters said, if the neural-scanners arrived where agreed to, and the bandwidth and power needs were present, the results could be discussed at tomorrow's meeting, and with the team's consensus, ended the call.

Faulkner called Bennett in California..."Do you **know** what time it is here, Jared? I thought Dr. Mahoney was covering the night shift?"..."He is Dr. B...but I need a favor...a BIG one" and asked Bennett to contact the PK research teams and get the scanners to the nearest of the countries in question, then gave Bennett the latest, apologized, and went up to the President's bedroom.

For the previous 2 decades, Russian internal and external political power had been refocused; exclusively concentrated in the offices of President and Prime Minister...a kind of power sharing duopoly with different, and significant, duties and powers...oil (and to a lesser extent, natural gas) was driving it all. Russia had new found wealth, expansive wealth, (oil had been periodically scarce since the beginning of the new millennium, mostly because of the production disruptions of the American Iraq war, and the following carnage when they withdrew to a marginal force, but beyond that, the perpetual political and tribal instabilities in Africa...war and strife were good for the oil business...scarcity strangles demand, and price responds accordingly...and the Russian oil fields were protected, and producing...certain powerful parties in Russia had a serious stake in flaming the violence of the world, so they did)...and with these petro-dollars, Mother Russia had modernized it's military, built and conducted a lucrative international arms business, offered shielded financial schemes protecting powerful international clients from United Nation's and watchdog agencies interference...and officially, they had admitted to their President, Alexander Kuzhav being "incapacitated", but unofficial reports were leaking that both men were down, as the Prime Minister was not in public...the FSB, the morphed millennial apparatchik from the cold war era KGB, now pushed mercilessly for destructive military intervention into the rebellious region of Chechnya...Russian arms sales, including thousands of armor-piercing grenade launchers and shoulder fired anti-tank and anti-aircraft Seyssna missiles, had been diverted by sophisticated means to the Chechyan rebel groups who were waiting for the inevitable attack...so they were well prepared...the Chechyans believed that at the highest levels of Russian government, Prime Minister Bolchenko was the only one they could trust and negotiate with...Bolchenko had distant relatives who were Chechyans...but now, and they had confirmation, that Bolchenko was unconscious, the Kremlin reign of terror would surely begin.

The FSB were pushing the story that the Chechyans were responsible for this global calamity. And they wanted to punish them for it...they *wanted*, in fact, to punish them for a lot of things...

Ufi Granjeau came to, walking with the others...single file...in a sun and shadow, heavy with humidity, jungle...he had lived in a place like this as a boy...thick, rich,...and predatory...with many dangers...many...

He turned to see who was behind him...the space immediately behind him was empty...and then Myanmar's President, Sai Thein Tun, they recognized each other...greeted.

"How many times have we done this?" asked Tun, "I am thinking four times...maybe more...I remember four" said Granjeau...he suddenly bumped into Ashley, who had just arrived..."sorry Mr. President...you were not there but a moment ago..." Ashley looked at him, then at Sai Thein Tun..."do either of you know what is going on?"..."we were just remembering how many times we have been together now...

I am thinking four...but you were not with us in the first one I do not think...it was a cave in...very awful"...Ashley then remembered the confrontation with the thugs in the slum in Rio, and the emergency vehicles rushing to a cave-in..."yes" he said, "it was the rock face, the..."...he never finished..."*Run*...go back...*RUN*"...yelled voices from in front..."hurry... *turn*...go...*GO*"...everyone turned and ran...the ground was slippery, muddy, but no one fell...some of the group were old, but they did not fall off the pace...one leader, the Chinese President got caught in heavy brush, thick and thorny vines...he was struggling, bleeding...frantically trying to get himself free as others rushed by...as Ashley came up to him, he and Granjeau reached in, pulled him out and back into the flow...

Ashley was aware then, that all of them were dressed in khaki fatigues, and had rifles and machetes...he himself had cartridge belts across his chest, and Granjeau had a belt full of grenades...they were in some kind of jungle conflict...Ashley could hear loud cracks and pops coming from behind...things were whizzing by and ripping the large leaves above their heads. Everyone kept running.

Stephanie Angelo awoke with a shudder...she had been dreaming...an unendurable cab ride in Boston...a cab with a huge backseat filled with screaming, crying children and her...she sat up...two other women were in the bunk room with her, the duet were snoring away..."so, we really *do* snore ...and make quite a racket about it" thought Angelo with a smile... she checked her watch...9:12 am..."oh, that's too long" she found the duly appointed bath facilities, showered, dressed, went out to the small kitchen area where coffee had already been made...and pastries and sliced fruit left...there was cream and sugar and White House coffee mugs and napkins...."what a place" she thought to herself...there was a note on the table..."breakfast is provided for all in the WH kitchen...whatever you want...CO'M (Coughlin O'Malley)" O'Malley himself had caught several hours on his office couch (he often did)...a pillow and blanket always at the ready in the corner.

Angelo also found the latest reports on President Ashley, ...in addition, she reviewed other summaries collected from the consortium Dr. McMaster's had organized...basically the same information...they were all unchanged. O'Malley had included an unusual report from Cote D'Ivoire physicians about their patient, President Ufi Granjeau... President Granjeau was now *writing* while he was unconscious...the content was not included in the report...but the physicians identified the material character of the writing as "substantive"...but of particular interest were the results, including the initial comments from Faulkner, of Ashley's neural scans, and the official report now back from Stanford... after she read it, she was astounded.

Angelo headed upside to O'Malley's office...and then, hopefully, the WH kitchen...she had hardly eaten since yesterday morning. O'Malley was hushed over his phone just back from the Cabinet Conference Room and... she waited by the door...he waived her in...

"ok Lucas...but get back to me if it does...thanks" and hung up. "Well, good morning Doctor...I trust you slept about as well as the rest of us?"

"Yes...thank you...very quiet down there...look, I've been wanting to speak with you about my role in this...now that Jared Faulkner is here,

I think you likely have all the expertise you need in one package..." she was hoping he would say no...we need you...

"Well...I suppose so...but actually, in accordance with Protocol-6, there should be 5 of you here at the moment...I stopped Gaiter from making all the calls,...oh...and McMasters was called to Ottawa...see we're accustomed to redundancy in the White House...it's everywhere in the executive branch...so *no* doctor...you are called to serve right here until this crisis is resolved or passes or whatever...please sit, I want to ask some questions if you don't mind...*Catherine...*" O'Malley's secretary popped in..."breakfast? Doctor...you have not eaten...I can tell by the look on your face...Catherine will call chef with what you want...they'll bring it up here...that ok?"

Angelo gave her wishes to Catherine who left the room..."and hold the calls Catherine for about 10 minutes please"...he turned back to Angelo... "comfortable?"..."Yes"..."coffee?" he got up to pour himself some from the corner carafe..."Blue Mountain...it's all I drink in the morning... James Bond's favorite, I might add..."..."love some thanks"...he prepared it as she wanted and returned to the chairs..."So,...you and Dr. Faulkner do *not* believe the President is in coma". "No, we don't...but before we get started with that, Mr. O'Malley, may I say a few things about the anatomical aspects of the brain? How much do you know about this marvelous orchestrator of ours?" She gestured with her eyes upward toward her forehead.

"Well, not as much as I probably should, given the circumstances... can you give me a brief overview?"

She gently folded her hands over her crossed legs. "Yes I can. The human brain is approximately 90% water and weighs roughly, as an adult, about 3 and a half pounds...but (and astrophysicists may disagree) it contains within its borders as many neurons as there are stars in the Milky Way... about one hundred billion give or take...in other words, a lot...and what is a neuron anyway? What does it do?...Well, for our purposes, let's just say that a neuron is a communication cell...in the brain...basically having 3 parts (I'm simplifying for the sake of time here) a cell body, and 2 end points, a dendrite and an axon...both ends can become very complicated with multiple terminations...but for simplicity sake, let's say the dendrite end receives information, and the axonal end transmits information all in an interconnected mass of millions of other neurons in specific neuronal networks...all powered and buffered electrically and chemically by a number of agents operating, for the most part, flawlessly from one second to the next...now, back to your question regarding coma...let's differentiate what we know about different measurable states or conditions of consciousness...and while I'm at it, let me say a few things about sleep and sleeping...do you have a pad of paper?" O'Malley slipped out to Catherine's desk...came back with a legal pad...

She broke the body of the page into 5 blocks and began drawing what looked like long repetitive peaks and valleys and pauses and squiggles in long tracks...she did this, in different patterns in the blocks..."back in the middle of the last century, early neuro-scientific research finally settled a serious misconception about sleep, a word which comes from Germanic origins by the way" Angelo smiled..."using crude diagnostic tools by today's standards, the collected data confirmed that sleep was not the abbreviation of most brain activity it was assumed to be, but it **was** characterized by **different** activity levels, mostly without the lo-co-motor movements from the rest of the body. REM and non-REM are coordinated together in a person's regular sleep cycle. Most people are now familiar with these terms, but in truth, they are not nearly a century old. Neurons from the brain stem on up all the way to the frontal cortex behave differently in these oppositional states...I bet you are unaware, Mr. O'Malley, although your brain is not, that in certain non-REM periods, huge sections of your brain's neurons are firing synchronously...the only time they co-ordinate and consistently do that, a kind of global pattern of activity...like an idling engine or waves at the beach...but our initial tests on the President are showing unusually long REM periods, and even in this short time (since yesterday) these REM benders are *increasing* in duration, and when REM is in process, the motor neurons essentially lie dormant, un-stimulated, which would explain him not moving at all at this point...but let's look at what I have drawn on the pad here...these" she pointed, "are patterns of measured electrical activity in different states of consciousness...This is not a debate about *what is* consciousness...we'll not resolve that here...but what we *have* done for example, both Dr. Faulkner and myself, independently, and without input from each other, is to assess the President with what's called the Glasgow Coma Scale or GCS3...it is a series of numerical assignments given to (physician) observed responses to specific external stimuli and also, independent, patient-generated activity...like making sounds for example...well, long story short is Stephen Ashley does not pass the GCS based on observation...according to the results, even with the updated categories, he suffers from severe coma"...she paused, expecting a comment from O'Malley, which did not come...she continued, "but *that* is not the entire story"...she rested the pad on her lap...pointing to the first hand-drawn box..."these are representative waves of activity which correlate with large scale or summary post-synaptic activities in the brain... we measure this large scale activity with electroencephalography equipment...mostly externally, and in the President's case, externally, and compare the results, mostly while we stimulate the patient in various ways, with control values..." O'Malley interjected, "the wires I saw coming off his head..." she nodded, "exactly...now, I brought the equipment we are currently using at MGH in Boston, one machine is under beta-testing because it has not been approved for clinical application although the information gathering capacity is levels of magnitude greater...and the neuronal network measurements are of a precision we do not currently have in clinical practice...and I also brought a standard digital EEG as well...the President has been tested, under duplicate conditions with both...and I also reviewed the results gathered by Dr. Jackson before my arrival...now, back to the waveforms..." she pointed again to the top block..."moving from top to bottom...Delta waves, then Theta, Alpha, Beta, Gamma...all measuring corresponding electrical output generated by the brain while it is doing *something*...but not the same thing..." "fascinating" said O'Malley...Angelo pointed to the next to the bottom waveform..."I would expect to see this or a variant similar in **you** as you're actively concentrating on this conversation...the Beta form...your neuronal network is generating low-voltage activity in specific anatomical locations of the brain...different voltages generated by different areas of the brain...the EEG then amplifies these different signals, and outputs them as deflections from a stylus or digitally in the representative wave you see here...when measured, post the GCS scoring, President Ashley's electroencephalogram is showing extraordinary *Beta* activity... and when I ran the EEG-2, there are waveforms I *cannot* identify...so I sent them back to MGH for analysis."...Angelo paused, thought a moment..."another thing, Mr. O'Malley", Dr. Angelo was intent on keeping his gaze..."the language of the brain, it's cerebral climate you might say, expressing through its neurons, is extraordinarily distributive...sweeping electrically in broad symphonic movements...and an individual neuron may sit some orchestrations out as it were, returning at appropriate moments to add its uniqueness...neuroscientists can stimulate a wide array of these individual and neural assemblies to significantly improve certain conditions, even some types of coma outcomes...in fact, Dr. Faulkner has developed several breakthrough techniques...and the more we analyze and evaluate Stephen Ashley's current neural firing patterns, the more likely we will inch closer to proposing an intervention...which may lead to a solution." Angelo broke off the eye contact, and continued, "by the way, do you know or might Dr. Gaiter, if President Ashley has *had* digital neural examinations previously?...and where the results might be?"

O'Malley was not certain but the President underwent batteries of tests with both of his yearly (two) medical exams when he assumed office..."Gaiter will know..." he said.

"Cough", it was Catherine, "10 minutes...and the Secretary General's office at the UN wants to patch you in to a conversation with the Secretary...can you take it?..." O'Malley nodded and mouthed "thank you" to Dr. Angelo..."Yes, Catherine, patch me in..." Angelo stood up to leave, O'Malley said "I would like to hear more of the results from Boston when you get them..." It would be mid-afternoon, 3:12 PM EDT, before the Neurology & Neuroscience Center at MGH had sent it's official analysis of the first Angelo EEG on Stephen Ashley. Ed Winthrop himself had written the summation of interpretation and discussion..."Findings inconsistent with observable condition. REM activity extra-normal. Activity levels across all wavebands high to very high. Occasional unidentified waveform action. Artifact a possibility. Electrical cycles indicative of superior perfusive effect. This brain is not in any coma that we yet understand"...Dr. Winthrop added that the MGH team had banked these results against the considerably significant data store of known neurological pathologies at the General with no success...Dr. Bashir spoke for the team when he said "this brain [Ashley's] is more active than mine...and I would be very keen to find out what the hell is going on in there"...

"Of course" nodded Angelo..."I'll be upstairs and then downstairs" and left as her tray from the kitchen was just coming in...

O'Malley picked the phone up and sat behind his desk..."Mr. O'Malleys?" said a voice..."yes, I'm on"..."the Secretary is speaking with Spain and Portugal and would ask you to give the status of the President? Can you comment on that sir?"..."yes, I can comment"...so he did...appointed officials in both governments were very nervous about sitting adrift without their own top executive's..."well, our doctors here in Washington are convinced this is *not* coma, and that the President is in no danger at the moment, and has not been...we have not however discovered the cause of this illness as of yet...I realize that the situations are somewhat different, between our country and yours, but continuing the machinery of government is a key to lasting out this crisis...the people must be able to rely on the power structure, the *institutions* of executive government at the highest levels...even if the figurehead is missing at the moment... we are all extremely competent at what we do, and I'm certain, moderate decisions and actions can be directed even now...by you...you are the proxy for the President and the Prime Minister...above all, be the comfort to the people...this is an unprecedented event...and the people need to be told it will be all right...and I believe it will be."

And with that O'Malley got beeped..."Fitch in SR...please come"..."May I suggest we stay in contact thru the Secretary General's office, gentlemen?.....and pass any information which may be helpful to each other...I like a single point of contact...much more efficient and reliable...I have to run...so keep in touch, ok?" everyone agreed they would, and that the SG's office would be the best single point of contact.

Before O'Malley could get up, there was another call...this time from the Ambassador to Cote D'Ivoire...O'Malley called up the name and details on his PC, and he remembered the briefing earlier speaking about the Ivory Coast..."Gerard...how are things holding up over there?"...Gerard Chabot, a career diplomat had been to the Presidential palace, he had something interesting to share about the condition of the President, Ufi Granjeau..."Coughlin...I'm not sure what to make of it, but as I've heard nothing reported quite like it, I think I should pass this along..."

And he told O'Malley everything he had learned while at the palace...he had even been allowed to see the President...who remained unconscious.

O'Malley was standing now as Chabot spoke...completely silent...mesmerized by the words emerging from the receiver.

"an amazing piece of news...don't you think?"...O'Malley shook himself..."yes" and paused..."Coughlin?...still there?"..."yes, still here...letting it all sink in...what do *you* make of it?"..."no idea to be truthful...but I witnessed it myself...that's all I have for now"...

"Mr. Ambassador...best to keep a lid on this for the moment...ok?"

"Absolutely...no one would believe it anyways...I'll keep you posted"

The chief of staff hung up the phone and just stood there staring into space.

Late in the previous decade, in early 2008, Bell Laboratories had successfully transmitted over 2400 kilometers more than 16 terabits of information in 1 second using 164 wave division multiplexed channels modulated at 100 Gbit/s...this would be the range of transmission and consumption muscle required to do what Faulkner was proposing using the BK series diagnostics...these were *f*MRI, PET, and digital EEG-2 capable machines all incorporated in an absurdly small and improbable package...this was breakthrough diagnostic medical technology, technology driven by nano-miniaturization applied in a totally unique manner... but Faulkner was not just asking for 1 second,...he was demanding minutes...possibly longer...5 multi-scan neuro-analyzers generating gargantuan amounts of data then sending trainloads of these diagnostic bits across the net dominating huge swaths at a time...what he was proposing would dramatically test the new, public, dynamic optical mesh transmission network now a heterogeneous network (he would need clearance from a couple of Federal Agencies, but his idea would synchronize 5 neural scans all terminating at the White House...he would also need help, heavy optical engineering help, which, fortunately for him was not far away in Murray Hill, New Jersey)...having showered, quickly eaten, attended to the President, and reviewed current data collected, he was now giving an update to congressional leadership meeting in the cabinet conference room...*"if* we can do this...if, by constant comparative recording, we can establish that something is going on, *in concert*, beyond our scientific understanding, then next steps relative to political interventions can be better formulated, it seems to me...because right now, the states of the world are beginning to get very edgy by the looks... at least the news reports...maybe we can make a case for caution...for deliberation...if what I suspect is happening here, my advice is sit tight... watch and wait"

"Thank you doctor" interjected Sen. Will Clemons disdainfully, Clemons, Faulkner would learn later, was an ally of the Vice-President, and Chairman of the powerful Ways and Means sub-committee on technology, "I *am* convinced, like a growing number of my colleagues in the Senate, that something potentially very dangerous *is* going on...and *my* recommendation, and I am introducing this on the Senate floor tomorrow, a rare Sunday in the Senate chamber, is that the President, legally, temporarily, be considered "nesciens sui...unconscious" of his duties, and therefore unable to execute the office of President, and further, that all responsibilities and functions of the Presidency be transitioned to Vice-President Hadley Willis at the hour of noon tomorrow..." Faulkner immediately did not like this man, and his patience with this line of thinking was fraying...so he asked a question...

"ok Senator, speaking as a non-governmental official,...let's say the Vice President assumes the Presidency...and let's say he signs several Executive Orders to do this or that in an escalating world environment, and let's say, certain wheels are put in unstoppable motion...and then Stephen Ashley wakes up...what happens then?...if he disagrees with the actions the Vice President had taken in his window of opportunity, how can he reverse something which then cannot be stopped?...say, a surgical military action or something?...to *protect US interests*...who answers for that Executive Decision?...huh?...we may find ourselves in the middle of an extremely difficult position to resolve...I have to ask you what are you rushing this for?...from what I'm hearing, other governments remain in holding patterns, not in active power transitions...sounds to me like an agenda opportunity...so answer my question...what happens then?"...

Clemons thrummed his fingers on the long cabinet room conference table..."you are hypothesizing Doctor...just like you and your assistant Dr. Angelo have been doing all along from what I can see, but to answer your question...you'd have to go to diplomatic wrangling of some kind to straighten it out...but this is a congressional issue now, not a medical one".

"I urge caution, and for this administration to wait" pleaded Faulkner... "please...oh, and Senator Clemons, Dr. Angelo is *not* my assistant as you have suggested, and my sense is, it is a good thing for you she is not present to hear you infer it"...and left the room.

O'Malley left as well...immediately called Carson in Legal..."Paul"

"yes Cough"..."how are you coming?...Clemons is going to introduce something in the morning in the Senate...a kind of interim resolution permitting the VP to take charge...likely circumventing the established legal pathway...do we have legs to stop this kind of thing or not"...

Carson sounded like he was turning pages..."Paul?"..."yes, sorry Cough...I believe we have legs, yes..." "Something we can throw at the Senate tomorrow prior to the resolution?"...

"yes, the OLC will be done by then...it will be finished tonight actually... so you can read, and the Secretary of State...you want Jack to review it, ya?"..."Just staff for the first run Paul...ok?...no one leaks it either...how many of your people are working this?"..."basically all of us...I will hammer the lid shut down here...don't worry, this team is solid..." "ok Paul, I'll look forward to it...thanks"...O'Malley got beeped as he shut his cell... it was Fitch..."come down to the SR...asap".

O'Malley swung by his office...picked up official faxes from dozens of US Embassy's...disorder was on the increase around the world as extremists both inside and outside governments were fanning old suspicions and ethnic strife...with the absence of an established global explanation for this "event", local hatreds were flaring wildly, and distrust and ugliness were sprouting...the world was beginning to come apart...fast. This was just the kind of chaos Faulkner was referring to, thought O'Malley, "we absolutely have to stonewall this as long as possible...and hope these international medical teams can figure out a cure, or the intel folks find the trail of who did this", and added to himself, "if that's possible".

Some new personnel were in the Sit Room when he came in...the FBI's Bill Sacks was talking in a videoconference to New York...Lisa Cash, a member of Shep Collin's second team, Team NightLight, was on the screen..."yes" said Cash, "we have 11 members confirmed *in* New York, on surveillance at numerous locations during the protests (Cash was referring to an environmental extremist group)...we do not identify *any* of those 11 within the perimeter established at the UN...that has been checked and re-checked...no dice..." and she continued the log on "persons and organizations of interest"...O'Malley asked Fitch quietly what was the issue?...Fitch slid him a brief...the cover read...**"Fire of God"**

Patricia Fitzsimmons was in the clearing with about 50 other leaders when Ashley and Granjeau and the Chinese Premier came running out..."Bloody poor form is what I say" she said to Ashley coming up..."we should keep moving shouldn't we?" he said looking back... "I suppose, but what the onions for?, I mean we're all getting flushed in this one too...that's the way I bloody see it"...Ashley took a moment now...a measured moment...and really looked at the others...most of these folks he had never officially met...Washington keeps it's visits and visitors at an arm's length since the attempt on the previous President...he hardly knew these people...but he knew who they *were*...the recognized leaders of all the people on the planet...and just us...he thought...no aides, no staffs...nobody...he saw Jorbin then about 50 meters away at the edge of the field...where the jungle crept right down, dark and heavy...Jorbin was yelling into the overgrowth and started backing up...others started running...Ashley slowly headed toward Jorbin who was still backing up and gesturing...and then, without warning Jorbin was cut down...rapid thwacks hit his body...Ashley could not identify what had just happened, it was too fast...Jorbin was still weakly gesturing as he lay crumpled... he was attempting to speak but his voice faltered...his mouth moving... then fading...to nothing..."*Petr*" Ashley called out and hit the ground, his rifle now un-shouldered, ready to shoot. "Petr...can you hear me"... Ashley started crawling on his belly toward his fallen friend. More bullets whizzed over his head...some cries coming from behind. "*Bastards*" it was Fitzsimmons yelling...and she rattled off her own rifle directly into the jungle..."*Bloody bastards*"...

Ufi Granjeau was crawling right behind Ashley...the grass was 2 or 2 ½ feet tall and thick...it was good cover. "Mr. President" whispered Granjeau, "I have grenades"...they were almost to Jorbin...Ashley lay still as more bullets flew toward the back...then he reached the Finnish President. "Oh God...they've cut him to pieces...".…but despite his wounds he was not dead...he turned his head slightly, opened his eyes..."Ahhh, it is you Stephen, and Ufi as well...coming to help me..." They were both around him now...one on each side. "you must not fire your weapons...no grenades" Jorbin looked at Granjeau, "why Petr?"..."who is doing this?... why do they want to hurt us?..." "it is us." whispered Jorbin..."we are killing us"...and breathed no more.

Government troops had begun to move inside Russia toward Chechnya and inside Angola toward the border with the Democratic Republic of the Congo. Angola would now use the present crisis in leadership as an excuse to punish and pillage its neighbor, the DRC with whom it had had long standing animosity…"we will attack before they do" said Chief of the Army, General Kumo Badinga…"they have done this (meaning the rendering of the Angolan President unconscious)…and we will finish it"…

These were the two most critical meltdowns in progress around the world, but by no means the only ones…the entire of central America was saber rattling…extremists were in the streets in every volatile capital in the world…they were watched closely by either the country military, or the riot police of the cities…but the tensions were growing exponentially…and information about who was responsible was pointing everywhere…no one could be trusted, especially long-standing enemies. This was exactly the kind of worldwide catastrophe which some terror groups had hoped for, and predicted, and their apocalyptic message was resonating…"the world is coming to an end…infidels must be converted, or they must suffer"…it was spreading virally over the internet in video and blogs and instant messaging.

The intelligence communities were beginning to see the worst possible scenario's…the use of $21^{st}$ century weapons of annihilation, especially biological weapons…man-made viral organisms to which there were few if any antidote's…delivered by canister, shot with shoulder launchers into major cities and international air hubs…the plague would be incubating before anyone knew what had happened…and worldwide involvement in a matter of hours. In the background, Fitch and his colleagues were gamming the only solution that mattered, the survival of America. Everything else was irrelevant.

O'Malley had quickly reviewed the brief Fitch gave him, "You think *they* are behind this?"...

"The Mossad have shared this information...I checked with Langley, the internal middle east bureau...we don't even have these guys on radar... completely new to us...they also sent digital images...about 60 in all... we're not sure that all these faces are part of this group...but we are building a database on them...getting into *our* contacts, who are different than Mossad, to confirm certain things...we're passing the digitals on to New York anyway...parallel tracking this"...Fitch took a long moment rubbing his eyes...he had not slept since this broke Friday morning... Langley had the latest pharmaceuticals for this kind of extended focused activity (not the stuff Faulkner had however), but the brain still rebelled some no matter what..."sorry Cough, I'm clinging a bit at the moment."

O'Malley nodded, furrowed his brow a bit, "to pull something off, of this scale, would require months of planning, preparation...dry runs...all that, not to mention the agent used...hell, we still, nor does anyone else know, *what* is causing this...why it is so selective?...the cable shows are parading 'experts' who suggest this is only the first wave for gawd sakes...all kinds of authority chains will be targeted next...military, financial, religious, on and on...could this Fire of God group actually have done this?...do they have the logistical where-with-all?" he stopped for a moment, took a deep breath..."or, could they be fronting a much larger, richer, more sophisticated adversary?..." O'Malley was a huge James Bond fan in his earlier years, and suddenly remembered SPECTRE, the organization determined to rule the world, and a common foe of Bond's.

Fitch, for the first time in all this, looked wide-eyed...O'Malley could see fear..."the intel people have possibly missed something of epic proportions", thought O'Malley..."and it is setting in now just how big a miss it was..."

"As you say Cough, nobody knows what's causing this...we can't afford to rule anything out...a high-tech bio-laboratory...an engineered viral organism...all of this is front burner stuff at the moment...I don't underestimate Mossad...if this is something hot as far as their concerned, we'll pull our levers too...and see what happens."

"they really said this...'this time we will kill the dog...and take them all if we can'?...what do you think it means? The conference?..." Fitch shrugged.

"We're trying to confirm if any of them were there...things will shake very fast if we find that they were...I'll keep you up on it..." and Fitch was called to the corner by an aide...

"excuse me Cough"...

Shep Collin's graveyard shift group, Team NoLight (which was working overtime, allowing the incoming team to catch-up) was officially just handing off to their day counterparts, Team DayLight, when the images came through from Langley, where Mossad had sent them...60 in all... mostly young, middle eastern, Jordanians, Syrians, Lebanese, and a few Palestinians.

The quality of the images was excellent...Collin's piped them immediately to the terabits...and picked up where NoLight left off...they had flagged several candidates from the extreme environmental group ERF (Earth Reaction Force) who had marched, and then, unexpectedly, one of them showed up at an official diplomatic function...she was gowned and escorted...so FBI was checking all that out...tracking the threads...in addition to the 60 images and short bios, Mossad had sent asterisks on the Syrian and Jordanian delegations, noting the Lebanese as well...implying infiltration, not collusion...so Collin's had the diplomatic corps from each country re-examined, with definitive biographies laced together on each member, this time, getting additional comment from Mossad.

Collin's had been part of many investigations...domestic and international, and he had good instincts...and after putting all these pictures up on "the arc" (the wall used to follow the arc of an investigation), and associated known biographies, he began to sense that somewhere on this wall now was the who...still remaining was the what..."but first things first" he thought, and returned to the official delegate lists from Syria, Lebanon and Jordan, sifting and comparing.

Jorbin remained motionless, and from what Ashley could tell, not breathing...but he continued to call his name..."Petr, Petr" and then, forgetting the danger, began to get up. He was in a low crouch reaching for Jorbin when the first bullet hit him...it was a shoulder hit, which drove him up and back at the same time. More slugs rifled into his chest as he folded back, landing hard on Ufi who pretty much caught him and bore all his weight (Ufi Granjeau was all of 5 ft 6 inches and very slight...Ashley was almost 6 ft 1 inch and 200 pounds)...but while he broke Ashley's fall, he could do nothing for his wounds. Ashley was wretching and struggling for air, but it was no use...death was hovering over him as a growing shadow. They locked eyes as Granjeau made the sign of the cross with hands covered now in Ashley's blood, on Ashley's forehead, lips, and heart..."as is our way" he said, and recited in a whisper, the Lord's prayer...as Ashley slowly closed his eyes, and slipped away.

Elizabeth Ashley was a year older than her husband. A Yale graduate in economics, with a minor in classical music...he graduated from the University of Chicago with a degree in political science, with a minor in languages. They were a talented couple, married 14 years, 2 children, a governorship, a collegiate teaching position, and now, center stage to the inner storms of world politics and international policy when Stephen was elected to the Presidency...and through all of this, including the recent harrowing and stressful primary and general election campaigns, from the times she was a little girl, Elizabeth suffered with first an undiagnosed, and then second, an untreated, bipolar disorder...for the past 5 years she negotiated, at great emotional and physical cost, the dueling knife edges of mania and depression...and Elizabeth's mania flowered richly with psychosis, hallucinations and voices...it was an ensemble cast of horror...her meds and therapy with the doctor (sometimes over secure video) barely kept the disorder from shaking loose, but the wolves were always there, always waiting...and *this* thing that was happening to her husband, to her *world*, threatened her in ways she never imagined... even with the medication, she could feel the gears slipping, the engine racing, the tires wearing down...she caught up to Stephanie Angelo. "Dr. Angelo...may I speak with you a moment?"...they had met the previous day amidst the battery of unearthly events..."yes Mrs. Ashley...how are you holding up?"..."well, that's what I'd like to discuss...can you join me in my office for a few minutes?...after you check on the President perhaps?" "yes ma'am" Angelo checked her watch..."say 15 minutes, in your office?"..."perfect...I need to see Jill for a few minutes...so that will be perfect" and both left in opposite directions.

Mrs. Ashley went to Monroe's office in the West Wing...stopped at the secretary's desk, Jennifer Eisle..."Jen...can Jill see me for a moment or two?..." "Yes Ma'am...I can buzz you right in"..."Thanks"...

Jill Monroe had the entire global map covered with push pins...she turned as the First Lady came in..."morning Ma'am"..."morning... gracious, what is all that?" impressed by the busy map...but the map images seemed alive somehow, even threatening...she held back..."all the confirmed unconscious heads of state...every single country in Europe, North, South and Central America...Australia, New Zealand, most of Asia, most of Africa, most of the Middle East...it's simply an event of unprecedented scope.

The New York Times is reporting this morning that seven countries have had coup attempts...but none successful...and another where the original Prime Minister was replaced, and now the replacement is un-arousable as well...same as Slovenia...no one knows what to make of it...CNN has been having apocalyptic forecasters from all over the world wading in on this...place is gone bughouse"...Monroe switched her focus away from the push pins and 3M sticky notes all over her wall back to the First Lady..."what can I help you with Mrs. Ashley?" Elizabeth Ashley was "dual tracking" as she had come to understand it...haunted by voices and visual hallucinations, and paranoia, but also, moving along another, separate, fully normal track, and at the moment she was thinking at the 30,000 ft level as Monroe outlined the severity of the situation...she had been listening and getting briefed by her own staff of course, but until now, her focus, almost exclusively, had been the President..."yes Jill, there is...at last night's press briefing...nice job by the way"..."thank you Ma'am"..."the terrorist question...what is the latest intel on that...have you heard?"..."yes Ma'am I have...we have FBI teams in NY working round the clock, in addition to CIA, Secret Service, the State Department, the Pentagon, other national state intelligence agencies...hundreds of leads are being followed...there are promising developments in the middle east, and NY is collating data like no one else with their multi-terabit computer banks...but nothing to pin a tail on yet...I believe they *will* find whomever is responsible, and sooner rather than later...with all these intel teams, and I mean international intel teams, the culprits will be discovered...and a restorative treatment will be found...I firmly believe that from what I am seeing and hearing"... "no breakthroughs that you have been briefed on though?"..."no Ma'am...not yet."

"Ok then...I'll just swing by from time to time or send Li Ming, if you don't mind...I'm pretty anxious about all this...as you can imagine"...

"Certainly...and have Li call me on the cell, either way is fine...I'm getting briefed with staff, and the cabinet, in about..." she glanced at the clock..."about forty minutes, then we'll patch another press conference together"..."thanks Jill"..."yes Ma'am" and the First Lady headed back to her office.

Elizabeth Ashley looked every ounce the competent, engaged, sound intellect and pillar of strength...but she was sick...very very sick.

"Oui, tres bien" said French President Pierre Mondot, "this is more like it...bright sunshine, blue water...the beach sand is like our Riviera...and with palm trees too...magnificent", and gave a kissing motion to his fingers, gesturing to the sky...it was an idyllic setting.....the sun high in the sky... greenery was lush, peppered with all manner of flowering flora... and no one else except them...for as far as they could see in any direction..."Like a holiday, eh?" said a voice...then laughter...leaders shaking hands...but Ashley had noted the last time they were together, that this friendliness now being shown, had an undercurrent...a kind of suspicion, of doubt...he looked for Jorbin...not here...not *yet*...but he saw the Chinese Premier and went over..."Mr. President"..."Premier Ho"...they bowed to each other...and both men smiled easily. "What do you make of all this?"..."a compelling question...one with unclear answers"..."how many gatherings is it now?"..."I have counted five...but none so beautiful...or so pleasant"..."I think, I missed the cave in...or I do not remember it...but I do remember *hearing* about it...I was close by...incredible as it sounds"..."No, I believe you are right...not everyone was there"...Jorbin came walking up then..."Petr...so good to see you"..."it is good to see you Ho Fong"...the Premier turned to Ashley..."This man, the President of Finland, put himself in the path of enormous falling boulders in that cave-in to try and protect me...he **did** protect me"...

Ashley looked at Jorbin. He did not know this man. Only from some state dinner at the White House early in his administration...he had been to China...had met with Ho Fong on several occasions, and both governments were well acquainted...but Finland...what did he know about Finland?...he knew he had never been there...or **any** of the Scandinavian countries...all he could think of was cross-country skiing... or ice hockey...and blonde women...it was cultural ignorance, and worse, cultural stereotypical thinking...(Petr Jorbin was the democratically elected President of Finland...a country on the easternmost flank of the Scandinavia triad of Norway, Sweden and Finland. Its easternmost border was shared with Russia, Norway and Sweden to its north and west, respectively. Jorbin's country now stood at approximately 6 million souls...and he was in his first elected 6 year Presidential term...now in its 4$^{th}$ year.

Jorbin was somewhat of a tragic hero to his countrymen...winning 2 gold medals for Nordic skiing in the 2002 Salt Lake City Olympics, and more recently, for losing his only child, his beloved Elle, to bone cancer in 2009. For weeks, neither he nor his wife Tarja could be seen in public... and when they did emerge from their sorrow, they would spend hours at the Helsinki Children's Hospital, visiting the families and the children fighting cancer...closest aides spoke privately that he was a deeply changed, and changing, human being...and how could he not be?...but Stephen Ashley knew nothing of this)...he turned to Ho Fong, "Premier Ho, I was hanging just below President Jorbin on that huge rock face... the climbers below us had already plunged into freefall, and people above were yelling for Petr to cut the rope...which he **could** have done... but he refused...I heard him whisper to himself that he would not do it... and then we were gone"..."I was far below the 2 of you" the Premier said, "and came off the mountain like a feather in the wind"...and laughed so heartily they all joined in...the three of them...shaking their heads and laughing...

"You must tell me, my friends, what is all the laughter?"

It was King Faisud of Saudi Arabia..."you are all looking well, gentlemen" and bowed and smiled, slapping Jorbin on his massive shoulders.

Ashley thought to himself, "this is extraordinary"...and others pressed in toward the happiness.

Stephanie Angelo had completed another EEG-2 test, and had it on hard disk as she carried her laptop to the First Lady's office about 5 minutes late…"you're late Doctor"…"yes, sorry Ma'am"…"one of the things I can't seem to get used to here…the clockwork, the precision of the place…if there is a defining element in the operations of the White House, it is punctuality…here, it is the lifeblood of every office and action and I still can't seem to get completely used to it…" "no Ma'am"…"you know how it can function that way?…the principals (members of the Presidential administration) have every detail of their day taken care of for them… no cooking, no cleaning, no choosing what to wear, what to read, you have personal time, I don't mean that…I mean, your *official*, executive branch everyday pulse…it's all dictated to you…efficiency is the rule of law…and that is something I **can** appreciate, it is also the lubricant of economics…" "yes Ma'am…you wanted to see me?"…"Yes, I do…but I see you have brought your laptop…news about the President?" she folded her hands and widened her eyes…"In a manner of speaking…we have tested Mr. Ashley, er, President Ashley, several times now…Dr. Faulkner wants constant monitoring, which is a good idea obviously, and essentially why we're here, that is, beyond ruling out certain things neurologically…but anyway…" she spun the laptop around and opened it, pushed a few keystrokes, and an image popped up…"this is the EEG just finished…he is in deep REM sleep according to this wave pattern…a remarkably active, intense, REM period…yet these waves here…" she split the screen into 2 images, pointed to the top imagery…"**these** waves should, theoretically, not be present…these come from different perfused brain geography, different anatomical structures which are *not* active at the same time these structures are…" she pointed to the bottom screen image…"honestly Mrs. Ashley, I have never seen this combination of brain performance… and it is flushed with activity…I would almost call it aggressive activity…

remarkable...I have sent the entire digital representation to MGH for analysis..." Elizabeth Ashley lingered on the images..."I am bipolar, Dr. Angelo"...there was a long, uncomfortable pause..."and I feel like my wheels are coming off....."

Angelo instinctively stood up...went over to the First Lady and half-squatted in front of her. Taking her hands in her own, she said, "I know Elizabeth, I knew shortly after we met...and I am going to help you."

"I have been reading about you, Dr. Angelo"..."please Ma'am, call me Stephanie...and I confess, I'm a little intimidated by all the surroundings to tell you the truth"..."that makes 2 of us, then...this is a formidable building when it comes to history...I'll give you the personal tour if it works out...but as I said, I've been reading about you...our staffs gather all pertinent information and compiles it so everyone in the executive branch will be well prepared, well informed about who they are meeting with and any political bias and so forth...you are not active politically?" ..."no Mrs. Ashley, my work consumes most of my time...free or otherwise"..."not married, no significant other"...Angelo shook her head no..."but you do have a brother...and *he* is bipolar...is that true?"..."Yes... he's a year younger than I am...college graduate...working on a master's in public health..." "according to my notes here though, he's not active in the field...and you have not been in contact with him for some time... why is that exactly?"..."Mrs. Ashley, I thought we were going to talk about you, yes?...why the interest in my brother?"

"Yes, I do want to talk about myself, and the hardships of this condition... but my interest in you and your brother gives me a kind of lifeline...a thread...hope, Stephanie...that's what I see here, and feel from you...you have not been in contact with him, because he is in hospital, and does not want to see you...and it is breaking your heart"...Stephanie Angelo's eyes were welling up now...she was shaking her head and looking down..."you are responsible for your brother, and his condition took a very serious turn...a life-threatening turn...and you took the steps necessary to protect him, and move down the road toward wellness...you have saved his life"...Elizabeth Ashley paused for a long moment, then added..."and I need someone to save mine"...Angelo looked up, the First Lady was sobbing...

"I take the medicines, I see the doctors regularly, but in my head,

I am going a thousand miles an hour, or not moving at all...I am doing everything I can at this very moment, to project calm and control, but I am anything but...I hear voices...they tell me things..."

Angelo had no idea...nor did the nation. The knowledge, in the press and around the world, of what a mentally ill First Lady would do to this Presidency was incalculable...so it was smothered...Elizabeth Ashley would "go deep" if her illness flared up...so no one, except only those closest to the First Lady and President really knew the truth. "what prescriptions are you taking?" Angelo shifted from afflicted family member to competent physician....this was, after all, a very big reason why she had entered medical school in the first place....to understand the nature of mental illness....to evaluate and build on the body of evidence in the field on how the brain functions, and more importantly, why it does not function, or functions as a compromised organ. Elizabeth Ashley, having prepared, handed her a detailed list of medications...some had been discontinued by her attending physician's, new ones added in their place...even noting novel therapies with psychiatrists that had been employed over the years...but the effects were not lasting. "You understand, Stephanie...you have lived with a loved one with bipolar illness, we have discussed hospitalization, I have been, on at least three occasions...all quite some time ago...since the advent of some of these new meds, it has not been necessary...but I feel it building, surging, trying to get out...I need your help..."

Stephanie Angelo thought for a few minutes...and then said, "Mrs. Ashley...yes, I do understand it...as much as anyone who does not have this illness *can* I think...not arrogance either...I have dedicated a considerable portion of my life to understanding it...and other illnesses of the brain...which of the White House physicians are managing things for you?"..."Dr. Simon...he is not resident here, I mean on staff here...I see him at his office...as discreetly as possible..."

"Alright, I would like to speak with him if possible?"...

"Yes, Li Ming can make those arrangements...I'll buzz her to set that up"..."and Mrs. Ashley, I'd like you to accompany me back to see the President"...

"Of course" ...

"Give me a little time...I want to talk with Jared, er, Dr. Faulkner about his test readings"...she got up to leave...the First Lady was sobbing again...

"I feel like I'm coming apart..."

"Elizabeth, I'm going to order some meds of my own...which will not interfere with what you are already taking...not contra-indicated in other words...I'll have Li Ming get the order out and express delivered back here within a half an hour...I'll be back before then..." and gave the First Lady a gentle and compassionate hug.

"I'll be back as soon as I can" she said, and exited to see Li Ming.

In no time she had reviewed the meds the First Lady was taking..."enough to put an elephant down" she thought, "the First Lady always appears so serene in public appearances...these pharmaceuticals might have quite a bit to do with that...but I see none of the meds which I would order based on my practice with BP"...she checked with Li Ming...

"Ms. Ming"...

"Yes Dr. Angelo…a pleasure to meet you" she stood to shake her hand…"strikingly beautiful" thought Angelo…

"I have read up on you…we all have, and Dr. Faulkner too, since this all began…very impressive resumes…the both of you"… "nice of you to say Li…can you tell me if anyone on staff checks the med intake, the daily intake of medications, and when…prescribed for the First Lady?"… "Well, I am responsible, and when I'm not here, Lindsey Zeleny covers…why?"

"Not sure…but I want some bloods taken with these blood levels checked" she handed her a list…"in addition, there are a few pharmaceuticals which I think the First Lady will profit from, but I first need to know where she is blood level-wise with this other stuff…is that a can do?… say…asap?…and at the very latest, within the hour?"…"sure…that can be done"…"ok, also, I would like these new meds ordered and delivered from wherever the White House gets these things"…"that's usually from Walter Reed or Bethesda…they send someone right over…they'll do the blood work you need as well…we do have some meds in the med office here, but not these, I can tell already…ok I'll make the calls"…"thanks Li"…and then Stephanie leaned closer, quieting her voice…"Mrs. Ashley is in some rough rapids at the moment…we need to calm the waters for her…those meds will help greatly"…"yes ma'am…I'm on it…and I'll beep you…" she handed Angelo a beeper, "if things get dicey"…Angelo liked her already, very competent…she took the beeper…"good", she said and left the office.

It would be 12:06 EDT when Dr. Angelo left, she had spent about a half an hour with Mrs. Ashley… "oh my goodness" she said checking her watch, and left quickly to find Faulkner.

O'Malley made several international calls, to embassy's, state capitols, even business leaders, gathering and sharing information...

"the Prime Minister's physicians have allowed the PK-3 diagnostic helmet to be placed on the Prime Minister, but only after a House of Lords member agreed to the test himself"...he was speaking with Sir Richard Cowell, Minister of Security for Britain, and a good friend of O'Malley's..."all went chipper...the technician, hell, the doctor, Ph.D. in Neuroscience, had Lord Singleton in and out of the contraption in no time...and with jolly good visuals if you ask me..."

And then Patricia Fitzsimmons was tested...the results sent via compressed video signaling to the twins in Stanford per Faulkner's instructions.

"So Omee, when will we hear anything?" Cowell played games with names all the time..."I expect that Dr. Faulkner or..." he checked his notes, "or Dr. Bennett will be getting back to you Sir Richard..."

"And what exactly are they looking for?...do you know?"

"Not exactly...Dr. Faulkner said something in his summary this morning about abundant white matter involvement...mean anything to you?"...

"Nope, not a toot's worth...alrighty then, I guess we'll wait for the Alice in Wonderland twins then"...

"Yes Sir Richard, I guess we will."

# GMT 3:50 PM Saturday / IST 5:50 PM Saturday (Tel Aviv) Israel

Ehud Lessar had just been informed by Mossad agents in Damascus that at least one and possibly two members of Fire of God had been part of the official Syrian delegation to the UN Conference the previous weekend..."details please" he requested, "photographs and background information...as soon as possible"...since the Peace Accord with the Palestinian government, including the troublesome Gaza, not majority ruled by Hamas any longer, but still, Hamas remained an unruly, if difficult, piece of the negotiations...the Accord, like so many before it, was on the verge of coming apart...this time when the crucial issue of Jerusalem finally seemed to be resolved to the satisfaction of all parties, radicals on both sides, right-wing Israeli's and Palestinian extremists, who seemed to be waiting for just the right moment, fomented so vociferously, that the fragile fabric began unraveling, it was then, that the breakthrough came from an unexpected source, Saudi King Faisud himself partnered with the Palestinians as the economic safety net for *all* the Palestinian peoples...Faisud said he would "remove the economic obstacle to peace", as conditions were dire, and had been for months (some would say years)... people had been barely *subsisting* in Gaza, especially Gaza, even though Israel had been relaxing the substantial economic, military, and cultural restraints in place for so long...because of Faisud's safety net, the parties at the peace table agreed, it would no longer be either government's policy to blindly and aggressively respond to the other, when and if terrorist attacks occurred, as they inevitably would...they were starting to work together, at lower, more significant, institutional levels than ever before, in relationships like Lessar and Mustafa...so the problems for Israel came mostly now from Syria, and especially, southern Lebanon, stronghold of Hezbollah, proxy for Iran.

So Ehud could continue building on the valuable information started from Mustafa...and hopefully connect the dots...

The Mossad had several theories of what was going on...and one of them put the Syrian ambassador right in the thick of it...this unconfirmed report of Fire of God agents flying to America as part of the Syrian diplomatic delegation would turn the heat up for clarity...for truth... Mossad would send Ehud to Damascus that very day.

Jared Faulkner was reading international summaries left by O'Malley as he drank coffee from what was now, a second carafe...updates on the conditions of the world leaders...the latest EEG-2 prints from Dr. Angelo's testing first thing this morning, and 2 more incidents of confirmed leaders succumbing to the malady..."jeez" said Faulkner to himself..."none of this makes any sense"...and headed downstairs to the Situation Room.

"Sorry Doctor...no admittance at the moment...security team in session"...a Marine in full dress, and side-armed stood by the door...his partner, just down the hall at the second entrance..."ok, no problem... just needed my laptop is all..." Just then, O'Malley and Fitch came out the door..."Dr. Faulkner...been out here long?"..."no sir, just a couple minutes"..."we are finished, Captain" O'Malley addressed the Marine... "Yes, sir...the doctor may retrieve his laptop then?"..."of course...there are several on the side tables...probably bunched with them".

Faulkner went in. A mix of military and civilian men mostly, but Barbara Jefferson was present, and someone else he had not met...not US...she had some kind of ID around her neck...and a military escort, her own military...he could see now they were Russian, and likely from the diplomatic corps here in Washington...they walked by, she smiled, the officer did not.

The room was tense when he ambled in with his coffee and reports to grab his computer...people were gathering their papers, belongings..."they cannot be serious about this" said one of the unrecognized civilians speaking to a CIA type, "this will inflame the entire region...several independent states will likely be drawn into it...damn"...Faulkner kept moving, found his Apple, and exited quickly..."Thanks", he half-turned to the Marine at the door and headed up yet another flight of White House stairs.

Dr. Gaiter would have some interesting results in the morning blood values which he would discuss later with the team, but he was at Walter Reed Medical at the moment...speaking with Chief Pathologist Captain Dr. Jerome Burns..."so you've found some irregularities when comparing these results to last month's?"...the President has routine blood testing, on a monthly basis since it was discovered he was developing early signs of elevating PSA (prostate specific antigen)...which was not familial..."yes, we have, a host of small changes...nothing but cocktail talk when taken individually...but together, show a kind of system variance albeit slight and arguable"...he handed Gaiter the results...Gaiter studied them for a few moments, and nodded his head..."yes...I see that...JB, did you have the metals test run?" ..."readings any minute...they take different filtering processes, and we got hamstrung on one of the machines...but it's fixed now, and outcomes are forthcoming...coffee?"...Gaiter checked his watch, "ya...I will"...and they headed for Burns private medical library, with the soft leather chairs...coffee and pastries were always sent up from the Walter Reed kitchen when Burns was in-house.

Mustafa had discussed this Fire of God cell before...the team closest to President Aswari had suspected the cell of probing the larger Presidential guard for alliances...they were trying to convince a guard member or two that the politics of the President were a betrayal of Palestinians, and making all Palestinians a laughingstock in Israel...he was "a dog" and deserved to die...they wanted to have access, to penetrate the Presidential ring of protection...by turning loyal Palestinians with the devil's rhetoric...this alone was enough for Mustafa...but there was more...once the cell membership in Damascus was digitally captured and sent to Mossad...and then on to Washington and New York, the terabits would hit on 2 faces...multiple times...moving freely within the Syrian delegation, and beyond. Mossad would discuss with Washington, possible next steps, but Mustafa would not wait...he was assigned to protect the President, and he had failed...they all had...

There was one particularly poisonous member of this group, clearly a high ranking member, possibly the leader, who had approached Mustafa's point man for dignitary visits..."a dangerous man" said Bashar Taqir, the contact thru which all diplomatic visits on Palestinian controlled soil would proceed..."unpredictable...with the face of a goat"...but the man was *not* to be underestimated...the car bombing earlier this year which had taken the life of the Jordanian President's daughter had been claimed by other groups, but the intel which Mustafa had, pointed straight to this group, and very likely, *this* man, Ala Abu Halaq. Mustafa decided it was time for a "visitation" from the S5, the small "closed fist" of the Presidential Guard...a crack team trained in several capitols in virtually every necessary element of urban warfare and hand-to-hand destruction...their favorite brand of "discipline" was Korean subak, "empty handed" which gave the team every advantage because they carried no weapons...it had given them access to some of most notorious terrorists...a grave mistake.

Mustafa requested permission, after giving his reasons, to send the team to find the Fire of God cell in Amman...the mission was approved...

"if you think they have something to do with *this*" said Ahmad Samir, his superior, and handpicked second in command of the Presidential Guard by the President himself, "then we will send **everybody**" Mustafa assured Samir that something *was* going on with this radical group, and head-of-state assassination or worse, this, was what this mission was all about...and S5 would do the job for all of them..."My contact in Mossad also believes this" Samir said he wanted word, and would be at the compound with the President...Mustafa headed back toward his office..."the fire *is* coming my friend..." he said to himself looking at Halaq's photograph..."it is coming".

Faulkner ran his tests again after examining the President...the Stanford twin supercomputers, Tweedledee and Tweedledum, to his astonishment, needed more information...Bennett had e-mailed the results from last night's test about 2 am PST...<u>inconclusive</u> ...despite a commentary from the neuro-science department...Faulkner was puzzled by this...he believed he had indications in the results of substantial white matter activity...in addition to Beta waves off the scale...but what did it add up to?...what did it mean exactly?...anatomical storms of extraordinary and unprecedented strength and depth as measured by the *f*MRI...a combination which frankly, Faulkner, as a neuroscientist, had never seen before...apparently neither had the Tweedle's...he sent the second set of results in addition to Stephanie Angelo's EEG-2 test earlier in the morning...and there were considerable differences...the EEG Dr. Angelo recorded was focused, energetic, fertile with powerful brain perfusives and electrical activities...Faulkner's was showing a passive brain... a brain at rest... what was going on in there?

The REM activity which Angelo measured showed a nearly fully involved brain, which was highly irregular under these conditions...under *any* conditions... and the President remained unconscious... yesterday he would have believed some kind of drug involvement, but he had checked and double-checked the blood analysis done so far for ingested or abnormal chemistries... none detected.

Faulkner would make a call...he had a hunch...a big one. The call he would make was to Dr. Benjamin Alexander, the renowned psychoanalyst...and more specifically, a respected international authority on sleep and dreams...is it possible the President's brain, *all* their brains could be looping over and over in some kind of dream state?

This is what the data was showing...virtually constant REM...but how can this be happening?

Faulkner had no explanation...he was hoping Alexander would.

He called O'Malley to inquire of any objections.

"Where does he live?"

"In Virginia per the phone number"

"OK, I'll get the Service and FBI on it... if he's clean as far as their concerned, we can bring him in."

"It's possible he's at a conference somewhere, but if he's home, we could use his expertise for sure."

Dr. Benjamin Alexander, now in his early seventies had a long and distinguished career as psychiatrist and psychoanalyst to scores of the Washington elite for four decades. The FBI actually had a file on him, but it was noteworthy only for whom he was treating, not for behaviors of his own.

When he arrived at the West Wing entrance, he presented as a short and somewhat portly gentleman in his tweed jacket and light woolen trousers. One of his hallmarks was the ever present bowtie, pipe and tobacco pouch.

With hair thinning slightly and a very generous grey beard he walked with a slight limp... the fortunes of age and a deteriorating left hip.

"No smoking inside the White House I'm afraid, Doctor" declared the agent dropping him off.

"To be expected, young man. If I have a moment, time permitting, perhaps I can enjoy a smoke in the serenity of the rose garden... not in bloom now of course, but still of interest." And thanked the 2 agents who had been assigned to retrieve him.

O'Malley was notified he had arrived.

Dr. Faulkner was talking with Bennett via the Sit Room when Angelo came in...he waved her over..."so why didn't the modeling work do you think?"...they were discussing the possible root causes of the "indeterminate" conclusion by the twin mega-computers...

"I've been over this with the modeling team here, Jared...the algorithms *should* work...Dr. Werner brought up a possibility, which, after reviewing the data, may be correct...the speed of inflection and deflection on the trace programming mimics normal brain electrical speeds...President Ashley's speed is slightly out of range...faster...with variant speed accelerations...hard to believe, but true...his brain is operating milliseconds ahead of profile, our algorithms can only compensate so much...that's the explanation which seems to fit...we've measured these patterns discreetly, and they are skewed beyond what we have ever seen here...nothing in our banking exists for comparison...truly astounding..." "Nothing?...nothing at all?...what about the larger resource library...the international data?" Faulkner found it as astounding as Bennett did..."we're looking into that now...you know, when we got the call from Dr. Gaiter to send someone, and after a few questions and the answers he gave, I honestly expected a diagnosis of stroke or heart attack...good gawd, the stress of the damn job is enough for 3 people...anyway, that's what I expected you'd find, but...this is a **real** mystery Jared...almost surreal...I'm sure you feel it too" Faulkner paused before answering..."Thanks Malcolm...call me as soon as you have anything...I mean anything...and I'll keep you posted from this end..." Bennett said he would, and ended the call.

Stephanie Angelo was sitting close by, but respectfully far enough to give Faulkner some talking room..."Doctor"..."please, call me Stephanie...I'm swamped as it is with protocol and formality...the White House beats with it"…"yes…I've noticed"…"any updates from the super comps?"…"incredibly, no…that's what we were talking about, Malcolm Bennett and myself…heard of Malcolm?"…"I have in fact met Dr. Bennett…he chums with Ed Winthrop, my boss at the General…"…"and I've met Ed…small world, eh?"…"smaller all the time…so, what's the scoop on the readings?"…"Dr. B says out-of-scope…the algorithms won't run the comparisons against the modeling…Ashley is too fast…his brain…too damn fast"…"forgive me Jared, it's not the equipment, right?…I *have* to ask… first thing I'm asked if a test bombs back at the General…everything running properly?…no software problems?…when was the last time you ran controls?…etc., etc…so I apologize for asking"…"no, it's a good point…I will double check…but for argument sake, let's say it checks out…can you explain what the hell we are recording in there?…*faster*?"…he emphasized the word…"the whole show doesn't make any sense…I mean, when we look at the perfusion changes, my gawd, it's like new channels have opened up in the brain…mega-perfusion…the blood in his brain is raging…*EVERYWHERE*" and raised his voice…

At that moment, O'Malley came into the room…walked briskly over to them…the Situation Room was at full staffing as the White House was gathering and collating for summary briefs, all the events occurring around the globe that were being reported specifically about this every-nation catastrophe…"I need to speak with both of you, please humor me by coming over to the corner there where we can talk in privacy"… the 3 of them went to the far right corner, away from the traffic and busy staff.

"something has been brought to my attention…and I've been sitting on it for awhile…I called Jeremy Fitch at the Agency to get his take…he suggested pulling you two in…"…he looked intensely at both of them…"you cannot share this information with anyone…is that clear?…at least not until it is made public knowledge…" They looked at each other. "Mr. O'Malley…is this a security issue?…national security?"…Faulkner was slightly uncomfortable with the scenario..."I have no idea, to tell you the truth...but I must cover the bases on this...do I have your words?"

They both shook their heads yes...O'Malley took a deep breath and exhaled..."I had a call from our ambassador to Cote de Ivoire this morning, our time...he shared an astounding account of actions transpiring at the Presidential Palace...he was a witness in fact...the President of that country, Ufi Granjeau, unconscious like the rest, has been writing..." Angelo jumped into his thought stream..."writing?...this man is unconscious you said...didn't you just say that?"..."yes, I did...but he's been writing...something extraordinary...suffice it is to say, his doctors recognized what was happening, and got him pen and paper...he's left-handed apparently...the same side his IV was placed in...but they managed, and he started writing...while unconscious mind you, I'm still trying to get my head around this...while *UNCONSCIOUS*...writing the same thing, the same sentence over and over...*Non temere*, WE ARE ALL OK..." ..."what was that again?" asked Angelo with incredulity..."the Latin translation of the first part is, *Fear Not, Non temere*, WE ARE ALL OK...Ambassador Chabot confirms it, saw him write it...I'm at a complete loss...is this a coincidence?...what the hell does it mean?"...Faulkner looked at his watch, and then back at O'Malley..."it *means*, Mr. O'Malley, that we need to get one of the BK's on Ufi Granjeau...as soon as possible".

O'Malley's beeper lit up, it was Catherine... "Dr. A in office."

"Dr. Faulkner, Dr. Alexander has arrived, can you join me in my office?"

"Actually, I really have to go up and check the equipment...Stephanie reminded me that whenever there are 'abnormalities' in the test results, first thing to do, prudently, is re-check the equipment... so let me do that, and then we can all meet with Dr. Alexander... and that's another reason we should be operating properly, we don't want Dr. Alexander pointing that out as soon as he arrives."

The two men left the Situation Room at a brisk pace, heading up the stairs.

Catherine was being thanked for just serving him coffee as O'Malley came in.

"Well, good morning Mr. O'Malley"... Alexander stood up and extended his hand. "It appears from what the news people are saying is we have a worldwide crisis on our hands. How can *I* help?" and lifted his slumping shoulders a little. O'Malley liked him immediately and explained the situation from the Chief of Staff position... "I'll leave the science to the attending doctors"

"I see" said Alexander when O'Malley finished. "This is excellent coffee by the way... Thank you again Catherine"... he boomed just the way O'Malley did when speaking to his secretary in the outer office. It brought a smile to O'Malley's face.

"I would begin by asking to see the President if that is possible."

He commented on some of the artwork and architecture as they left the office and headed for the residence.

S5 took little time entering and leveling the Fire of God cell in the south of Amman. Splitting up a mile or more from their destination, all five members took different routes and approached the apartment where this armed group moved and plotted from...the Jordanian security force kept an eye on this dangerous cabal, but they were locals, not foreigners, and some were merchants and merchant's sons, so the security force only kept them under observation...all men of the group were tied to the Abu Abdallah mosque very near the nerve center of their work, the apartment. This would not be easy...the plan was for each man to come up and enter the building from one of 3 entrances, all guarded...dressed casually and hopefully, drawing little suspicion. When the point man knocked on the door of the 2nd floor flat, the others were already in position, with 2 lookouts dispatched and their bodies hidden.

A man in his early forties answered the door..."Blessings my friend" said S1, "I have been told in my prayers to visit my brothers with a donation and ask for literature...I am seeking ways to honor my children, killed by the friends of the Palestinian Authority...the Jewish pigs...if I have come to the wrong house, I beg your forgiveness...I do not know the area well"...he held out a loaf of fresh baked bread and 2 date sweet cakes..."for your family"...the man inside the door looked at him a long moment, asking him to turn around, which he gladly did..."yes...you are have come to the right house"...and stepped halfway into the hallway, looking in both directions, and the stairwell...there was no one...he extended his arm to enter.

S1 moved slowly into the room...men were sitting on either side of the door...7 all told...with handguns, and a Kalishnikov on a small table...

there were laptop computers and a large stationary computer in addition to cellphones, and boxes of printed materials for distribution...he stood holding the bread and cakes, bowing his head slightly as he met each set of eyes that were now fixed completely on him...the older man closed the door behind them..."what is your name?"... "Yahmoud Basat...my family is in Gaza"...this was in fact his real name, but not where he lived...he lived in the West Bank...as did the rest of S5. One of the men already was at a laptop pumping in his name...

"you are not in our files, Yahmoud Basat" said the man, standing and turning toward him, they all stood now, "we have every Palestinian name and address in Gaza...*you*, are not here...why is that Yahmoud?"... Yahmoud handed his host the bread and date cakes, and before anyone could react, he exploded at the man asking the question, breaking his neck cleanly...a split second later, the door crumpled and flew inward as the rest of the S5 team came splintering in...it was over in seconds, not a shot was fired...7 men were on the floor, most of them dead before they could react...Yahmoud, who did not kill the man who had let him in, picked him up roughly and sat him in a chair..."how is your memory today, my friend...I hope for your sake it is clear and sharp..." and with that, the interrogation began.

A few hours later, Mustafa received four laptop computers, and the hard drive from the stationary computer...he sent them on to the technical team for analysis...after the S5 de-briefing, the written notes, and re-corded interrogation they brought back he took to his desk for review... he was satisfied with the information extracted from the operation, but the prize, the leader of the Fire of God, was not in Jordan...he was in Syria, in Damascus...Mustafa would now contact Ehud by cellphone... and give him the news.

Stephanie Angelo had returned to the First Lady's office and was walking the long hallway now back to the President's bedroom. "have you ever been comprehensively psychotic Mrs. Ashley?...the world making no sense whatsoever?"..."yes...high school was the first time...several times since...my last year of college was the worst of it...hospitalization for several weeks...laboring under sledgehammer medications for some time after...and then, into the slipstream of life again"...Angelo nodded..."and now?...is psychosis crowding in now?"...Elizabeth Ashley stopped and stood moving her foot and gazing at it...then looked up...she was void of affect...no emotion...no expression..."I believe", and took an uncomfortably long pause..."I'm almost ashamed to say it, Doctor, I believe that the President is not my husband...he's a copy of my husband...a duplicate. "...Stephanie Angelo knew that this woman was expressing profound illness, engaged in a monumental struggle for her mind....and, as she looked quickly around, was thankfully relieved that they were not in earshot of the Secret Service...After more details, and a few questions, Stephanie Angelo was getting a better picture of Elizabeth Ashley's medical needs. Angelo was not a psychiatrist, but worked with dozens of them at MGH and elsewhere...and typically, *they* were the one's coming to her for counsel about certain things...asking her thoughts about "wrinkles" in the clinical pictures of patients they were treating...and she would almost always help nail the condition down.

Angelo, after living for years with a very mentally ill brother (and a parent), possessed a "facility", a gift for putting disparate damaged neurological pieces together to form a sound and accurate clinical judgment...but more importantly, a solid treatment plan. She was forming something in her mind now about Elizabeth Ashley...and she would very much like to test her with the new EEG-3 she had brought with her from Boston... and, if Faulkner would agree, the BK-1 he was using on the President.

Behind them, an aide to Li Ming was carrying a small package toward the First Lady's COS office...Angelo was guessing the meds she had ordered were here, and waited to be beeped...as if on cue, her beeper lit up, "Meds here...bloods back"...

"Mrs. Ashley, let's return to your office for a few moments...I believe some of the prescriptions are here"...and gently escorted her to the couch outside the office..."I'll be but a moment"...the prescriptions were all there...five in all...and the blood work was back..."these blood levels have barely *any* therapeutic value...except the veterinary tranquilizer of course" Angelo looked up at Ming and smiled..."she's not even in measurable range on this one" and went on through the labs..."ok" she took a moment, punched in a few numbers on her lab calculator, then looked solemnly at Li Ming..."ok, I'm changing a few things...I have 3 new prescriptions I'll need someone here to fill quickly, and deleting these previous 3"... removing three of the new meds and handing the replacement scripts to Ming. She handed Ming one of the remaining prescription bottles. "This first one is a 200 mg dosage spread evenly QID throughout the day, taken with food, but start today, preferably as soon as possible... and this one, 20 mg. in conjunction with the first, they have a synergistic effect together, and for the moment, we'll wait until I get this new med just off trial from MGH for the positive psychotic symptoms, it is a very promising new medication, here is the name of my colleague at MGH who will send them via med transport to Washington...MGH does it practically on a daily basis, with tissue samples and blood work on the return flight from teaching hospitals down here, but I trust Mr. O'Malley can speed up the delivery process considerably, yes? I'll ask my colleague at The General to send 3 months' worth down" Ming nodded..."also, a liquid multi-vitamin with Omega-3 fish oil and plenty of Vitamin D... let's make sure she has 3 tablespoons today...spaced apart, and this 3rd script is to help her sleep, it's very good...any questions?"..."no Ma'am" Li

Ming had written it all down in shorthand. "please order her some food from the kitchen, I want her to start right away with this regimen...and let me know when those other scripts come in?." ...Li Ming nodded and picked up the phone, hit 3 buttons..."Jack?...Li Ming...please send up to the First Lady's office a good sized brunch for 2...and including some fruit and pastry please...asap...ok?"

The chef would do it himself..."10 minutes, max"..."thank you, very good...you need to be with her...ok?...I have to check on the President... oh, the First Couple have 2 daughters if I'm not mistaken?"..."yes, Elise and Renny"..."I'll want to send some blood work off to MGH later... the President and the First Lady...k?" Li Ming nodded and would have someone on stand-by.

Angelo softly approached the woman sitting with her hands folded on the couch in the hallway...and sat down beside her..."Mrs. Ashley... Elizabeth...there are several medications which I have ordered for your condition...Li Ming will help you to take them during brunch... and something for later to help you sleep at bedtime...I'm going to see the President, and if you wish, later today, we can go to see him together... ok?" Elizabeth Ashley looked gravely worn...psychically exhausted..."yes" she said whispering..."fine"...Angelo patted her hands and shoulders as she stood up...stretching into Li Ming's office..."she's *NOT* to be left alone...play classical music...Mozart preferably...no stress whatsoever... this will be difficult under the circumstances, but please manage it..." Angelo locked eyes with Ming...they nodded to each other, and Angelo moved down the hall.

Faulkner had finished checking his equipment...he turned as she came in..."checks out...no glitches...and you're not going to believe this but, the Chinese Premier, Ho Fong...wait, let me back up...the Chinese director-ate of medicine or security, I don't know which one, would not allow our researchers even into the Presidential complex at first...we had to get the US Ambassador, and several researchers in China who know our work to confirm its safety and so forth...so that took almost too long, our people were ready to ship over to India, but there was final agreement and Premier Fong was tested...one guess as to what the Tweedle's came up with?"

"His brain waves were phased beyond the controls...speedwise...just out of range...ya?"..."ya...just like Stephen Ashley's...I've asked for a comparison between the results from both men...and conclusions...from the neuroscience *team* at Stanford, not the super comp's...and I think MGH should weigh in on this as well..." Faulkner looked around the room, the Service agent stood not five feet away, Dr. Jackson was busy comparing data on the President's vital signs and lab work over the last 40 hours... "Dr. Jackson..." Jackson stood and came over..."yes...what is it?"..."I am thinking we are moving into a prolonged period with the President...we may want to add nursing and at some point physical therapy to get his extremities moving..." ..."rightly so, we have requested a full nursing contingent starting " he checked his watch, "any minute now...coming over from Bethesda...and it will be round the clock, 2 nurses per shift... and we are reviewing fluid management, catheterization, etc...and, whether within a certain time frame, the President should be moved to either Walter Reed or the naval hospital...both have suites to accommodate the chief executive...so contingencies are being firmed up...there is legislation being introduced in the Senate chamber this morning as to the legal status of the executive branch under present circumstances...looks like the VP will be taking over...by tomorrow"..."tomorrow...?"..."yes"...Faulkner cringed and got ready for another test. He also contacted the closest team to where Ufi Granjeau was..."yes Paul (a graduate student), you and the team need to get to the Ivory Coast as soon as possible, and contact the US Ambassador...then over to the Presidential Palace or whatever...ok? We need to get Ufi Granjeau tested...as far as any telecom limitations, I'm hoping Dr. Ehsani, you know him from the Labs...I'm hoping he can crunch some numbers on the fly and come up with some algorithm to get that info into the data stream without breaking up...call me when all

that is set, ok?...and we don't have much time Paul...a few hours at most...
good luck." And Faulkner ended the call.

If the Africa team could get that done within a few hours, then all the
functioning BK's would be online and monitoring (except one, which
they were having trouble with)...the US, Canada, Great Britain, China
and the Ivory Coast.

Two months previous to this worldwide "event", Chinese Premier Ho Fong had hosted, in Bejiing, a breakthrough series of negotiations between Pakistan and India, two countries who shared borders with China...the talks focused on the seemingly unresolvable status of Kashmir. It remained *the* flashpoint in the tense relations between the two countries, with nationalists from both sides pushing their governments into continuous strife. Premier Ho, in an extraordinary gesture, invited the foreign ministers from both countries, with their respective delegations, for exploratory talks. Ho himself would participate, showing both regimes, and the world, in what serious regard he held his neighbors...and how important peace was to him personally, and for the entire Asian sub-continent. By the end of the eight day visit and discussions, a framework emerged...new ground upon which to gingerly walk forward, and a resolve by all sides to meet again...a success by all accounts. For the first time in decades, real progress had been made...much due to Ho's continued presence and encouragement.

He renewed the invitation for another round, this time inviting the Prime Ministers to an official state visit...and opportunities to step closer to a final acceptable status for Kashmir. With the issue of Kashmir and the constant threat of border confrontation finally diminishing, Pakistan could effectively address the internal troubles in its northern provinces. Ho had sent signals at the negotiations with the foreign ministers that China was ready and able to deliver aid in whatever form to Pakistan, to help.

But all the leaders were "as good as gone" now, according to more than one news source...the world had to move on...to a different collection of presidents and Prime Ministers and premiers, etc…and the question was being asked everywhere…on all news channels and internet sites…"what happens next?"…

Upon arriving at the President's bedroom (Alexander had some difficulty with the stairs, but gallantly forged them), he was introduced to Dr. Gaiter, Agent Wheeler, Drs. Angelo and Faulkner.

"I'm very pleased to meet you all"...extending his hand to each... "May I approach the President?" Gaiter escorted him to the bedside. Alexander stood there a long moment without speaking.

Then, looking up, he watched the EEG tracings for several minutes. No one spoke.

Angelo finally broke the silence. "Dr. Alexander, I have all of the President's EEG tracings which we began yesterday morning and have broken the classic stages down for time in that stage, etc., synching them with general observations of the President." Alexander crossed the room and stood over her shoulder as she ran the synopsis. His current EEG was also running in a separate window so he could get a general sense of where the President was, and is now, regarding brain activity.

"Quite remarkable I should say... and no unusual electromyographic potential has been noted... this is highly irregular. The tracings show enormous time is being dedicated to dreaming... to REMming, more and more as this progresses. He is dreaming right now... and has been for nearly 3 hours... also, without being indelicate, I did not notice any notation of erectile stimulation during any of these REM periods... is that correct?"

"No erections noted" Stephanie Angelo glanced at Agent Wheeler.

"No Ma'am... not that I noticed" Wheeler was blushing. Alexander told him that both male and female experienced sexual flushing, or engorgement, during REM.

"Of course that passes with age, and is not a luxury of mine any longer, but the President is in his sexual prime I would say...this is highly irregular physiologically. Please note that, and identify it if it does happen... REM without sexual engorgement occurs only in serious physical disability. It is a natural phenomenon."

Alexander, with some effort, sat himself on the couch reviewing more of the data from Angelo's laptop.

"This appears to be a progressive expansion of REM... with very little time now spent in any of the other stages of sleep."

O'Malley asked, "How many stages of sleep are there?" He had forgotten some of what Angelo had already told him.

"Typically a human being experiences 4 distinct stages of sleep... you continue to have arguments over research about the front and back ends of a complete sleep cycle, but I subscribe to the classic 4. He then spent a few moments describing the 4 distinct periods experienced by every person when they finally begin a sleep cycle.

"Stage 1 typically is the initial stage... breathing slows, your body temperature drops, your muscles begin a relaxation process and the brain wave changes into an alpha type rhythm. Stage 2 deepens this entire physiological process... a person may experience hypnogogic dreaming at this deepening, which is nothing more than nonsensical imagery. Stage 3 continues the slowdown, heart rate, blood pressure, musculature and so forth, until finally the person falls into Stage 4 which is the deepest and longest period, and that which separates human consciousness most completely with the surrounding world. This combined cycle lasts roughly 90 minutes or so.

The person then progresses upwards from Stage 4 into Stage 1 again, and the process begins anew. As the process unfolds, somewhere hovering around Stage 2 is where REM and dreaming occur... the dreaming can be short or lengthy, with each person experiencing 5 plus REM dreams per full sleep cycle...

I say that while also noting that dreaming *does* take place in non-REM sleep as well... there are considerable studies showing a distinct difference in the quality and temperament of the two dream states... REM being the more aggressive state and non-REM being the more passive... or, if you like, REM being the more contentious, non-REM the more quiescent."

Alexander once again approached the President.

"Well, the *classic* characteristic of REM sleep remains active in the President... his eyes are rapidly moving under their lids, confirming what I was just seeing on the EEG. I should also like to know, for as long as this phenomenon goes on, whether this rapid eye movement accompanies the EEG readings of REM... if not, that also would be a radical departure of physiology. By the way, since the reporting of this event on the news channels never seems to get it right, how long has the President been like this may I ask?"

O'Malley checked his notes. "I cannot speak to before the monitoring began, but he went to bed sometime after 11:30 Friday evening.

The extended REM periods, as you call them, I expect have been building since then."

"Extraordinary" declared Alexander. "I for one have never seen anything like it in all my years of practice."

Jared Faulkner had reviewed all the measured REM periods and, with Dr. Angelo's concurrence, mentioned the unusual spike just as REM began. He brought it up on the screen for Alexander to see.

"Initially it crossed my mind as artifact, but it is a marker preceding every REM period. Have you any idea what it is?"

Alexander saw the spike over and over as Angelo spliced the REM's together.

"No idea... yet another piece to what is becoming a remarkable puzzle. I have never seen such a marker on any of the patients I have studied or treated... but I would label it immediately." He thought for a moment.

"The Angelo-Faulkner Shift is what I would call it." And he smiled at them both.

"And we have seen the EEG's of some of the other nation's leaders as well... it is there too."

Alexander had to sit down. "This isn't possible. This just isn't possible."

He began reaching for his pipe and tobacco... and put the pipe to his mouth but did not light it. He looked over at Ashley for a long moment, then at the EEG tracing his mind.

"It has just struck me... the brain consumes enormous quantities of energy when awake... REM is a close kin to that state... for a brain to sustain prolonged periods of REM *without* the energy it needs would likely induce a catastrophic atrophy of cells, of neurons... they will literally burn themselves out. I would suggest increasing the glucose administration with continued blood sugar monitoring... this will be a balancing act of sorts until something turns in his condition...I expect, but this is most unusual, and will require a most unusual regimen of support... do you agree, Doctors?"

Gaiter, Angelo and Faulkner all shook their heads yes in unison.

"Good... this will protect the President to a substantial degree."

That was *it*, thought O'Malley. "Whoever has done this, the endgame is to render the global leadership permanently disabled. A virus or something is continually amping the brain until it exhausts itself, essentially becoming a dysfunctional mess. I have to speak with Fitch to get the word out...and to McMasters to spread the word medically. This is like something out of science fiction...I hope Dr. Crosby and her team can identify something and recommend treatment...and quickly. I'll get an up to date from her in the SR later" he noted that and turned to Alexander. "Thank you Doctor... this has been considerably enlightening... and if you care to smoke, I'll have one of the agents escort you to the veranda or garden area. Also, can you remain awhile longer? There are other questions I, or we, might have."

"But of course, Mr. O'Malley... I am at your service." They started walking out. "20th century literature is replete with the treatment of dreams (Alexander put his arm over O'Malley's shoulder in a fatherly kind of gesture)...with substantial careers built upon their expression...I am thinking of Kafka and Ionesco, Picasso, Dali, many composers and writers of all types, engineers etc., the list is, well, quite long indeed. Dreams are fascinating to discuss, and to see how they impact our world through the expression they get from the dreamer..." He paused for a moment then whirled to the other doctors..."in fact, if you recall, Doctors, it was Dr. Otto Loewi who first discovered that neurons communicate with each other by way of chemicals, now known as neurotransmitters, Loewi contributed quite a bit to understanding their roles, won the Nobel Prize and so forth, but the key piece was that his insight into the process came to him *in a dream*, actually 2 dreams because the first time he woke up and wrote it all down but the next morning couldn't read his own writing...so the very next night it happened again...and he woke up, stayed awake, wrote down an experimental technique to prove his theory, and went to his lab and successfully demonstrated that synaptic signaling was orchestrated by chemical messengers, not electrical ones as had been thought and widely accepted. He's been known as the Father of Neuroscience as these things go…" Alexander smiled and scratched his head as he glanced at Stephen Ashley again…then asked for an agent to escort him to the garden for a pipe full.

And with that, O'Malley excused himself and headed out of the residence.

The White House Office of Legal Counsel had finished, after several rewrites, the brief O'Malley had requested to stall any transition process of duties and powers, titled: The Constitutional Protection of the Office of the President as Regards the 25th Amendment...whereas the 25th Amendment aptly describes the *procedural* transition, definitions and conclusions provide, some, if not much, interpretive room. Senator Clemons had prepared, after some delay, and each senate office would receive, the legislation he would introduce at 3 PM EDT, unless, the condition of the President improved, or competing legislation was introduced before that...Clemons was the powerful Chairman of Ways and Means...he was not to be trifled with, and certainly not upstaged on such an important matter as execution of the 25th amendment...but O'Malley had done something better, he passed to the Senate, *and* the House leadership, the concluded brief from the White House OLC...a particularly erudite passage determined that the current status of the President was expected, based on the best medical assessment, to be transient...no authorization to replace was therefore necessary or prudent...in matters of grave national security requiring action while the President was unavailable, the sum membership of the cabinet could, in truth, consent to a course of action...their power was an extension from the Oval Office due to their Executive branch affiliation...and so forth. It was good enough, and cast enough doubt on the constitutionality of Senator Clemons' legislation that senators would pause and give the situation time...and time is all O'Malley wanted...

Stephen Ashley had come to the conclusion, that he really did not *know* any of these men and women...oh sure, he had met a number of them, some more than a few times, but never informally, never like this...no one had ever met like this...on a basic human to human level, this was fantasy. He looked intently at the formations around him...the entire Central American leadership group was laughing and playing some kind of hand game...there were natural groupings, some in twos and threes, some larger...there were a few singles too, human beings, off to one side, politely listening at a distance, or facing away altogether, toward the sea.

The Prime Minister of Israel was one of these leaders...and the Russian President...and now he realized, he too had drifted from close contact with anyone...there was a kind of rhythm, a flow, in the global affairs of states, where certain heads of particular states always bore more scrutiny, more criticism it seemed, it was historical, and much depended on regional or even global political positioning...he felt a hand on his shoulder...it was Pope Gregory II.

"I expect you are wondering why I am here Mr. President?"...Ashley did not exactly recognize him...he was not officially dressed...he looked more like an Italian café owner...Ashley had met the Pope twice, once in Rome after a G8 conference, and once as the visiting titular leader of America's and the world's 1.3 billion Catholics...Coughlin O'Malley very much liked this man, a Bolivian Cardinal, raised to the Papacy on a legacy of a Nobel Peace Prize, tireless work on behalf of Bolivian and South American poor, and his extraordinary holiness..."Pope Gregory II?"..."Yes, I am amazed myself"..."Wait" said Ashley, "you are an official head of state...isn't that so?"..."so it is my friend...I have been speaking with King Faisud, and Petr Jorbin...we are thinking we are not all passed from the world just yet...something else is going on...something with great significance..." "but I'm a Congregationalist"...and with that, the Pope laughed mightily..."Petr is an avowed atheist, King Faisud is Sunni Muslim, I am Catholic, and so forth...there are many stories here Mr. President...I do not think this is about religion"...and he laughed some more slapping Ashley on the back...

General Ushkya was in charge of the land forces now moving toward Chechnya...he was staunch anti-independence military from before the official breakup of the Soviet state, and he would not fail in putting down the heinous plot he had come to understand, and so launched by Chechnyan "freedom fighters"...Ushkya and his commanders had been told that evidence existed which implicated Chechnyans in a wider global plot focused on the world leadership...Ushkya was told to give that information to every soldier to inspire the comrades to fight for the Premier and the President ...he was a man burning with revenge, his oldest son, a lieutenant in the old Soviet Special Forces had been killed in car bomb remotely detonated while he was on mission in Grozny... and these rebels against the motherland would now pay...all manner of military firepower was available, and he was resolved to use it. The plan was astonishingly simple, worked and re-worked as intelligence agents tracked the Chechynan terrorist top military and political people. Ushkya had the locations, the safe houses and offices locked in to his tanks' GPS tracking systems and helicopter gunship systems with powerful Argos missiles. Ushkya knew this first assault had to be extreme...a defining blow...and had to be immediately followed by a massive ground operation. Chechynans were well entrenched, fortifications laid years ago, simulations run over and over for this very kind of thing, which they knew would eventually come. This world event had given certain elements in the Russian political and military structure the excuse they had been scheming for...and unbeknownst even to Ushkya, FSB agents had designed, and were in place with his soldiers, to release an engineered virulent biological organism into Chechyna...and by their calculations, a total in excess of 58% of the civilian population would ultimately succumb. This plan would sacrifice likely 25% of Ushkya's invasion force in the process, but to effectively blame Chechynan terrorists for this bio-logical weapon, precious Russian lives would have to be compromised.... no outside investigative body would be allowed close enough access to determine the real cause until the crisis had passed, if ever.

And Ushkya was readying for zero hour.

Bennett was excited when he reached Faulkner…"Jared, we have reviewed the scans again, the team…and we did some input changes on the super's…we found that if we run the algorithms on specific *segments* of the brain activity, and not an in-total run, we have stretches of normal activity…the algorithms are unable to make sense of the speeded up segments, so we are eliminating those sections from the interpretation… this brain is as normal as yours or mine…except in certain segments…and the time-lapse might be a millisecond or two, but they are interspersed throughout the end-to-end scan…that's why the Tweedle's kicked it out… couldn't make sense of the time distortions…that's what we think anyway…and it seems to hold up when we cut those sections out…normal EEG-2 measurements" Bennett paused, as if he were thinking whether or not to continue…

"there is something else…" Faulkner, who was sitting, had his head down now, supporting it with his right arm and hand on his forehead, elbow on the knee…he looked in pain.

"Malcolm…what?…for gawd sake…what is it?"…Faulkner could hear excited voices in the background…"Jared…Stephen Ashley is showing anatomical changes"…Faulkner fixated on a speck of something on the floor…"this is almost too difficult to believe Jared…but, and we have looked at this a dozen times or more now…Frank Stapleton first noticed it…but, from the beginning of the scans, as we coordinate them with the electrical activity, we can literally watch white matter changes from beginning to end…the white matter congestion has increased by .6 %… and the pace accelerates, in concert with the electrical frequency…this, frankly, is extraordinary…no one here has ever seen anything like it…"

Faulkner waited, thinking..."Malcolm, have you looked at the Chinese Premier's test results yet?"..."no Jared, we were in the middle of this...I wanted to be certain before I called you...the Premier is our next task...the team is very wired up here...this is a revolution in neuroscience, we are all revved up..." ..."I have a suspicion what you'll find...but...oh, do me a favor?...Dr. Angelo has contacted Ed Winthrop at MGH...please send the data, and your conclusions on President Ashley to that team...ok?"

Bennett said he would.

"Thank you, good work Dr. Bennett...pass my appreciation on to the team...especially Frank...damn...this is getting stranger by the minute."

Stephen Ashley. 47th President of the United States. Favorite son of the State of Missouri. Harry Truman country. Republican. Cautious moderate centrist on foreign policy, a populist, even progressive on domestic agenda initiatives, but fiscally responsible about it...he would drive the fat out of legislation and get it, lean and muscular, to the intended ends... that was his record as governor, and the public appreciated it. He was 2 years in now to his first term, and already was losing his stomach for the Washington power heads and their minion armies of pocket stuffers... this place was rife with people buying and people being bought...he longed for his days back in Big Mo...back where your word still meant something, where the money trail never went very far, and could be followed pretty easily, rooted out...not so here. He rode a tidal wave of popular support in the general election, but found he could make little headway against this mountain of lobbyists and seasoned corporate lawyers, "ghost" writers of much of the legislative agenda...lawyers owned this town...not the citizenry at large...and few were driven by service to the public good...he would get done what he could, and leave after one term...

Coughlin O'Malley did not want this to happen. He had known Ashley for 20 years, from their time together around Missouri courtrooms and the Missouri statehouse, and he knew that the changes which had already started to take hold in the dark places of Washington, would continue... the country **would** bleed itself of the foulness bubbling in Lobbytown... but it would take time, and a President who would finish the job. Ashley was that man. He knew it. He would push and pull the extraneous bits of executive branch protocol to the limit to protect the President...he did not understand, no one did, what was happening with this world event to state leaders...but he was strangely not afraid...and he believed

Ufi Granjeau…"they were all ok"…and that something extraordinary was occurring…something, about which, he only had an inkling….he paged to find Dr. Angelo…she was reviewing test results with the MGH team. She met him in his office, 15 minutes later.

"You're getting the hang of this place" said O'Malley as she came to his doorway, "fifteen on the dot"…he motioned to his sofa, "please…

I am interested in what you can tell me about dreams?…and I promise to keep quiet"…

"I know Dr. Alexander is here, but I would like to hear what you have to say. We can all discuss this topic together later… if we have time."

## Stephanie Angelo's Monologue

"Let's see", and she thought for a moment how to start with an answer...

"if we examine the international research on dreams, about the only thing we can say with certainty is that dreams are self-actuated. They emerge from no single identifiable physiological source or process, and require a kind of puzzling interplay of diverse neurochemical compounds to be sustained...the kind Dr. Faulkner and I study all the time...but in our line of work, we are looking for pathology mostly, and backtracking, usually, till we find origins...but I don't believe this is possible with dreams...these exist as multi-tasked phenomenons, parsed from different organic regions. They are complex visual, auditory and sometimes tactile experiences, sprouting up when the brain relaxes its' comprehensive sensory grip on the exterior world. There are embedded cues of course, remembered sights, smells, sounds, touch, emotions, all combining in a kind of unconscious kaleidoscopic batter deep in our brain while the rest of our being recovers in sleep."

O'Malley was smiling..."unconscious kaleidoscopic batter...quite an image"....and he sat back in his chair..."doctor, please continue"

Angelo took a sip of water before she went on.

"Historical accounts are rife with the cultural significance assigned to dreams. Great literature uses dreams. Religions, as you know, speak frequently of them. Tribal spiritual rites and milestone passages to adulthood are often centered around dreams. Native Americans of the southwest in particular sought to induce dream-states with natural psychedelic compounds. Psychoanalytic therapy has focused a great measure of importance on the interpretation of dreams.

Neuroscientists like us for example, examine the various waveform results of EEG tests, as we've done with President Ashley and the others, as we search to determine brain wellness or pathology...and in these current cases, we can find nothing which we could pronounce as pathological. Dreams are not my specialty Mr. O'Malley, and I'm jumping around some, but let me just try stay on track and finish what I was saying... invariably we see in EEG results portions of what is known as rapid eye-movement sleep or REM. Dr. Alexander was just talking to that somewhat upstairs"...O'Malley nodded..."and the periods just before and just after... this is the brain time for dreaming, and perhaps a human being's deepest differentiation from full consciousness. And Stephen Ashley for example, is showing far more numerous and durational REM periods than are normal...far more. But as regards his complete EEG, and not just these excessive REM periods, we can compare the measured electrical discharges from his tested brain against enormous data banks of identified conditions, and we have done that, hoping we could steer a proper course of intervention. The electroencephalogram, Mr. O'Malley, is a centerpiece tool for a neurological diagnostician like myself, perhaps validating observable symptoms or doing the exact opposite...and in this case, completely befuddling us. As I have said, and Dr. Faulkner has said, high normal results across the board...except for the REM segments.

In cases like this one where the EEG provides inconclusive results, then magnetic resonance imaging or MRI may be required. This is that remarkable little scanner Dr. Faulkner brought with him...I had heard a lot about it, but had not seen it myself before yesterday...but the machine gives extraordinary pictorial accuracy, and 3-dimensional mapping, a tool with which our teams could view the anatomical structures of the brain "in action" as it were, and recommend something...and with all of this gadgetry, the schematics that the brain spits out in those bizarre waveforms I explained to you yesterday, and the technology of magnetic resonance, we cannot provide **any** additional information about the **process** of dreaming except that it is happening...and happening a lot.

Dreams are experienced some time of some part of every single day, I believe Dr. Alexander mentioned a floor number of five, and most of the time we barely remember them, and rarely, unless we are in therapy, even discuss them. There exists no substantive evidence to my knowledge, that any one culture, or any one race, or any specific geography influences incidence or duration of dreams. It happens to all of us.

Our brains seem to **need** them. Whether they are purposeful to the waking brain remains an open article of neurological and psychiatric debate.

We don't actually know **what** they are, and in that sense, they remain one of the final frontiers of brain understanding...I expect that since we have seen and continue to see the prolonged REM periods our leaders are enduring, we may wish that we could speak better to the issue...but we can't."

O'Malley asked Mrs. Freitas, who also did not leave the White House, and was, just now, up from a short nap in the WH sleeping quarters, to call Reverend Sloane and Father Buckley. He would like to speak with them as soon as possible...O'Malley was Catholic, Ashley was Congregational... the mix made for great discussions. O'Malley, while strangely reassured in his mind, as to the "final" outcome,...he was also the White House Chief-of-Staff...and he had to follow his instincts, and they were good, always had been...and speaking with Reverend Sloane and Father "Buck" would help him a great deal.

The President and Cough often played chess after hours to relax... Ashley was the better, more comprehensive player, but O'Malley typically feigned his way into advantageous positions, delaying outcomes and occasionally beating Ashley...O'Malley had learned years earlier how to squeeze into and out of tight political and legal spaces, leaving little or no shadow behind...with this event, there was no way he could negotiate his skill set, no measure he could take of his adversary...for the first time in a very long time, Coughlin O'Malley felt unable to move the pieces on the board...he could not help Stephen. He headed back to his office by way of the Oval Office...he slowed, lingered...he started thinking about Missouri...and what a wonderful state, "the heart" of the nation...then speeded up...leaving it all settling there, in the empty room.

Everything changed in an instant. They were not on the beach. It was pitch black. They were, again, on an ancient wooden ship...in a galley of some kind...it was the belly of a slave ship, and they were shackled and stacked like sacks in a wet, dark place, pitching and heaving in an angry sea. Ashley was stuffed in the middle position, on his back, on the bottom of a 3 tiered rack of human misery...Ashley strained to look around...all of the leaders were naked and groaning from the discomfort of the wooden pallets they were strapped to...and the stench and awful air. Ufi Granjeau was chained to Ashley's right, Petr Jorbin to his left. Jorbin appeared to be sick...coughing and wretching. Granjeau raised his head, "they will come for Petr...throw him to the sharks...his sickness might spread to the rest, ruining the lot to be sold...the Chilean President was thrown off a short while ago...I could see through the opening here... right into the sea...hundreds of miles from land of any kind". Ashley cringed as a whip cracked behind and to his left...there was a moan, and a hideous laugh following...urine was dripping from the pallets above him on to his face and head..."Ugh"...and he turned as much as he could away from it, held his breath. Chains began rattling, like links were being pulled through holes...his left arm was jerked hard and secured so he couldn't move it...Petr Jorbins' body was forcefully yanked from the pallet, and was gone. Ufi raised his head again, "Petr seemed sick from the beginning...it's too bad"...they heard a splash to their right...

"he's gone"..."What the hell is happening Ufi?" whispered Ashley...

"I think King Faisud was on to something when we were in the jungle"...

Suddenly the ship rocked violently, sending leaders at the aisles tumbling off, garroted by the chains..."men started hollering for help, but above deck there seemed to be some kind of evacuation going on...voices were leaving the ship...boats were being lowered...it took minutes, but the ship definitely pitched forward...water could be seen now...it was rising rapidly...“we are sinking...free us from the chains...*FREE US*...” Ufi Granjeau could hear the voices from the small boats cursing and arguing...all their cargo, AND their ship was a total loss...

Stephen Ashley relaxed, and remembered the cliff, and the battle, and the jungle...“Ufi...”...“Yes Stephen”...“What did Faisud say?”...“He said we are being taught lessons...” Ashley pondered this, as the sea lapped his legs...“Yes...but are we in another life?...has the world come to an end? Is this our future?” and then the ship, fracturing and cracking, tipped high as the bow plummeted, sending the slaves, still shackled to their berths, deep into the sea.

# Petr Jorbin's dream

Petr Jorbin was surprised to find himself seated at a small table overlooking the bottom of a popular and bustling downhill ski run. He was in the lodge behind a giant plate glass window. It was beautiful weather, and children of all ages were skiing and taking the chair lifts to a vanishing point high on the mountain. There were 2 hot chocolates with fresh whipped cream in front of him at the table...and equal portions of his favorite Finnish pastry Tiikerikkakku (Finnish Tiger Cake). A roaring fire in the lodge fireplace finished the ambiance. This is exceedingly pleasant, he was thinking. He looked around for the other leaders. Fong or Granjeau...or Ashley...he recognized no one...but the Lodge was very full. They could be anywhere, or not here yet? There were children with parents and grandparents. "Children" thought Jorbin...and looked down and let his sadness move into his mind. Suddenly, he heard a voice, soft and sweet ... "Papa"...Jorbin was afraid to move...afraid to look up. He shuddered, like when he was on the edge of hypothermia as a boy...the intense physical shaking...the uncontrollable shaking...

Still he did not look up. And then, *her* hand...Elle's soft beautiful hand touched and rested on his. "Papa, I am happy to see you here...and hugged him until her embrace stopped the shaking...she smiled. "You are only visiting I know, but still, it is warm and good, ya?"...Jorbin stood up, turned and wrapped his enormous bearish arms around his only child. He was sobbing. Tears streaking his strong Finnish features..."we miss you so much Elle...so so much."

"Yes Papa...all of the children and young people here have died young... all the skiers you see out there have not been re-united yet...only those of us in the lodge have had that comfort...and *every* time you visit, I will be here...shall we have our hot chocolates?" "Yes" said Petr, hugging Elle again, "Yes. Yes we shall"...

# Dr. Helen Crosby's Team

By the time the full list had been checked and re-checked by the Service and FBI, a total of one hundred and twenty eight people either travelled with, met at the UN, were part of specific security details covering the conference and reported to superiors who migrated in and out of the Presidential circle. All of those identified had to be located, communicated with, and either travelled to Ft. Dietrick or had visits from personnel from Crosby's team with security present. Each person had several tubes of venous blood drawn from their arms, iced, and brought back to Crosby's labs for analysis. This collection process took a number of hours to complete...luckily, everyone was still in, or had returned to, the Washington area since the news broke of the global calamity.

The bloods were clearly marked with name, date, time drawn, etc., and were systematically being tested in the Level 4 security lab where all personnel were gowned, masked, shielded, and purified air continually circulated... highly calibrated chemical, bacterial and viral sensors were situated throughout the premises. If something foreign or unrecognizable at the molecular level were present in the air, the sensors would alarm and seal the facility.

The testing room was separated from the computer room by non-permeable materials, especially at the cable ports to and from the rooms.

It was here, in *this* lab, that some of the most sensitive biological work on the planet was being done...and that all came to a screeching halt as Operation: Aladdin's Lamp 128 vials of human blood analysis proceeded. Crosby had her team re-calibrate every diagnostic tool and run controls through them all...if there was a vector and/or an abnormal organism or particle in any of this blood, their machines would find it, their microscopes would photograph it, their super computers would posit corrective actions. It was just a matter of time.

187

# GMT 9:06 PM Saturday / EDT 5:06 PM Saturday

Jared Faulkner was standing at the President's bedside monitoring his equipment. He had already called the Ivory Coast team and they had successfully worked with Dr. Ehsani so the testing results on Ufi Granjeau would transmit properly. Every team was "standing by" for his single conference call message: Record Now...then a follow-up message: Stop Recording. Two simple commands which would set in motion a first of its kind medical-telecom experiment of unprecedented proportions. He was waiting for the signal, the Angelo-Faulkner Shift which Dr. Alexander had named. Then, at GMT 9:12 PM (Saturday) / EDT 5:12 PM (Saturday) he saw it...the spike which heralded the beginning of a generalized REM experience. So, with phone in hand, he hit the button.

Exactly at **GMT 9:13 PM (Saturday) / EDT 5:13 PM (Saturday)**, Faulkner sent out the Record Now call. All the teams had coordinated previously on a dry run...all BK's began recording and transmitting immediately. Five mobile neural PET and fMRI scanners, compiling, compressing, and transmitting colossal amounts of medically sensitive data across 3 global time zones...cumulatively thousands of miles apart from one another... by way of an unproven optical mesh network ...terminating at the USA White House Situation Room and its towering data storage facility. Faulkner was anything but assured this would all occur seamlessly.

But it did.

The entire group of leaders, all 184 of them, found themselves sitting in Epidaurus, the theater in ancient Greece...an all stone engineering marvel where speakers could be heard, without shouting, in all sections... even if the theater was filled to capacity, with thousands of listeners...

They were all sitting together, looking down into the center of the performing area, where a single unrecognizable speaker stood looking up at them.

"I expect you have figured out by now that you are not dead"

"Finally" thought Ashley, "some answers"..."but that you are not quite fully alive either...you are in a kind of **ανασταλούν ζωής**,(he spoke in Greek), a suspended life...a dreaming...together, and separately...but these dreams are unlike any that have before existed...you need to answer the question **why** you are dreaming...and **why** you are dreaming together"...the speaker looked directly at Ashley, at them all, eyes to eyes at the same time..."I am not here, I'm afraid, to provide answers...all to your disappointment, I'm sure...you," he gestured grandly to them all, "the **collective** you, will do that...you are the **only** ones who can...but I have one final thing to say, and encourage you to regard my words with solemn assurance, as you will hear them only once...*you do not have much time*"...and he was gone.

And as they all turned and stared at one another, they each began to fade, escorted by the warm ocean breezes...into nothingness.

He was not supposed to be here. Stephen Ashley knew that much. The scene was like something out of a Civil War re-enactment...except, the numbers of people were in the hundreds, with more coming from every direction. He was at attention, in some kind of regiment. Union colors.

They were about 25 yards from what was serving as a kind of platform, for speakers and such. Several companies at least, with dozens of ranking officers standing to one side, closer to the platform. He looked around. This place looked very familiar. The small buildings, the church, the hills to his back...and the field. Ashley suddenly became very uncomfortable. He looked to the hills again, then back to the church. A chill ran up his spine. This was the killing field. This was Gettysburg. He strained, looking for modern day equipment...cars maybe...television trucks... anything.

He started taking in the uniforms, especially the shoes...a pair of modern boots or something...there was no hint of the 21$^{st}$ century anywhere.

Even the murmuring language was skewed...no terms he was familiar with.

The man to his right had a weeping injury of some kind to his neck... and all the men were unshaven, very hard looking...very worn looking. This was not some re-enactment somewhere. This was real...some kind of solemn occasion. And it was Gettysburg, the battlefield itself...and these men were the soldiers who very likely fought here. He racked his brain for dates, and was sure the year was 1863. Fall. The leaves were well into their change. The air was cool, with a warm sun. The grizzled veteran to his left spat a wick of tobacco juice on Ashley's boot..."pardon" said the man, and looked down, adjusting his powder bag. There was a bad smell lingering in the crisp cool air...Ashley noticed that some of the better dressed women were holding handkerchiefs' to their noses and mouths...the worst of the odor was coming from the west. He looked that way. The burying had still not been completed...horses were pulling mounds of dirt loaded on skids... and a dozen or so men were clearing and shoveling into unseen places.

Ashley suddenly became aware of a speaker, a short man of considerable vocal strength...saying that this was a great victory, a just victory, a victory at great cost...the man was Edward Everett, and the crowd had been swelling while he spoke...it numbered now, by Ashley's guess, in the few thousands...he turned his head looking behind...the hills still carried the battles' devastation...the stands of trees splintered by cannon fire...he remembered Chamberlains' charge and strained to look that way when suddenly he was quietly called to attention by the regiment commander, "Soldier, face forward", Ashley turned as Everett was just finishing his remarks, withdrawing to his chair.

Ashley scanned what he assumed to be a collection of dignitaries on the stage until his gaze abruptly stopped at the man seated in the middle of the platform. The man rose...slowly came to the front. It had been barely 5 months since the battle had been fought...*this* was the dedication, the consecration of the nearby cemetery grounds...the figure about to speak was Abraham Lincoln. Lincoln scanned the crowd and assembled guests...resting his fatherly gaze on Ashley for a brief moment, Lincoln nodding slightly...then, the great man spoke:

**"Four score and seven years ago our fathers brought forth on this continent, a new nation, conceived in Liberty, and dedicated to the proposition that all men are created equal.**

**Now we are engaged in a great civil war, testing whether that nation, or any nation so conceived and so dedicated, can long endure. We are met on a great battlefield of that war. We have come to dedicate a portion**

of that field, as a final resting place for those who here gave their lives that that nation might live. It is altogether fitting and proper that we should do this.

But, in a larger sense, we cannot dedicate—we cannot consecrate—we cannot hallow—this ground. The brave men, living and dead, who struggled here, have consecrated it, far above our poor power to add or detract. The world will little note, nor long remember what we say here, but it can never forget what they did here. It is for us the living, rather, to be dedicated here to the unfinished work which they who fought here have thus far so nobly advanced. It is rather for us to be here dedicated to the great task remaining before us—that from these honored dead we take increased devotion to that cause for which they gave the last full measure of devotion—that we here highly resolve that these dead shall not have died in vain—that this nation, under God, shall have a new birth of freedom— and that government of the people, by the people, for the people, shall not perish from the earth."

Lincoln returned to his seat. Ashley felt the hair on his neck bristling and his knees weakening. He struggled to gain some hold on himself as the crowd, so silent for so long, suddenly erupted in cheers...in thunderous applause. Ashley looked to the veteran on his left again. The soldier remained quiet, looking down, tears streaming down his face.

Damascus was a dangerous city. It was a network of criminals, weapons dealers, religious extremists, and governmental spies...often, the same people...Ehud and 3 Mossad agents were using intelligence they had paid for, with money and promises, to 2 key Baath Party intelligence agents... very high up in the government structure...they were given addresses, 4 in all, and likely meeting places of Fire of God members, including Ala Abu Halaq...the suspected leader. The Mossad agents would break off from the team, they did not travel together, but always stayed within visibility of each other, as they moved...this time, because of urgency, they would travel solo...into very fortified areas...with lots of eyes watching from lots of places. They carried no weapons...not for recon...but they did carry 2 small handwritten lists...grocery and bakery items, they were asked to get "for the family"...and sufficient Syrian pounds, enough and a bit more...for charitable donations to Hezbollah social causes, one being a charity for orphans from the Israeli-Arab ongoing struggles.

The rendezvous apartment for all was a rental property in the back alley behind a furniture shop in southeast Damascus...Israeli agents had used it for years...they paid extra to the landlord, and no questions were ever asked...it was quiet, with roof access, and 2 exit routes...the place had been specially modified and stocked with weapons....with nothing seen, ever.

Ehud was the 3rd of the four to return. Ala Abu Halaq was staying deep in Hezbollah controlled northwest Damascus. He was moving freely and without concern for his safety. Only one bodyguard. The Mossad agent sent to the address had actually passed Halaq on the street, even giving him a slight nod as he passed, carrying his groceries back to the Mossad apartment. He did not look back, he did not stop, he kept moving, nodding to the men, ignoring the women.

They would use 2 vehicles, a small pick-up to locate Halaq, and a sedan, to get him...creating an accident with the truck as a diversion. The agent in the truck would park and wait until Halaq emerged from his apartment and call Ehud and the others...when it happened, the accident drew many onlookers, and emergency personnel in a matter of 10 minutes... by that time, the bodyguard had been killed and left under a car, and Halaq had his wrist broken, and was whisked away...the Mossad agent who had caused the truck accident became part of the growing throng who were yelling and cursing, and moved easily away and back to the apartment in no time.

Halaq had been sedated, and put in a trunk, loaded on the back of a different truck, packed with other furniture and was heading toward the border, in 26 minutes. Ehud, with all the necessary border papers, was driving. He called Mustafa. "We have the piece you were looking for...we will review its authenticity, and send along to you shortly"...

**<u>Operation: Alladin's Lamp</u>** had recently pulled in data sent by the RCMP in Canada...several of the delegations visiting the UN Conference had in fact traveled by train to New York after landing on international flights in Toronto. The Syrian delegation was among them. Shep Collin's team had now processed the RCMP data and hit on several faces...matching photo's sent to New York from Mossad in Israel...Collin's cellphone lit up as he headed into Manhattan after a few hours sleep..."Sir" it was Lisa Cash..."we have 7 individuals meeting repetitively, as a mass, and as pairs and triples...we have all of them at one time or another visiting the off-area which will be the main meeting room for the July Arab-Israeli peace conference...this was designated as a restricted zone, but all of them entered, 2 even seeming to role play, and exiting in what we have determined to be a suspicious manner...we do not see a material exchange of any type, but this clearly could have occurred in restrooms or delegation lounges...these individuals have been identified through official documents"...and she started to give the names...but Collins stopped her..."this sounds like a breakthrough Lis, please have a complete briefing ready if you can, and transmittable to the folks at the White House, before our next scheduled call..." he checked his watch..."which is in 58 minutes. I'll be there in 15" and ended the call.

Collins had his coffee in one hand and a another brief under his arm as he made his way into the team conference room...Cash was busy at one of the terminals selecting still photos of the front and side profiles of the suspects. She turned as he came over..."7 suspects sir...6 definitive delegations...Syria, Egypt, Jordan, Palestinian Authority, Lebanon and Saudi Arabia. All men of course, low to middle security clearance, nothing higher than level 2, but the actions to unauthorized areas are furtive and secretive...we are just now running the official personal biographies against a host of security data...this should not take long..." she slid him a complete to the minute brief on what they had found on these men... he read quickly, and leapt to the photos...these were digital splices of faces and figures lifted from archived data...he stopped at the 6th page... folded the brief open...now took the other document he had brought in with him...flipped pages until he came to a man's face...folded it open on the conference table...they showed pictures of the same man...Ala Abu Halaq.

The call with Fitch and the White House would start in 6 minutes.

Lisa Cash began her report via secure teleconference to the WH Sit Room...Fitch was chairing the proceedings..."yes sir", she was responding to a question about Halaq, "...he was regarded as an official delegate, assigned to several conferences according to the UN log we have...he had a Level 2 clearance...moderately high...access to lots of people, he was in attendance for the entire weekly session period...as were the other suspects"...*suspects*...Lisa Cash had said it...they had identified suspects... and these suspects were on the inside of the most significant gathering of heads of state in history..."Lisa", it was Fitch, scanning some brief from Langley..."alright, we have these men on the inside....we might first assume there are others, a wider group...then eliminate that assumption if possible...how much of the official itinerary can we realistically review?... and how much digital can the UN share?..."virtually all of it, sir...and we have already started cross-checking these faces with that data...with exactly what you suggested in mind...how many hits do we get with the same men or women during the week...meetings, casual conversations, frequencies to particular areas within the UN official designated areas... and we are vetting the remaining members of the Syrian delegation... these men did not get there on their diplomatic credentials...they have none...someone else is involved from where we sit...so we are chasing quite a bit"...Fitch turned to Barbara Jefferson, "questions Madame Secretary?"...Jefferson turned to the screen, "Ms. Cash, Barb Jefferson here, you and your team are doing are a remarkable job, and may be on the verge of unraveling this global mystery...I don't need to tell you of the continued urgency...the world is catching fire...we need answers...fast"... Cash was unfazed..."yes Madame Secretary...we *know*"..."OK then folks... let's get together in 4 hours...or sooner if alarms go off...thanks... Fitch out" and Jeremy closed the call. O'Malley stood at the back like he mostly does, leaning against the "military wall"..."what do you think, Cough?... think this will lead somewhere?" Fitch had discovered what Stephen Ashley already knew, O'Malley had great instincts..."yes" said O'Malley, "I think it will...just not where you might expect"...and left the room.

The Secretary of Defense Edward Crawford placed an urgent call to O'Malley's office... "Cough...we are seeing significant military build-ups by two major powers...in Russia, several divisions worth of troops and logistics heading rapidly toward the Chechyan capital, and also, India is fortifying positions all along the Pakistan border...we need to convene the Cabinet and intelligence at the White House as soon as possible...our people in Russia are telling us this is the prelude to an offensive operation, not a defensive one...nothing yet as to Indian intentions...neither capital has informed our in country embassies, nor leaked anything through covert channels...

"Ok Ed, I'll get the cabinet and NSA/CIA in one hour, Vice President Willis will preside...I'll get channels open to NY even though these are only movements at the moment, the UN needs to be made aware..."

"I'll have briefs for everyone at the meeting" said Ed, and ended the call.

Fitch placed a secure call to the Mossad lead man on this, Ehud Lessar.

"We have video of several Fire of God members, inside the UN Conference, including Ala Abu Halaq...multiple meetings, some in restricted areas within the UN. We do not as yet have confirmation by video, or sniffing devices, of chemical or other detectable contaminating agents...but the team is still working this...but the main thing is, we have them *there*, and interacting all week long. The information you provided was solid. We will have a full report to you within the hour."

Lessar listened respectfully...he was thinking to himself, "I must have been, at times, just across the room from some of these men, that's how close they were"...Fitch finished and thanked Lessar and Mossad on behalf of the Agency, and the United States, and ended the call.

Ehud was still not satisfied...Mossad would interrogate Halaq with the latest pharmaceuticals...the entire proceeding would be recorded and would last almost 5 hours...the pharmaceuticals, "the brain busters" as they were being called were relentless...it did not matter the amount of effort the injected person garnered to withhold information, once the drugs started to work, you simply could **not** stop talking as they slowly separated the layers of your consciousness...the things you were doing, the things you were thinking...this drug combination (which was highly classified) created no unpleasant side effects, no pain, no psychic breakdowns...it just completely "unlocked" your secrets and your life... you just kept talking...no one even had to ask you a question...it just all came out. And Halaq was no different. He spoke about his children, his family, his brothers, his friends, and most importantly, his plans... he hated the Israeli's...his father was killed, and his uncle, in the Arab-Israeli War...fighting for Jordan...dying for Jordan...and he wanted his revenge. He had wanted it all his life...and not just his revenge, but also his father's revenge, on those Arab regimes, all of them, even his beloved Jordan who now capitulated with Israel...who made peace. There must never be peace. The plan, of which he was the architect, required agents in the diplomatic entourage of every target country...an enormously patient and far-reaching plan...years of quiet work...seeds planted... nurtured...and finally harvested. The "harvest" was scheduled for July...the UN sponsored Arab-Israeli Peace Accords...the leaders would be killed there, on American soil...America would be blamed...in fact, the initial Al-Jazeera news reports would say the assassins were American killers... all the "martyrs" would have American credentials, American papers...

the world would be thrown into chaos. The Fire of God had six initial targets...the Prime Minister of Israel ("the dog"), the King of Jordan, the Presidents of Lebanon and Egypt, the President of the Palestinian Authority, and finally, the most powerful living figure in Sunni Islam, the King of Saudi Arabia, King Faisud.

The International Economic, Climate and Human Right's Initiative was the "dry run" of this plan...where all those delegations were present, the agents in attendance, the entire scheme oiled and perfected...

Ehud Lessar lacked the names however, Abu Halaq would only name them in alias...the last of the 4 laptops taken from the Jordanian safe house and given to Mustafa held the key...this is what Lessar needed to bring this thing full circle...

Mustafa had notified him that the hard drive was encrypted, and he was sending it on to Tel-Aviv...special courier.

Mossad's internal tech unit was busily running de-crypting algorithms on the drives when Lessar came into the lab.

"Anything yet?...Liev?" Liev Heslam was the guru in the IT group, and had several programs running on the 4 confiscated hard-drives when Lessar suddenly popped in.

"Yes Ehud, we will finish this..." he checked the clock on the corner of his screen..."in about 3 minutes."

Lessar stepped into the corridor to make a cell call...when he returned, Heslam and his team **had** finished.

"Ehud...two of these drives have lists and lists of citizens from various cities and towns...enormous files...and plans of needed community action programs...some military equipment schematics and so forth...we will have to evaluate how much of it is meaningful information for us...

but *this* drive..." Heslam brought Lessar to terminal 2 in his lab bank..."it has much on the personnel you are interested in..."

Heslam's team had unlocked the actual deep biographical information on all the players and diplomatic contacts working with Halaq and the core Fire of God cell...but Lessar had this information now, and capitols throughout the Mideast (and beyond) would shake when the truth was known. Fire of God had "friends" as high as the deputy foreign minister of Syria and Saudi Arabia's second in command of the King's personal security detail.

Lessar would call for a meeting with Shimon Davide, the director of Mossad about what steps should next be taken, and when...

Davide typically contacted the Prime Minister's office to secure guidance, but given the extraordinary circumstances, he consulted with his friend and previous PM, Tev Shi-el. Lessar would bring Shi-el up to date from the beginning, and then Davide would take over.

"The Americans have uncovered damaging information which may pertain to the current global crisis with our leaders, and if not, they have hard visual evidence which corroborates statements made to us by the FoG leader, Ala Halaq. They were planning a coordinated multi-assassination action to take place in July at the UN Arab-Israel Peace Conference in NY. We have acquired all the names, and names of critical contacts in key diplomatic missions...I am not sure how to proceed, but I believe we must act quickly...can you offer guidance?"

Shi-el spoke softly, as was his custom, and advised that all the information be given to the Fatah Party in the West Bank, to Lessar's contact, Mustafa.

This was something *they* had to do...**and be given credit for...**

Mossad and Israel should keep as low a profile as possible...and by all means, confide all this to the Americans, to CIA.

Davide would have Lessar do just that.

# Ufi Granjeaus' dream

Ufi Granjeau woke up soaked in blood and urine, his head pounding with pain. He was lying on a cot in a small plastic open-ended tent. The cot next to him was empty. The heat was staggering...100 degrees Fahrenheit or more. He sat up and put his feet on the ground...everything was muddy, wet from the rains. He slapped at a mosquito at his neck. He was nauseous and dizzy. He felt dehydrated to go along with it. Outside was a constant din of wailing and yelling. He stood up shakily and arched his head along the plastic as he exited the tent into the scorching sun. The scene was chaotic with refugees as far as the eyes could see in every direction. There was death and stench in the air. Open latrines lay just to his left. The old, the sick, the children, the pregnant mothers, the men... all were sitting, standing, laying, in mud. Flies were everywhere. The camp had a few larger tent-like structures, so Ufi headed for one of those. He was weak, moving very slowly. He noticed also that he was wearing a yellow short sleeve shirt with STAFF written on the pocket. There was another yellow shirt about 50 yards ahead of him with a large NGO on the back. Ufi called out but could not be heard above the crowds. His throat burned. "There are thousands of people here" he thought to himself..."maybe hundreds of thousands even". There was a large tent with a Red Cross insignia just ahead of him. He went inside. Hundreds of cots all with grossly debilitated people on them. Some were unmoving and had white bags over their faces. He stopped at one of these. It was a child. No more than eight or nine. Overtly malnourished. The child had died in the night. The mother had come and gone, leaving the body to the Red Cross. She had no strength, and 2 other children to care for. Ufi looked around. He spotted another yellow shirt at the other end of the tent. It was King Faisud. He was cleaning, as best he could, and placing yet another dead child in a white bag. Ufi heard him praying over the child as he worked. He looked up with tears in his eyes. "An abomination, my friend…just so many, every day…dysentery, starvation, malaria, even Ebola is here…the worst of the worst. We lost 2 of our own yesterday…the Slovakian President and the President of Peru. I have no answers for this…this child could be my grandson"…and returned to his work. Ufi said nothing. He simply placed his hand on Faisud's shoulder and went back to the other child to perform the same ritual.

As he stooped, a woman from Medecins Sans Frontieres (Doctors Without Borders) came up to him. I am Dr. Lecole Gauthay, and extended her hand. Ufi stood and introduced himself. "We already know who you all are in the yellow shirts" she said. "The total world leadership…but why are you here?…what can you do to stop this catastrophe? We have done this work for years, losing some of our best doctors and medical personnel to other horrors like this and now you show up…what is this about?" "We do not know exactly" replied Ufi, barely able to speak, "but with each passing experience it seems to be getting clearer…"

"What do you mean? This is not an experience Mr. President, this is real…people are dying, by the hundreds every day…they have been driven to this awful place full of biting flies and mosquitoes and parasites, by your wars…the gunmen know that sooner or later everyone here will die, so they can save their bullets. It's just a matter of time. So I ask you again, what are you doing here?"

Ufi hesitated to answer even though his sense was that these dreams were an unfolding revelation…something beyond important, beyond politics, beyond full comprehension. So he said, "we are being taught global and historical lessons…and it is my belief, that our personal survival depends on our learning them…by whom or from where, we have no idea." At this he coughed and doubled over.

"So you think you can stop disasters like this?"

He weakly held up his hand. "I think it is imperative that we do so."

With this, Ufi collapsed, convulsing and immediately started bleeding from his gums, nose, rectum and eyes. He struggled to speak but could not. Dr. Gauthay was bending over him telling an attendant that Ufi likely had Ebola and something else which was unidentified as of yet and struck just like this...lightning fast and completely fatal. They lifted Ufi to a now empty cot, careful not to move him too quickly to spread his blood to unintended places...they both wore face shields and elbow length plastic gloves.

He died in 16 minutes, bleeding out before they could even start intravenous fluid replacement.

Dr. Gauthay pronounced him and noted her estimated cause of death: "Rapid system wide exsanguination likely precipitated by Ebola virus and some other organism/agent as yet unknown." They placed a white bag over his face. She shook her head, walking away.

And over the same sequence of REAL time, in their dreams, where time had no meaning, all the leaders would succumb to one of a number of terribly painful deaths...in the course of several days.

**Summary Findings Dr. Helen Crosby's Team: White House SR, CDC
and CIA Headquarters via video-conference**

"Chief-of-Staff O'Malley, assembled physicians and security staff, etc.
We here at Ft. Dietrick have been working tirelessly (in addition to our
colleagues at the CDC who are also on this conference call) to unravel
this disturbing national and international event. We are able to share
initial findings, and that is what this conference is about." She looked
tired...having had 2 hrs sleep total for the previous 24. In the room
with her were two other members of her team which she did not introduce...O'Malley asked if she would please and what their function was.

"Oh yes, terribly sorry about that...to my right is Dr. Martha Rask, her
specialty is molecular vectoring and to my left is Dr. Ari Sundrahu, Dr.
Sundrahu's specialty is exotic bacterial diseases. Thank you Cough for
calling me on that, I apologize...just a little tired I guess.

Ok then...our techniques are the latest and on the front edge of bio-terrorism research. So let me say that right off the top...no one in the SR
room, to my knowledge, has visited our facility, but have no doubt, we
have the latest everything. Some of our results, as well as those from the
CDC will not be known for several days...reason being as even under ac-
celerated growth medium conditions, organisms on the Watch List and
others will sometimes take 24-48 hrs to express...so this is a summary
report as to what we have found, what we are looking for, and what can
be eliminated from consideration as an agent or agents, of interest. Let's
proceed then.

First, receiving updates on the President's condition every 30 minutes or so has helped us narrow our focus. There are no known bacterial or viral organisms which initiate responses such as those described (Dr. McMasters has also been in touch)...but we have not eliminated them from review or growth opportunity...we just are not aware of any with this particular type of behavior. There are parasitic organisms such as Protists or protozoans which cause conditions that fall within the purview of sleep disorders, I am thinking particularly of the so called "sleeping sickness" family of diseases, but we have ruled them out also because nothing of the kind shows up in the blood of the President or any of the 128 people who are on the list given to us by Mr. O'Malley and the Secret Service. Additionally, we find no common threads of trailing immune responses in any of the blood samples. So, if a carrier, a person, transitions into the agent or vector of transmission for any of the biologicals I have already mentioned, we would have evidence of immuno-response...both in that agent, and the President...and we do not. The possibilities as regards the use of nano-particulites is intriguing, however, no known research even borders the extent of ambition here. We would have seen directional research months ago and we have not... and if a metallic nano-particle had been used, the tests Dr. Faulkner is running in particular would have picked them up...and certainly larger MRI scanning done already on other leaders and shared with the CDC. So we ruling that out as a vector opportunity...just too damn complicated. There are 6 possibly 7 (the seventh is borderline) samples which garner interest for exposures to other un-related contaminations, so we will be calling those people back in for additional testing...but HIPAA regulations prevent me from discussing that any further on this call. So let me share with you what we *have* discussed internally as to what might be happening here (keeping in mind we, and the CDC still have some results we are waiting on).

First, that this might be a multi-stage process, with likely an enormous latency period...months, even longer to fully express. In such a scenario, a trip or signaling chemical may initiate the final stage. This could explain why all of them have come down with this at once. I cannot explain HOW this could have happened only that it IS possible. Organisms or molecules which penetrate the CSF (cerebral spinal fluid) and blood-brain barrier can take years to accomplish this feat...so we have precedence in nature regarding latency...the signaling stimulant for this expression is what is the difficult piece. Also, we have not discounted, nor should anyone, the possibility of protein infection, prions in other words...if the essential protein for sleep, more specifically for triggering REM sleep has been discovered in some obscure lab some place, and then tricked into misfolding so it's original purpose is altered in some progressive and deadly way, then we have quite a problem on our hands...we are theorizing here...but it would explain the lack of immune responses...a human protein, specific to the brain, changed slightly in appearance and function to alter its cellular effects, would pass undetected through the blood-brain barrier, and directly into its intended target. This is an elegant transmission model, as proteins are easily ingested through food and liquids...the only caveat to this theory is that misfolded proteins historically effect malformation and destruction of tissues they interact with (think CJD or Creutzfeldt-Jakob disease in humans or BSE, bovine spongiform encephalopathy, Mad Cow for ungulates, etc.)...so far, thankfully, we have seen none of that...isn't that correct Dr's Faulkner and Angelo?...no detrimental anatomical changes as yet discovered?"

Jared Faulkner, who was leaning toward a prion explanation himself (in his own thoughts) answered with a cautious note. "As of the moment, that is true, we have been unable to measure or verify deteriorating areas of the brains of those men and women we have tested." Angelo added, "all the electricals, except for the speeds, which are faster than algorithmically coded for, are showing no evidence of destructive disease...so I concur with Dr. Faulkner."

"Well, that places us at a crossroads of sorts..." said Crosby, "maybe we should think about taking some spinal fluid from the President? Sounds radical to most everyone in the room, I know, but it would be fairly routine for Dr's Faulkner and Angelo...just a thought. Anything to add?" she looked at her colleagues who both shook their heads. "Then I guess we'll entertain questions if there are any?"

They did answer some basic questions for other members of the gathered SR group, then O'Malley thanked them, urging a call from Dietrick or CDC if ANYTHING was found promising, and ended the call.

He thought about her comments regarding ingesting a pathogen like agent, a prion for example, and his mind shifted to the wait staff at the UN...but then he dismissed it as the leaders who were not in attendance were also suffering with this brain-driven illness...he was as baffled as ever.

It was freezing, it was dark, and the wind was howling...an ordinary Mongolian winter. Ashley stood up. He was dressed in skins of some animal...warm skins...only his face, which was exposed, was cold...but it was bitter. He heard animals snorting. Unable to see them, but knowing they were there......dozens, maybe hundreds. Someone was coming by..."hello" said Ashley to the dark..."hello" said the voice, it was Russian Prime Minister Bolchenko, "are you going in?"...Ashley looked around... not far away, he began to make out the outline of a huge tent of some kind..."yes" he said, "I think I am"..."shall we walk together then?..." and they fell in arm in arm, struggling together against the withering wind.

It was an enormous structure, a 21$^{st}$ century version of an ancient design. A Mongolian kibitka. A kind of round central house, with divided inner rooms for communing and sleeping...all made from poles and reindeer skins...and while the temperature outside was nearly 30 below zero with the wind chill, the inner rooms, the communal room, was a comfortable 65 degrees...with the central fire...the individual sleeping stations were even warmer, hung with skins to block all drafts, and layered with skins for coverings, you could sleep naked with no problem at all...an amazing concentration of warmth in such a hostile place...

Ashley and Bolchenko entered, and moved right hugging the inside of the outer wall...they came to another inner entrance, again, covered with hanging skins...they pushed them aside, and stepped in...the room was almost too big to believe, with men and women sitting on skins and talking...laughing and hugging...all around a central fire, where reindeer meat was cooking...

"Everyone" shouted a voice, "it is Bolchenko and Ashley"...immediately there was an uproar of applause and greetings..."we are almost all here then"...and more clapping...even a little singing...

Ashley took off his outer coat and mitts...he noticed an empty space beside Petr Jorbin, and next to Ufi Granjeau...he moved that way. The Israeli Prime Minister stood up as he approached, he was seated next to the Mongolian President, Gonchigiin Amaral, who had been giving some history of these structures, and the people who continue to live out here, in the steppes...the reindeer people.

They have shunned modernity for this simple and difficult life, tied to the world by their reindeer, which they herd and protect. The Prime Minister of Israel was smiling for the first time that Ashley could remember...a real, unforced gaiety brought by this place, and these people.

He was enthusiastic to share what he had learned, so Ashley listened and soon he too was infected with the enthusiasm these simple herders felt for life...just then 2 more figures entered the room..."it is President Fong and President Gonzalez (from Uruguay)"...again the room ignited. "just the Zimbabwe President" and just then, in he came..."we are all here then...a great thing is it not?"...and the cheering began anew.

There was music and feasting and much, much, good will...the fire was replenished, and after a long while filled with stories and the continuing building of emerging friendships, everyone was back at their place. The great room became gradually hushed, then quiet. Petr Jorbin, who had been mixing with everyone, suddenly rose at his place. "there is a different feeling at this one. I think you can all agree, that something fundamental is different about it, no?" there was widespread nodding and agreeing..."we, as a group, have been through many, what shall we call them?...dreams?" more nodding..."and through them all, we only glimpsed the feelings we are experiencing now...good will I must call it...a kind of happiness with each other...the joy of humankind...is this not what we are sharing here?, the delight of each other?...of humanity...all of us are the leaders of our countries, our states, yet the distances between us on our very small world have been as like an abyss...we live and act as if nothing and no one else really matters...we have been brought together, by who or what we may never know, brought together I think, to not just build bridges over this abyss, but to fill it, completely and forever... when we left, our leaderships had failed, war, the throttle of inhumanity persists...and not just with each other...we destroy our world as well.

I do not know how you view this thing we are going through in your heart, but I now see it in mine as a last chance...a chance for human beings to finally live in harmony and true good will...and in harmony with our world, which we are killing. Do you remember what the speaker in Epidaurus said?...he said we need to answer **why** we are dreaming... and why we are dreaming **together**...because there was no other way to reach us...no other way we would listen...we do not have a choice it seems about experiencing this thing, but we may have a choice about whether we wake up from it, what did he call it?...suspended life?...yes...it is the choice to change and live, to be re-born one might say...or perish like we did in the terrible dreams...but this time, for real...and why are we dreaming together then?...maybe we must all agree about this change... all or nothing...if you all agree, and I say no, I do not think any of us will wake up...and what about our peoples? what is happening to them right now?...we *must* get back...we must *all* share the one choice..." Jorbin looked unsteady for the first time, uncertain..."something also which some of you, perhaps all of you have experienced, are the dreams which seemed to be far more personal, more intimate...tailored to who you are, and your personal history...I have had several...all of them very powerful...but as to our collective dreams, let us reflect now on the lessons, the dreams, and talk this thing out as we must". Jorbin did not understand, but certain leaders were emerging in his mind...he knew these were the companions he would ask to share their sense of what these dreams meant...a dream reflection from the inside...Jorbin looked to Bolchenko...to his neighbor from the east to speak first..."I would ask Prime Minister Bolchenko to speak to us about the first dream, the disaster in the mine."

Bolchenko was a man about Ashley's size, and he looked magnificent in his skins as he rose......»Мое сердце согласились...

Ashley, for the first time heard the Prime Minister speaking in his native Russian, yet Ashley was translating it in his head as he listened..."My heart is agreeing with what Petr is saying, and I hang my head in shame for the contributions we as a country have made to our own, and to the world's, continued misery...it will not go on"...he waited a very long moment before continuing..."if you are familiar with the fathers of Russian literature, you will know that the metaphor, the literary technique, was a powerful tool for teaching...I was in the mine, with Farid Najib from Lebanon, and Eduardo Campos from Chile, both excellent friends (he bowed to them in turn)...the great shaft groaned many times...many warnings...and then it crushed us all...

The mine was a metaphor for our planet. And it cannot take much more before its peril is our own. That is what I see in my heart. Disaster on a scale unknown before...our own Lake Baikal, the jewel of Russia east of the Sayan Mountains, is a wasteland now...decades of excess and neglect... it has collapsed like the mineshaft..." And Bolchenko, emotional now, speaking of Russia sat somberly down, and wept.

Jorbin looked around, he asked Ufi Granjeau to speak about the second dream, the rock face. Granjeau stood, respected African League leader, and emerging world statesman, he bowed and addressed his fellow leaders...

"Thankyou Jorbin Président, et je suis également...

The same thing again...Granjeau was speaking in French, and that is how Ashley heard it, but in his mind, everything was streaming in English...

"Thank you President Jorbin, and I too am in agreement with your opening remarks, and with those of Prime Minister Bolchenko...I was below Stephen Ashley, and just above John Miller from Australia...we had no idea what to do...what to hold...what not to hold...I was just spinning there until John grabbed my foot, and pointed up to Petr...he was showing what to do, when to move, how to move and so forth...and then the awful yelling and screaming coming up the mountain...how did it all start?" the Cuban President spoke up, "an entire section of the rock face just gave way...three of us were hanging on it"..."ah" said Granjeau, "and now we know...but this lesson for us I think is the reliance we must have... we **must** have on each other, if we are to survive...helping each other, not betraying each other...I watched as Petr Jorbin was exhorted to cut the rope...save everyone above...but he did not do it" he looked down at Jorbin, who was now sitting, "he did **not** do it...we are all tied together in our world, are we not?...are we not all needing the one above?, and the one below needing us?...the great war in Africa now, all of us, the entire continent, has slipped off the mountain...huge swath of peoples perished...we have never healed the old wounds, the tribal rivalries...we have cut the rope, and have **not stopped** cutting it...it must come to an end... all of us who can stop this are here...now..." and with that, Granjeau sat down again, meeting many African eyes with nods and understanding.

The wind shook the kibitka with a horrific thrust as Jorbin stood and looked around again..."there are four dreams left to explain, the battle in the great ocean, the unseen things in the jungle, the slave ship, and the beautiful beach"

...before Petr could ask, British Prime Minister Fitzsimmons rose to speak of the battle dream...

"As I have been sitting here, listening, and before that, sharing and greeting you all, I am brought to my knees (and she did indeed, kneel down) to ask your forgiveness for the part the British people have played in the transport of war and cruelty in the world..." at this, several more leaders joined her on their knees, and then more leaders, until no one at all was left sitting...they were *all* guilty...all of humanity was guilty...they had all done unthinkable things...

They remained kneeling as she continued.

"I was on one side of a cannon emplacement toward mid-ship, Stephen Ashley was on the other", she looked over at him, "splintered pieces of the deck, bodies, blood, water, all mixing as the cannons blasted into the night...and then I was gone...literally blown away...I have been told how the dream ended, with the ramming and sinking...and I am reminded how stubbornly set we are to wage war, and profit from it...how with the stroke of a pen we set the great wheels of this killing machine to motion... and how often England has done it...but we must put an end to it...an end...we were all there, all busy with the cannons and the riggings...all blasting away and getting blasted...war is a monster that eats its children...have we not given it enough...? "...all the leaders were silent...heads down and nodding...some rose and came over to Fitzsimmons...hugged her...whispered to her...

Jorbin waited, this took some time because Britain had a considerable and expansive colonial history...and memories were very long...Jorbing allowed the leaders to retake their places...and then, King Faisud stood, he marveled how they all looked the same in their reindeer skins...he spoke to them in Arabic.

"ان نرى لكم جميعا..."

Again Ashley heard and translated...he was completely baffled how this was happening...but it seemed to be happening to them all...

"Greetings my friends, (the King bowed deeply), I am very happy to see you all...this has been an extraordinary experience has it not?...even in the cold (and laughed out loud)...as you know, I come from a land very dry and very hot, covered in sand...flush with oil...and I have always had dreams of the jungle...of the wildness of it, the untamed throb of nature at its core...I have reflected on this dream we have all had, and see this: the earth has come at us since time began with everything it has, the raw brutal power, the howl in the dark, the seen and unseen beast... and mankind has plundered it...mauled and pillaged it until it cannot stand...the jungle, the metaphor, to use Bolchenkos' literary device, is nature herself...using the dark unknown, she has nothing now to scare this profligate child...try as she might, the balance has finally tipped... man suffocates her...and with it, himself. What fools we are to do this, no?...This too, like war, must end...and we, you and me, must do it...that is why we are here...to restore the balance"

And the King sat down, drawing a great circle with his finger on the skins on the floor.

Jorbin, still seated, looked at Ashley..."the slave ship, Stephen...is there something you want to say?" Ashley nodded. He would speak. The American President stood and looked around...there were tears in his eyes as he spoke...

"My country has tried many times to spin the story of slavery...to say in many ways that the men and women and children were somehow *better* for having been brought here against their will...I have never under-stood that logic...we bought and sold human beings...***HUMAN BEINGS*** (and emphasized it because of his emotion) by the thousands...there is nothing but forgiveness to ask for......not explanations to give...not fancy reasoning's to try to make it sound better...nothing but forgiveness"... he paused and gathered himself..."and the lesson from the ship...it is a wider one, I think... It has to do with all the pieces by which human beings make up their lives...with freedom at the very cornerstone. I do not say that lightly. I know the conditions in our world as we left it...an absence of freedom at every level of societies...economic, racial, religious, political...we enslave each other...we have always done it...we will go down doing it...just like that ship. I agree with everyone that this time it feels different...like something is about to happen...let us not try to explain away the slavery we continue to support...let us end it"... and Ashley sat down.

Petr Jorbin then recognized the President of Indonesia, the worlds' most populous Muslim-majority nation, President Suraya Rakyat. He rose and bowed to them...and chose to speak in English.

"I do not pretend to understand what is happening to us. I do not pretend to know where or how this is all taking place...but *for* this to be happening, and to **whom** it is happening is of profound importance to our human family...indeed, to the very meaning of our species.

I have made the effort to be certain I have spoken to every one of you at some point in our shared experiences (in fact he had), and it is not lost on me, after the first horrors we were subject to, that all of us, each and every one has at some critical moment, put him or herself aside to help another...to **save** another. But I have something to say about a dream in which only I was present. A singular dream. There was only me and the dreaded monster Komodo.

I was stalked and attacked by this dragon, the largest predator in Indonesia, but this beast was 6 meters of relentless power...the largest I have ever seen, awful and terrifying. He stalked me for days and nights, finally running me down and ripping into my upper thighs and back... and then circled away...the damage done. I would weaken and die from the many poisons, the toxins and venoms from his mouth...he would wait until I became feverish, unsteady...and finish me off...which he did. And since that experience, I have come to see the dragon for what he really was...a metaphor for **my** greed and selfishness, my predation. It **was**," he paused, looked around the entire circle, "it **IS**, killing my soul, and my government...and I had lost all comprehension of it...but no more." He extended his arms outward, gesturing to them all.

"Each of these shared realities is likewise metaphorical...and, I think we should not let their meanings go un-responded to. When we come back to life, as I believe we will, I look forward to speaking and working with you all for a very long time. For we are no longer Presidents and Prime Ministers and Kings and Queens, though we will be that for a short time, we are now, disciples for our species...disciples of peace and hope."

The leaders stood then and cheered him over and over. This went on for a long time...finally quieting with the dimming of the central fire.

Jorbin knew the Chinese Premier wished to speak, so he introduced him last, to explain the beach dream...the Premier was not a big fellow...and stood aspen straight as he spoke...

"海灘是一個美麗的地方...

The translation continued in Ashley's mind...and the others.

"The beach was a beautiful place...the flowers, the warm ocean breezes...the peacefulness of it all...do you all remember?

(the leaders nodded)...this is who we can be, people at peace, in communion with the great oceans and the great skies...we have enormous gardens at the Beijing palace...ponds and flowers, fish and birds of all kinds...it is a beauty I sometimes wished I never had to leave...a tiny speck of the world...and it is so renewing there, so rhythmical...we have lost the rhythm, the ebb and flow, the yin and yang, and we must get it back... or we will surely perish..."

Premier Fong sat back down.

And with that, for a very long time they all just sat there gazing at the fire...the dreams were all seen and felt the same way...with the same sense of human hood...of community...and spontaneously, they all reached and gripped the hand of the leader next to them...a circle unbroken... and started disappearing...one by one.



of human hood...of community...and spontaneously, they all reached and gripped the hand of the leader next to them...a circle unbroken... and started disappearing...one by one.

219

Jared Faulkner had spent the entire night busily working in the Situation Room, or travelling back and forth to the President's bedroom where nursing staff were now monitoring and logging information. Dr. Weinstein was also present, and accompanied Faulkner down to the Sit Room several times to assist if he could.

Faulkner and Angelo had now taken 11 EEG's on the President, and had reviewed the results from several of the other leaders as well. They had agreed to meet in one of the West Wing conference rooms at 7:45 AM.

Angelo arrived with coffee for them both, and a little pastry. He smiled, thanking her for her thoughtfulness.

"I'm not sure I can even think it, Stephanie...but these results look hard and fast to me...what did John Adams famously say?...'facts are stubborn things'...there are sections from these different tests, and you know it too, there are sections which are **precisely** exact" and he emphasized "precisely". Neuroscience ultimately was about precision, and there simply was no way in the current purview of their field to explain what they were seeing, what they were *measuring*.

"When Dr. Winston is faced with the need for novel explanations, he heads for his recliner...but I don't even think his recliner will help with this one.

How do you want to handle this?...I've been tossing things around, and I know you have..."

"For one thing" said Faulkner smiling, "we cannot let anyone hear us" now he was laughing...

"it's too incredible".

Angelo was smiling too. It *was* too incredible, and she knew it.

There was a long, almost uncomfortable pause, as they sat there smiling at each other.

Faulkner had something of a reputation with the nursing staff and young interns back at Stanford, but it was all bluster. He was charming and flirtatious and even funny with the staff, but he was a driven man...not a ladies man. The brain was his playground, and suddenly, he was now engaged in one of the real mysteries of neurology, no, **THE** mystery...and he was doing it with a brilliant and beautiful researcher from MGH... someone, just like him...no time for dating, no time for liaisons...just hyper-focused on the brain. He felt a real blush as he continued to look at her. And she at him.

"Let's start talking then" started Angelo, "and see where we end up..."

Faulkner and Angelo were alone, in a small, glassed in, conference room on the ground floor, near Press Secretary Jill Monroe's office. Coughlin O'Malley was hurrying by when he saw them...he poked his head in.

"Anything you need doctors?..."

"Not unless you have a box full of explanations"...Faulkner was writing things down as he spoke.

"Well actually, we keep one in the bottom drawer of the Resolute desk in the Oval Office...every President has..." O'Malley smiled briefly as he said this.

Faulkner asked him to please come in, and kindly close the door.

"Something about the President?"

Faulkner stood up…"Dr. Angelo and I believe it is something about them *ALL* …"

That phrase burned in O'Malley's mind again…"we will get them *ALL*" He stepped in and clicked the door shut. He noticed also, neither of them had their laptops.

"Please sit down Mr. O'Malley…we have some pretty strange stuff to throw around"

Stephanie Angelo went first.

"Well, I must say, this case, regardless the patient…is just as baffling now as when I got here. I have been reviewing in my head all the tests we have run…all the comparisons, all the input from the Stanford and Boston teams, and have come to the conclusion, that although we can *measure* this, we have no idea **what** we are measuring. Oh sure, I can point to the waveforms and give you commentary. I can look at the anatomical scans, and rule this and that out from a diagnosis…but I don't think there is, or can **find** anything *wrong* with Stephen Ashley. Whatever is going on with him…with all of them, is, and I swallow hard when I say it, beyond medicine…it's beyond science. To spend such an inordinate amount of time in the REM period, *is*, abnormal as we currently measure it, but so far, no harmful effects that can be ascertained." She was surprised that O'Malley showed no response whatsoever…Faulkner was nodding…and picked up where she left off.

"First of all, the plane ride getting out here was wild…I've never traveled that fast in my life…I thought I was getting younger…you know, going back in time…"

"Yes, I know the feeling…military speed. Full-bore"

"Anyway, this is true truth, what Dr. Angelo is saying…we have used the very, very, latest equipment on the President (and some of the others), nothing exists anywhere that can give the comprehensive results the BK's can...and never, have we synched live testing like that...so many patients at once...at the same time...unprecedented Mr. O'Malley...a first. And you know what the damn results are telling us?...what the Tweedles and our teams are saying?...what we are concluding is that this group of human beings, and I believe we can extrapolate to the entire global set, that these human beings are 'conscious' at a much different level than we are.

Something like what Dr. Angelo has said, something *beyond* science is going on. This group we are measuring, Mr. O'Malley, are 'conscious' of one another...even interactive. I'm not sure I should even admit to saying this, but, those are the results. It's almost a science fiction movie...except that it is real...it is happening as we watch."

Faulkner nervously looked back to Angelo who now was nodding to *him*.

O'Malley stood up. "What we are talking about is dreaming, correct?"

"REM sleep, yes sir" said Angelo.

"Lots and lots of dreaming...and science can't explain it, correct?"

"Not presently, no sir...the abundance and persistence is unique in our data"

"OK..." O'Malley looked at them both, "I think it's time to bring in the back-up..." and thanked the doctors and quickly exited.

Angelo looked at Faulkner..."what do you think he means?...back-up?"

"I'm as anxious as you to find out"...

They kept at it, until they were both satisfied they had said and explored all the corners of their thinking.

"I've put **most** of it down on paper" and he looked directly into her clear, brown eyes..."so we can quickly shred it if we have to" and smiled... Faulkner put his arm around her shoulder (which she did not mind at all) as they headed for the residence.

"Unbelievable" he said as they left the conference room,

"just unbelievable".

Father Thomas Buckley was retired from full-time parish duty...he assisted now, where the greater diocese of St. Louis might need him on any particular weekend, keeping in mind his age and travel limitations. The White House had contacted him through his private cell phone number...known and used by Coughlin O'Malley...Buckley was an old friend....and spiritual advisor for O'Malley, who, in this business of politics, often found himself at a tangled crossroads of competing "truths".... he often called "Father Buck" to help him find his way through. The roles were reversed decades back when O'Malley, a distinguished defense lawyer at the time, took the case of this zealous priest who, once he had discovered the sexual abuse going on in the church he had been recently transferred to, became incensed, confronted and seriously beat the abuser, a priest in charge of pastoral youth ministries for the parish, restrained finally, only by several police officers, and two additional priests...Buckley almost killed the man with his bare hands. O'Malley spent long hours developing his defense, and with it, long hours getting to know Buckley..."a kind of modern day Peter", O'Malley called him in court..."a man of faults to be sure, but, infuriated by injustice and willing to act, but finally, fully, a man of faith and charity.....his religion, indeed his very life in Christ demands repentance for this sin he has committed, which he does now, and will do every day of his life, but he also has forgiven the abuser, and ministers to the needs of the children and the families of this tragedy"...the jury found Fr. Buckley not guilty of assault, and he and O'Malley became heroes for the oppressed and abused. They were, from that moment on, forever linked. O'Malley needed Buckley here, now, at the White House, and would send the Secret Service to get him if he had to.

Reverend James Sloane did not have the dramatic introduction that Buckley had, but he participated in an ecumenical advisory council in the early 1970's reporting on conditions in the poorest areas and neighborhoods in Kansas City, Missouri, and Kansas City, Kansas...it was there he caught the ear of a young councilman, Stephen Ashley. Sloane worked in the barrio, his ministry pulled back the covers on all manner of social and racial discrimination of the mostly forgotten Latino communities of both sides of the Missouri river...and he knew of the priest, Buckley, who was on trial at the other end of the state, in St. Louis, for acting against child abuse.

Sloane spoke fluent Spanish, his parents were missionaries to Central America, and young James and his brother, Mark, and sister, Sarah, were culturally rich, and linguistically adept. Kansas City had a large population of Spanish speaking residents and transients, moving north or northeast...there were criminal gangs, extortion rackets, depressed schools and housing...teenage truancy and teen pregnancy were exploding, and drugs, which were flourishing, brought violence, and death. James Sloane took the message of Christ's mercy into those streets, and spent days and nights with people "on the edge, on the knife edge" showing them the charity and love of a stranger...and a gospel of hope.

Stephen Ashley's family had moved to Missouri from Massachusetts, when his father had been transferred to St. Louis when he was a teenager...and everyone but Stephen's oldest brother, who had been killed in Vietnam, now called "Big Mo" their home...after college, Stephen, who stayed on in Kansas City, was encouraged to run for city councilman, and he did, and won...it was early in his tenure that the advisory council issued their report, and then that he had met Sloane...and both were Congregationalists....so they struck up a friendship...one which had lasted until this day. The Reverend had called O'Malley's secretary within 2 hours of his hearing about the President, asking if there was something he could do...O'Malley and Buckley, Ashley and Sloane... Coughlin was impelled to bring them together again, as they had been so many times over the years, in celebration and in sorrow...and now, in mystery.

When all the details were worked, both men would travel together, on military transport, touching down under Secret Service escort, just short of an hour. O'Malley met them both at the West Wing side entrance...

"Father, Reverend...it's good to see you both." He hurried them along to his office, where he had asked Faulkner and Gaiter to meet them ten minutes after arrival. Buckley was officially dressed, black pants, shirt, suit coat and white clerical collar...Sloane too was "Sunday dressed". Sloane carried a pocket Bible, Buckley, small receptacles holding elements of his faith's sacraments, and the Holy Eucharist...for O'Malley.

Faulkner arrived before Gaiter, who was finishing up the authorization to move the President to Walter Reed on Monday noon.

"I can offer you fresh coffee from the White House kitchen, or soda and bottled water from the fridge right here"...O'Malley grabbed a water for himself.

"Coffee would be welcomed" said Buckley.

"and for me" chimed Sloane as he pardoned himself for yawning.

Cough asked Catherine to call chef. Faulkner came in then as Buckley and Sloane stood up to greet him. Everyone exchanged pleasantries as O'Malley took the floor..."Dr. Faulkner and Dr. Angelo are anchoring the continual monitoring of Stephen's brain function"...O'Malley nodded to Faulkner, "he'll provide the latest details...in what so far, is a very perplexing situation"...Gaiter entered then, and after the introductions, they all sat on the office sofa and comfortable chairs..."Stephen is getting 24 hour monitoring and whatever this medical team feels necessary... the reason I have asked you both to come out is because I sense we are moving now beyond simply a medical issue...but..." O'Malley turned to Faulkner, "doctor, can you please sketch out the President's current condition...and options?".

Faulkner took about 8 minutes giving the best summary he could, asking Dr. Gaiter to add the rest. When they were done, the coffee (and pastry) was brought in.

Neither Buckley nor Sloane interrupted by asking questions until now, just sitting and listening. Buckley spoke first. "let me just say thank you doctors...given the raft of error-filled reports and opinions being trotted out out there, this is relieving news. The President's condition is far better than I expected...and dreaming so much."

Reverend Sloane then asked if the White House chaplain had prayed for the President... "No, Jim...there is no official WH chaplain..." O'Malley thought for a moment..."I think it's a good idea now though...let's finish our coffee and go up to see him."

Faulkner then told Buckley that Stephen Ashley was dreaming virtually non-stop....of an increased frequency and duration than he had never seen or read about clinically..."nothing recorded like it in the databanks"...this was a phenomenon he frankly could not even begin to explain. Buckley asked both doctors if this dream-state could be a manifestation or effect of some vector organism or chemical, like LSD or something?...Gaiter said all the leaders that they had been in conference about, and named the countries, all had shown no such trace vector... or injection point, etc. "There is nothing that is showing in any of the tests...and let me say, virtually every known and some novel tests have been repeatedly done on these folks with nothing...I mean NOTHING showing up..." Gaiter's frustration with the situation was showing, and he apologized. "I am at a complete loss to explain it...just like Dr. Faulkner said...an unexplainable phenomenon".

Sloane nursed his coffee, and cleared his throat to speak. "lots and lots of dreaming you say?"...Buckley looked over at him...slightly smiled...

he seemed to know what was coming. "from our vantage points, Fr. Buckley and myself, we have some pretty important references regarding dreaming in our work...let me share a few examples with you...the Old Testament, or The Torah as it remains in the Jewish faith, and the New Testament are filled with accounts of dreams and visions...dreams seem to serve different purposes for God than visions...Daniel and King Nebuchadnezzar for example...an ancient head of state, Daniel calls him the King of Kings of that period, all powerful in a military and economic sense, but is disturbed by a recurring dream which he could not understand...it was finally interpreted and revealed by Daniel, a servant of the Lord." Sloane talked of Pharaoh and Joseph, and before he could continue, Faulkner interrupted, "Joseph was warned in a dream, as I recall...to get up and leave for Egypt...for something terrible was about to happen...terror by one of the Herod's on all the children was about to be unleashed...and so, the family was saved"...Sloane added, "yes, not the same Joseph, but nonetheless, the Magi too were also warned in a dream not to return to Herod, Herod the Great, to be clear, and indeed, scripture tells us Herod had all boys 2 years old and younger, in and around Bethlehem, slain by his soldiers...in hopes of killing the Christ."

"Yes, and there are more" added Buckley, "dreams are a way to be spoken to when other ways do not work, it seems. We can only partially explain dreams, I mean the content...it is believed that God uses this time, not always of course, to speak to a resistant mind...God's voice in the murmurings of dreams...in those days, people believed that what they experienced in dreams was *more* real than what they experienced in their waking lives...and in scripture, we see especially how certain dreams came to change the course of human history..."

O'Malley stood. He had a smile on his face for the first time since Friday morning...he looked to everyone in his office in turn, and motioned to them all..."Let's go see Stephen."

The gathering at the President's bedside was prayerful and respectful and lasted as long (36 minutes) as O'Malley felt appropriate...they said the Lord's Prayer together, Fr. Buckley extending the Sacrament of the Sick to the President, and Dr. Alexander, who had left late Saturday but was called back again, was Jewish, and asked politely if he could recite the Jewish Prayer for Healing, which, he said, "was so helpful during my wife's illness"...so he did:

"God, hear my prayer,
And let my cry come to You.
Do not hide from me in the day of my distress
Turn to me and speedily answer my prayer.
Eternal God, Source of healing,
Out of my distress I call upon You.
Help me sense Your presence
At this difficult time.
Grant me patience when the hours are heavy;
In hurt or disappointment give me courage.
Keep me trustful in Your love.
Give me strength for today, and hope for tomorrow.
To your loving hands I commit my spirit
When asleep and when awake. You are with me; I shall not fear."

They all nodded in appreciation..."Thank you Dr. Alexander" said O'Malley..."that was quite beautiful."

Shortly after its conclusion, Dr. Faulkner paged Doctors Angelo and Gaiter, and asked them, in addition to the clergy and O'Malley, to join him in the Situation Room to view some recent developments regarding the President's condition.

O'Malley then checked with Faulkner if staff could be present, with particular thinking to have Jill Monroe there. Faulkner had no objections. O'Malley then sent word out via Julia Freitas that all central office staff leads were to assemble in the Situation Room in 15 minutes. O'Malley also asked Freitas to come. This could very well be the last briefing to West Wing personnel associated with the Ashley administration about their chief executive, and O'Malley saw no reason to keep them distanced from it...and Faulkner had no reservations whatsoever in speaking on this issue to staff.

Thirteen minutes later, everyone had gathered around the conference size table and the multi-wall bank of high-def monitors...the biggest one, just to the right of the speaker's podium. Faulkner seemed not to notice the growing crowd as he was busy reviewing on the embedded podium monitor, his presentation...for several minutes as the gathered invitees exchanged conversation, Faulkner focused on his work. Finally, satisfied, he looked up.

"Good afternoon folks"...a chorus greeted him in return. Many of the staff had heard Dr. Faulkner at some point the past two days, and clearly, there was an atmosphere of goodwill in the room.

"I have some synthesized imagery based on the ongoing testing conducted on the President as this crises has proceeded, and, after some help from the White House engineering team, we have merged most of it through the holographic software which is loaded on the resident super-computers just behind the back wall there" Faulkner pointed to the far wall. "Do you folks know the technology that's back there?"...people were looking now..."you access it from an adjoining room, not this one...place is lights-out stocked with the latest everything...including 2 tech's 24/7. I had not planned on putting this together, but when Dante..." Faulkner looked around at the collection of faces..."where is Dante?" Dante Espinal was not present. Faulkner took a sip of water, and continued.

"When Dante showed me the holographic capabilities, I have to tell you, my knees got weak" Faulkner smiled broadly..."and I could see where this might be useful...and given the results, I believe you'll agree."

Faulkner initiated a sequence from the podium which dimmed the room lighting and simultaneously brought online 5 separate projection sources from the 4 corners and the black 2 ft. orb hanging just above the center of the table. With another key he actuated a 3-dimensional slowly rotating 3 by 3 ft. image in the center of the room, below the orb, 18 inches above the table surface. It was a gleaming, electrically active image of the human brain. More precisely, Stephen Ashley's brain.

There was murmuring, even gasps...some staff members stood up...O'Malley himself, who had been to this room hundreds of times and seen dozens of new technologies here, had never seen anything like this.

Faulkner brought the oversized high-definition screen up behind him. Several rapid undistinguishable digital images came and went before stopping...the supercomputers had now aligned the hologram with the images on the screen. Faulkner could now proceed.

"What you are seeing here is a composite hologram of the President's brain...this has been done using the data compiled from the standard and next-generation EEG technology which both Dr. Angelo brought, and Dr. Gaiter had in-house...in addition, the results generated by the

BK1, which is my affectionate name for the mobile neural PET and fMRI scanner, have been integrated into this composite."

Faulkner took a wireless hand controller from the podium and moved closer to the screen. He advanced the stream of information slowly forward, describing what everyone was seeing.

"I have culled out in the first part of this exercise what we refer to as 'quiet periods', which for the neuroscientist is a gross inaccuracy as the normal functioning brain is never truly 'quiet'...but the intent here is to dramatize some rather unusual" Faulkner paused, chose different words..."no...*historically* unusual happenings in the recorded annals of brain science."

The room chattered with his words, "*historically* unusual"...everyone here was a best and brightest candidate in their particular area of expertise, and the phrase, and its significance, was not lost on any of them.

"As we proceed", said Faulkner, "you will notice in the holographic image, areas which will deepen and increase in the assigned color hues...this is accounted for by significant increases in blood flow and electrical activity. Also, at several junctions the image will split in two and separate, one above the other...this gives you an internal sectional perspective of what is going on bilaterally...no need to remind you, but all that you are about to see was occurring while Stephen Ashley, as far as we can currently determine, was asleep."

Faulkner then hit the play button, and the show started to roll.

It was clear that Faulkner had worked on this for some time, likely hours, as he had an accompanying audio commentary, pointing out when to view the screen, and when to look at the spinning hologram, and how the two were related. It was magnificent...the colors, the bursts of electrical convergence, the compelling physiology...and all the while, the words of the neuroscientist sprinkled it all. Faulkner would not "dumb down" anything, this was the human brain after all, *a* human brain, and all these other human brains were taking it all in.

Faulkner hit the stop button in the middle of a prodigious burst of light in the President's temporal lobes…

"I need, I guess, and I would like Dr. Angelo to comment, as well, but I need to emphasize the main players in this…this event…the main characters are the neurons…everything else, the chemicals, the structures, the electricals, all have their parts, but the neurons are the top bananas."

Faulkner waited for Angelo to comment, but she did not, she was too wowed by this extraordinary rendition of Stephen Ashley's brain. She simply shook her head…nothing to add. She admitted to herself that she never would have thought of doing this…nor had the energy *to* do it. This was not some dog and pony show put together by some salesman, this, to her knowledge, had never even been done before. Her admiration for Jared Faulkner, was taking off…and she was enjoying the ride.

"Ok then…let's continue…" The dreams, the duration of dreaming, clearly the richness of them as shown by the near total brain involvement, was all pointed out by Faulkner in the audio…then separating the two brain halves to show which side was likely doing what, and then *slicing* the brain into layers, as the BK1 had done, brought some members of the audience out of their seats with wonder. But Faulkner was taking them somewhere, laying the groundwork to end at a place in neuroscience where no one had ever gone before…

After 64 minutes, Faulkner stopped the illustrations, and terminated the hologram…the lights however did not increase the illumination in the room, instead, Faulkner squeezed nearly every photon of light out and spoke for the last time.

"We are nearly done…thank you all for being such an interested audience. This case, the case of the President, has brought us, the teams of clinicians working it, virtually to a standstill. Our goals, of understanding and healing have come to little where the rubber meets the road I'm afraid, which is charting a course of recovery...so, we remain stymied... as do other teams around the globe, working in their ways, to help their leaders...but even with the looming executive transition, we are not stopping trying to figure this out, and then, how to place the President on a path of improvement...you can count on that.

I have stopped here, because the place we have come to is completely uncharted territory...for me, or anyone else in this field. I am re-configuring the hologram to show only one thing"...the hologram re-materialized over the table...the shape of the President's brain was intact, but all the identifiable structures were filtered out...all that hovered there, was a mass of gray white illuminated matter...

"What you are seeing here are masses of glial cells, there are different types...they are far more numerous in our brains than neurons are, and have functions which neuroscientists have essentially categorized as supportive of the neurons...there are studies of course, which take the field this way and that, but nothing, essentially, to dislodge that supportive role hypothesis...what you have seen until now in this presentation has been fairly straightforward, except unexpected, certainly while the brain is sleeping...but **_this_** is something altogether different..." Faulkner left the sentence hanging there...much like the hologram, and started the last portion.

Seven minutes later, the image vanished, the lights came up to strength, and not a single person spoke in the room. They just sat there, none of them understanding what they had just seen.

Jill Monroe was giving her fifth news conference in 48 hours...it was wearing her down. The room, the East Room, was overflowing again... the White House was issuing additional press corps clearances with each passing conference.

Monroe walked to the podium.

"I have additional details on the President's condition, and then, will ask Dr. Jared Faulkner to give the neurological assessment." She plunged into the data even pointing to, and explaining, the segments (which Stephanie Angelo had helped her understand) of Ashley's latest EEG now up on the portable widescreen set up yesterday.

"We have information from Dr. McMaster's team in Ottawa which is included in you packets...those of you without one please see Christine afterwards and it will be provided. The situation remains essentially un-changed overall. The same reports from other capitals, London, Beijing, Canberra, Yaounde in Cameroon...to name a few...all unchanged, still unconscious."

She took questions for about 30 minutes before introducing and turning the podium over to Dr. Faulkner, who was, more than a little nervous at what he was about to say. Both he and Angelo agreed on the final conclusion, and after O'Malley and others (meaning CIA, Defense and Justice) had cleared it security wise but not without incredulity, he stood before the seasoned and cynical Washington press corps ready to share the most fantastic medical analysis any of them had ever heard.

Faulkner opened the bottled water handed to him by Monroe, and took a long swallow.

"Good evening ladies and gentlemen. I have some extraordinary conclusions to share with you tonight, and none of it, for reasons which will become obvious, is detailed in your packets." The room grew un-customarily quiet and attentive. All the network and cable teams were carrying the briefing live. Faulkner put his right hand in his pocket and pinched his leg, as hard as he could stand it. It was an old habit which helped him focus on the task at hand, whatever it was. And then he began.

"As you know, the White House follows protocols for virtually every contingency which affects the Executive Branch centered within it, and as Ms. Monroe has made clear in several previous conferences, this situation called for the Neuro-Protocol, or Protocol 6. Dr. Angelo and myself, as has been stated previously as well, were not the primary choices, the chiefs of our departments were, but as they were unable to make it, we are their proxies. You have all been given, previously, all the academic and clinically significant information about the two us, our schooling, our residencies, our scholarship, etc., so you know, we are not, as they say, chopped liver. We are serious researchers, serious physicians. The reason I want to emphasize that, and any of you can review our research to confirm, is that we have both, independently, drawn very much the same conclusions so far about this case, the case of President Stephen Ashley, and perhaps, by extension, the remaining unconscious leaders. And you will be startled by them."

Faulkner had them now...no one made a sound or moved a muscle in the room.

"Before I share the opinion we have arrived at, let me just say, that we have tugged at this puzzle with some of the finest researchers in the field, and the latest, most accurate technology. While Dr. Angelo and myself are here, we are both members of wider, independent teams, Stephanie from MGH, and myself from Stanford University Medical Center. And we have discussed, and sought additional information on our findings with those teams.

Since our arrival on Friday morning, we have conducted a battery of neurological exams and tests...in addition to the clinical work done by Doctors Gaiter, Jackson and Weinstein, and the labs at Ft. Dietrick, the CDC, Walter Reed and MGH.

We conclude that there is *nothing wrong* electrically, chemically, anatomically or physiologically with Stephen Ashley." Faulkner let the conclusions settle in before continuing...journalists were frantically writing. "The President's blood has been scanned and had samples sent to rule out nanotechnology contamination. All negative. Every blood test, within normal limits. No pathogens discovered. No untoward poisons or radioactivity. The President has not suffered a stroke or heart attack... the NSA has confirmed there are no radio or microwave transmissions involved in compromising the President...no untoward man-made disruptive influences that can be currently measured.

The explanation we have come to is no explanation. We have none. He is as healthy as you or I. There is no reason for him to remain unconscious that is within out tool repertoire to discern...every diagnosis, no matter how farfetched, has been considered and ruled out. But this is beyond medicine. It is beyond current science. And further, all the other leaders who have been tested using our BK-series technology are presenting with exactly the same conclusion. There is **nothing** wrong with them. At certain moments, which were synchronized, they appear to exhibit a *singular* consciousness, as astounding as that sounds.

The white matter in Stephen Ashley's brain has **increased** in mass, which is a historic development, or at least an unprecedented finding. We have recorded brainwaves never seen before, and in concert. What does it all mean? **This is**, and I choose these words *exceedingly* carefully," he paused then as if stepping off into space...**"a collective meta-physical event."** Faulkner stepped back from the podium, as the room erupted with shouts and questions.

239

Stephanie Angelo returned to the WH residence after the news conference. She wanted to look in on Mrs. Ashley, who did not attend. No staff were present (short of Secret Service), and never *were* after hours, unless specifically requested by the First Lady. Angelo found her in the second floor study, across from the Lincoln bedroom. She knocked softly on the open door jamb...

"May I come in Ma'am?"

"Oh", Elizabeth slid the book she was daydreaming about on to the coffee table.

"Yes, Stephanie, please do". She gestured to the chair, and sat back on the sofa.

"And, I'm feeling better, thank you very much"...she beamed as she smiled..."calmer somehow. My skin feels like my own, if that makes any sense...and I'm not brooding on the same thoughts over and over...it's incredibly exhausting.." she met Angelo's eyes in mid-sentence, "I'm sure you know...would you care for anything? tea perhaps?...I have a carafe of hot water from the kitchen and several types of tea..."

"Yes Ma'am...that would be lovely."

"Chamomile?...it seems to help me sleep...at least I've convinced myself of it..." The First Lady smiled slightly.

"Yes, chamomile is fine, and I believe it does have properties to help encourage sleep...one of my colleagues at the General swears by it."

"Stephanie, look at this..." Elizabeth held an exquisite 6 oz. cut crystal bottle with matching cap.

"The kitchen crew came up with this...pure orange blossom honey in this bottle...the crystal is from the Franklin Pierce administration...now *there* was a fish out of water, President Pierce...I've been reading about him... this library is loaded with historians' accounts of all the Presidents...but Pierce seemed to have a soft spot for the confederacy...he was in office in the mid-1850's...and being from New Hampshire, that put him squarely at odds with the abolitionists...needless to say, he had a pretty rough time of it...but as I was saying, chef found out I was reading up on him and located this cut crystal and now he keeps it replenished with honey...I just love the echoes of this place. Amazing."

After fixing everything as she spoke, she brought the tea and honey to the coffee table.

"Are you just coming from the news conference?"

"Yes Ma'am, Dr. Faulkner spoke at length. I agree with him that all that could be said, *was* said. He called this phenomenon a *metaphysical* event... we discussed the situation earlier today...and with our teams at Stanford and MGH before that...I'm afraid we are not looking especially competent in this crisis Ma'am, but the clinical picture is so confusing because it's breaking all the known rules...no evidence after 2 days of continued testing of health compromise...except of course that neither he, nor any of the other affected leaders can be aroused from sleep...very baffling... but from what we, and other medical teams we have conferred with around the world, neither the President nor the others, are, up to now, in any apparent danger." Angelo looked down, fingering her tea cup.

"May I ask you a question Ma'am?"

"Certainly"...Elizabeth added honey to her tea.

"Mrs. Ashley, you remember when you and the President retired on Thursday night?"

Ashley nodded.

"I remember thinking, and I know this isn't real, but it seems so very real when it is happening, I remember thinking that Stephen is waiting for me to fall asleep so he can leave through the window and meet the others...the other aliens...so I stayed awake for hours. When I finally fell asleep, Stephen was snoring away."

"Yes Ma'am...did the President complain of headache or chills or anything unusual?...anything at all?

"Let me see"...she sat stirring her honey swirling through the chamomile...

"Not that I remember no...he had a bourbon on the rocks, not at all unusual, around 10...and a little cheese, cheddar I think, and some crackers.

I went to bed before him, but not much...and he did toss a bit as I recall... but that has come with the job it seems...and when he finally went off, it was an uneasy sleep...like he was reluctant to give in to it or something... but then I slipped off myself and only when the alarm woke me up did I know something was wrong. Stephen always gets up to the alarm...and lets me sleep."

Angelo was making mental notes as Ashley spoke...she was calmer, more in control like when she appears on TV. or in public...she really is an elegant co-emissary of this office Angelo was thinking.

"I am not parallel tracking as much, so the meds you ordered, are kicking in somewhere up there" she motioned with her eyes to her forehead and smiled again.

"If I get, and more importantly, remain steadied like it seems I am, this whole thing is going to hit me, and hit me hard...the girls are with their maternal grandparents for the moment, but we are going to have to make plans...and how the Office will extend medical coverage if, I mean when, Stephen is no longer President...I would think no longer than tomorrow...I will be front and center for the inevitable press invasion... the 60 Minutes segments...the cable news trucks...I am going to need you Dr. Angelo...if these new meds can plateau me out of the ever lurking psychosis and mood swings..." She was beginning to career her thoughts like so many vehicles in a highway pile-up.

Angelo reached over and took her hand. "Yes, Elizabeth...I will take you as my patient for as long as we both think necessary. These new meds will blunt the more disconcerting parts of the illness, and level the playing field for you...or, as my brother says, 'rights my boat in the water like everyone else's'...we are very fortunate to live in such a time as this... pharmaceutically speaking."

"It is like letting the water out of the bath tub...the anxiety, the crazy thoughts, the fixations...and then the dark, dark, mental rooms in which we sit...yes, I can feel it all going down the drain. Isn't that amazing?"

Ashley looked at Angelo with those soft brown eyes, and clear, but still a little distant, expression of gratitude.

"I would like to go see Stephen and give him a kiss goodnight."

"Yes. Ma'am...I'll walk down with you."

It was 12:38 AM EDT Monday night as they headed down the hall.

MGH received the batch of the Presidential Family's blood sent high-priority by Stephanie Angelo, Attention to: Dr. Sara Candorro, a peer of Dr. Angelo's, her specialty was the controversial gene-intervention therapeutics field...using techniques she and her team, assembled from disparate academic and clinical backgrounds from the best universities in the Boston area, Harvard, MIT, BU, Northeastern, BC, in addition to the existing resources within MGH itself...they were "lifting and substituting" individual genes and entire segments and sub-segments in laboratory animals. They had the tools, both chemical and atomic, and they were building an impressive knowledge-base. Angelo, as a special favor, had asked Candorro if her team could scheme the blood of the First Family...Angelo was looking, or rather, having Candorro's team look at specific genomic segments in the First Lady and the children for flags of bipolar illness...and projected severity levels for the daughters. The President's blood was a routine run...looking for any kind of evolving discrepancies, shredding, in short, anything which might help to explain his puzzling condition...Dr. Candorro would run Stephen Ashley's blood herself...for the other's, she asked Dr. Ranjit Beswar to be the lead as he was the bipolar genomic expert...Candorro was viewing with the platinum of technological research tools, a 3$^{rd}$ generation Simpson electron microscope...the most powerful viewing tool in the medical research arsenal...she was looking into the code of life itself, the proteins, the amino acids...she was seeing all that...and something else. Incredulous, she switched the viewing template to the large UHD screen in the lab... she was hoping the screen image clarity would resolve what she was viewing...but it did not...she wasn't sure now exactly what to do...this was the

President of the United States after all...but she clicked several digitals off and reviewed them...just sitting there, by herself, for 15 minutes...and then sent the files via e-mail with an alert to her cellphone to Stephanie Angelo, flagged with High Priority..

O'Malley had been up until 4 am reviewing the now inevitable and necessary transition process. The Vice-President would be officially assuming the Office of the President at 9 am EDT, Monday, the 24th of March.

The Ashley presidency was over. Stephen Ashley had become a casualty to something completely elusive...an intangible agent...he and the others, victims of a devastating force. Security in all capitols of the world was now at the highest protective conditions...this, whatever it was, had to be prevented from happening again. O'Malley's hopes (and prayers) that this was somehow a temporary condition, a transient state, were now waning...but he made a note to especially thank Carson and the Legal Office for a fine job of stonewalling things on the Hill...for he thought this would all be resolved by now...either through some drug administration or something...anything...he walked then to the Oval Office, stood at the door...the lights were all turned off, still, he could see the outlines of two Service agents outside, under the portico...he slipped his hand into his right pocket...his rosary was there...O'Malley fell to his knees, and silently whispered his prayers for Stephen, the country...and the planet. Lying down finally, completely exhausted, he closed his eyes and slipped into sleep on his office sofa, and sleeping there, he expected, for the very last time.

# Stephen Ashley's Last Dream

Elizabeth was running away from him. It was downtown in some big city,and the streets were filled with human beings...with packages, on cell phones, dressed in business suits, passing in cabs. He called to her.

Elizabeth kept looking behind as she darted in and out and around the moving mass. Ashley got some sense that this was rush hour...people escaping their jobs, their colleagues, their work selves...leaving it behind and heading away...they all turned and looked at him...just as Elizabeth had, and started moving in her direction...all getting ahead of him, looking back, and increasing their speed. More poured in from the side streets and from shops...everyone began running now...hundreds,thousands...he could not see Elizabeth anymore. He stopped. The throng kept going...going...until everyone was gone. He was, once again, alone on an empty street.

He stood there. Unmoving. Minutes passed. Interminable minutes....but something *was* happening in him...Ashley was beginning to understand.

He put his head down...remembered Petr Jorbin...a man he hardly knew, yet Jorbin would not, had not, abandoned him...or anyone else who needed his help. Jorbin cared. He did not discriminate...he did not judge...wouldn't do the expedient thing, the self-serving thing...he wouldn't cut the rope.

Ashley suddenly became overcome...a wave shuddering through him... emotion, bottled up,...yes, abandoned for all these many years...and for why?...he didn't have that answer. And what about Elizabeth? Once his best friend and counselor, and he, hers, even through her compelling illness, nothing could come between them but hadn't he abandoned her too?...hadn't he willingly opened his arms to seduction?...the seduction of power?...the smothering certainty of it all as you were folded into obscurity?...and this change he supposedly was bringing to Washington, it wasn't change at all, was it?...it was tinkering child's play...he turned, looking everywhere and seeing no one, not a single human face, or hearing a single human voice...he fell to his knees, sobbing, heaving...crying out for Elizabeth.

Like a bolt of lightning, he suddenly remembered Ebenezer Scrooge, the miserly curmudgeon of the Charles Dickens's classic, A Christmas Carol,who is saved from a ghastly eternal trek by his coming to see himself for what he had become...and pledged to the spirits that he **would** change...that he **would** celebrate charity and good will every day of his life.

Ashley began whispering then as Jorbin had... "I will not cut the rope" and said it again, with emphasis..."I will **not** cut it"

Ashley collapsed as he spoke this, right there in the street...and woke up, whispering those words, in his Presidential bed.

At 7: 13 am Dr. Gaiter sent O'Malley a text message on the beeper, O'Malley had just started to make his morning coffee after a scant and restless 3 hours sleep or so..."POTUS up, call me please"...an instant later the cell buzzed in his hand..."Coughlin, the President is awake... he's asked for Finnish morning cake, whatever the hell that is, and wants to see *you* asap, ...I've never seen him so animated...you'd better get up here...he wants to see Elizabeth, and a call placed right now to President Petr Jorbin of Finland before he does *anything* else...can you imagine?... before *anything* else...

Cough, who the hell is Petr Jorbin?"

O'Malley was already half running up the residence stairs and turning the corner at the top when he heard Ashley shouting to Allan Wheeler how happy he was to see him. A small bank of Service agents were gathering at, and in, the bedroom doorway.

"Allan...have I ever even *called* you Allan?...for gawd sake" said the President looking momentarily pensive..."I don't think I have..." he reached out and hugged a clearly startled Wheeler...

"Allan, I mean it...the President is happy to see you...thank you so much for all you do for me...for *us*."

Wheeler was blushing but smiling now. "Yes sir...thank you sir."

"And who is this?" Ashley was looking at Stephanie Angelo. She extended her hand..."Dr. Stephanie Angelo sir, from MGH,...er...Massachusetts..."

"General Hospital"...Ashley finished the sentence. "Is someone sick?"

Ashley looked around...he still had 8 or 9 EEG wires hanging from his head as Angelo was recording when he suddenly woke up. She had motioned to Gaiter to come and look at the readout as "something significant" was happening, and then, Ashley simply woke up in the middle of a sentence... "will *not* cut it"

"Well" said Ashley, holding his hand out (which was bleeding slightly because he had pulled the I.V. connection out) and shaking Angelo's, "it's a pleasure to meet you doctor." He turned toward the door..."hey guys"... he waved to the gathered agents and gave his head a little shake, flopping the wires all around...he was having a great time of it.

Gaiter was about to start talking to the President and begin explaining what had been going on the last 3 days, when O'Malley came in.

"COUGHLIN" the President roared... "do you have any idea how much you look like Pavel Ragussus, the President of Hungary?...it's quite astonishing really." Ashley gave a quick look and a wink to Wheeler as he put a bear hug on O'Malley..."really, Cough...so good to see you" he whispered...

He turned then to everyone...composed himself.

"I have been away. I think most of you know that...I'm not sure how long exactly, but my knee is still tender", Ashley lifted and flexed his right leg...he had twisted it exiting the limousine 5 days earlier..."so it's not too long, and I'm still in the White House I see...I'll be interested to find out what you can tell me about it all" he turned to Angelo as he spoke it..."but what I can tell *you* is, everything which has characterized this administration is about to change. I expect we will begin to see substantial worldwide change as well.

You know, when I was a younger man, I did a great deal of reading about our Founding Fathers...what an extraordinary group of human beings they were...I often wondered *how* such a remarkable idea, *this* idea" he gestured grandly..."the living document it is, our republic, how it came to pass...yes, there was this fire for independence, this passion to determine their, our, own destiny, but the hardships, the sacrifices...I honestly don't know if I would have been up to it" he paused, seemed to meet them all with his eyes..."and then, the *how* of it all...the meetings in secret, the assemblies in Philadelphia...the Articles of Confederation... the Constitutional Conventions...the *vision*" Ashley raised his voice as he spoke it, then softened again..."the *shared* vision...no, *more* than that, the dream...I could never quite grasp it...but I can grasp it now. We all will have much work to do...much..." and the President grew distant... glassed over slightly...they waited for more, but he was somewhere else...

O'Malley filled the moment then, and simply spoke for them all, "Mr. President, it's good to have you back, sir."

Ashley looked up, locked eyes with O'Malley.

"Cough, take me to Elizabeth please."

# Epilogue

Thirty-three percent of a human beings life is spent sleeping. When a human is not conscious and interactive, they essentially, "cease to exist"... they are isolated from everyone and everything, and, as few other times, utterly alone.

Sleep, and what happens there remain, one of the last frontiers of science.

There may be a time in the future, when even our dreams can be comprehensively recorded in 3-dimensional representations and played back for our amusement or education...but not yet.

What has happened in this story "goes quite beyond the human mind", and I appreciate the readers attempts to reconcile the beginning to the end...that is to say, to make sense of it all. I **can** tell you that the entire global leadership all recovered from their "dream" states...and those who were targets of coup attempts (8) while they were "incapacitated" all survived to re-assume their positions. The approximate time turn from beginning to end was 72 hours...just 3 days...yet in that time, the world staggered as never before in recorded history...suddenly, and without warning, the world was without rudders...without their elected or appointed or by whatever other means, leaders, and surged toward hysteria and panic, and easily could have pushed terrible buttons, or launched horrific missiles, or marshaled invasions, because it thought and then acted as if there was nothing else to believe in...as if there was nothing else to give it balance. Luckily, or by design, this did not get very far.... and the leaders emerged, not exactly as they were before....not exactly.

And what Dr. Sara Candorro found in the deoxyribonucleic acid of Stephen Ashley, and what she sent photographically to Stephanie Angelo, can only be described as "medically mystifying, unexplainable"...

for there, mixed and intertwined with the human double helix, was **another** helix, almost opaque in the films, a ghost image of light....at first she thought it was "shadowing", or impression-fade, or some trick of the technology she was using...so she did it again...and finally a third time but it remained...an unmistakable aurora,..and Angelo saw it too, and then Faulkner. Faulkner stood for a long time gazing at the impressions, trying and failing to understand what he was seeing...he finally called it simply a "purity and elegance of revolutionary importance"...asking Dr. Angelo to send them to the Situation Room and the ultra-powerful screening technology contained there...he remained fixed, joined by Angelo, at the screen for over an hour.

Afterwards he quietly proposed (as they exchanged private cellphone numbers) that he and Dr. Angelo lead a team to continue investigating this phenomenon the press was simply now calling, "the dreams". They would speak privately with O'Malley, and possibly the President.

Faulkner had a strange and powerful sense, that something more, something equally incomprehensible, was coming.

"What I am saying is that these human beings are 'conscious' at a much different level than we are...I can only speculate here...but something extra-ordinary, in every sense that word can be understood, is going on. The group we are measuring are <u>conscious</u> of one another, **even** interactive."

Something was **behind** this unprecedented event, even moving **within** it... and Faulkner had made up his mind he would not give up until he found out what it was...if he could.

# Acronym Legend

| | |
|---|---|
| GMT | Greenwich Mean Time |
| EDT | Eastern Daylight Time |
| PDT | Pacific Daylight Time |
| POTUS | President of the United States |
| COS | Chief of Staff |
| SRV | Socialist Republic of Vietnam |
| VP | Vice President |
| WH | White House |
| WNL | Within Normal Limits |
| SG | Surgeon General |
| NSR | Normal Sinus Rhythm |
| CBC | Complete Blood Count |
| USMC | United States Marine Corps |
| MGH | Massachusetts General Hospital |
| EEG | Electro-encephalograph |
| DCA | Diagnostic Comparison Analysis |
| NIH | National Institutes of Health |
| CDC | Centers for Disease Control |
| VIP | Very Important Person |
| NTK | Need to Know |
| CIA | Central Intelligence Agency |
| CNN | Cable News Network |
| SR | Situation Room (White House) |
| RCMP | Canadian Protective Policing Detail |
| NSA | National Security Agency |
| CIC | Commander-in-Chief |
| UN | United Nations (New York City) |
| PM | Prime Minister |
| NYPD | New York Police Department |

| | |
|---|---|
| FBI | Federal Bureau of Investigation |
| IT | Information Technology |
| PET | Positron Emission Tomography |
| fMRI | Functional Magnetic Resonance Imaging |
| CLC | Chief Legal Counsel (White House) |
| DHS | Department of Homeland Security |
| PDD | Presidential Decision Directive |
| WTC | World Trade Center |
| FSB | Federal Security Service (of the Russian Federation) |
| DARPA | Defense Advanced Research Projects Agency |
| DNA | Deoxyribonucleic Acid |
| CAB | Chemical and Biological (US Army, Ft. Dietrick) |
| AP | Associated Press |
| NBC | National Broadcasting Company |
| FPC | For Public Consumption |
| PC | Press Conference |
| IDF | Israeli Defense Forces |
| REM | Rapid Eye Movement |
| DPS | Deep Pressure Stimulation |
| BSL-3 | Biological Safety Level 3 |
| WHCA | White House Communication Agency |
| WHMO | White House Military Office |
| LED | Light Emitting Diode |
| MIT | Massachusetts Institute of Technology |
| BK | Boris Karloff |
| FRR | Face Recognition Resource |
| R&D | Research and Development |
| DPW | Department of Public Works |
| UHD | Ultra-High Definition |
| OLC | Office of Legal Counsel (White House) |
| FoG | Fire of God |
| DRC | Democratic Republic of the Congo |
| ERF | Earth Reaction Force |

| | |
|---|---|
| IST | Israel Standard Time |
| EET | Eastern European Time |
| EO | Early Out |
| SSRI | Selective Serotonin Re-uptake Inhibitor |
| GCS | Glasgow Coma Scale |
| ASAP | As Soon As Possible |
| GPS | Global Positioning System |
| NGO | Non-Governmental Organization |
| HIPAA | Health Assurance Portability and Accountability Act |
| CSF | Cerebral Spinal Fluid |
| CJD | Creutzfeldt-Jakob Disease |

# Acknowledgements

I understand this is desirable, perhaps even necessary, to include an acknowledgement page...but for me, it is a most difficult exercise to complete...separating out individuals and/or groups who have influenced me in one way or another is indeed a promethean task...but I **will** do my best, keeping somewhat within the bounds of convention, to acknowledge particularly important names and personages.

So, first of all, I would like to thank my family...especially my wife Sharon, who remains my wisest counsel, truth teller, and best friend... and, like most men, I neglect, more often than not, telling her how much I love her.

To our three children...generous, caring, and meaning more to me than I can ever express here.

As regards an acknowledgement particular to the book...I would like to thank Rebecca Fee and Sally Fitzgerald...the first-proof readers of an early, early sketch, of the story...they did not discourage me, and for that I am very grateful. Dr. Kelly Rose, who took those first tentative story steps, and kicked the horse in stride...thanks so much.

I would like to thank my "final" group of readers: Cathy Spinney, Ronald Beauchain, Ed Tivnan, and Pat Emiro (who sadly, passed before finishing the manuscript)...without each and every one of them, I could not have moved forward. My gratitude abounds.

A special mention must be made to my friends in Leadership, a program run out of the University of New Hampshire Institute on Disability (Institute on Disability/UNH/UCE), especially Beth Dixon and Frank

Sgambati, among others, and the miraculous work done there...thank you.

Especially fond appreciation to Don Moore (and his lovely wife Ahdrah) for actually editing this second release (which needed it badly)...thank you so very much, Don.

Finally, an extra special thanks to Jack Farrell, SJ, DST, who has been a part of my life since nearly as far back as I can remember. His charity, generosity and kindnesses will never be forgotten.